For Whom the Book Tolls

Also available by Laura Gail Black

The Antique Bookshop Mysteries

Murder by the Bookend
Bound by Murder

For Whom the Book Tolls

AN ANTIQUE BOOKSHOP MYSTERY

Laura Gail Black

CROOKED
LANE

NEW YORK

Published in the United States by Crooked Lane Books, an imprint of The Quick Brown Fox & Company LLC.

Crooked Lane Books and its logo are trademarks of The Quick Brown Fox & Company LLC.

Library of Congress Catalog-in-Publication data available upon request.

ISBN (hardcover): 978-1-64385-451-9
ISBN (paperback): 978-1-63910-304-1
ISBN (ebook): 978-1-64385-452-6

Cover illustration by Mary Ann Lasher

Printed in the United States.

www.crookedlanebooks.com

Crooked Lane Books
34 West 27th St., 10th Floor
New York, NY 10001

First Edition: September 2020
Trade Paperback Edition: March 2023

10 9 8 7 6 5 4 3 2 1

For my mother, Linda Myers
(1942–2002), who showed me the
limitless universe held within the covers
of books and who encouraged me to
share my own stories with the world.

Chapter One

I sat in my car, squinting into the darkened alleyway. The streetlamp my uncle had mentioned seemed to be burned out, as no light cut through the moonless night. He'd said we weren't supposed to park behind the businesses, but an eerie chill skittered up my spine at the thought of parking here in the assigned lot at the end of the street and walking up the alley in the dark with only a flashlight and a duffle bag to protect myself.

Uncle Paul might think this was a nice, quiet little town, but my recent past had left me more than a bit jaded and skeptical. However, I couldn't guarantee I'd be up and about before morning delivery trucks might arrive. Last thing I wanted was to cause problems for Uncle Paul on my first day.

I squared my shoulders, grabbed my duffle and flashlight, and got out of my car, wincing as the sound of the doors locking echoed across the parking lot. Sweeping my flashlight along the side of the old warehouse-cum-historic shopping district, I spotted the stairs up to the second floor, where the soaring upper space had been converted into apartments.

A sliver of moon popped out from behind a cloud, shining enough light for me to avoid tripping over residents' doormats and

1

potted plants as I carefully aimed my flashlight at the numbers on the front doors. There! 205. A breath I'd not realized I was holding whooshed out, and some of the tension in my shoulders slid away.

I stooped and groped under the doormat, hoping I wasn't grabbing a bug or a spider. Dealing with a bite wasn't what I had in mind for what was left of my night. My fingers brushed metal, and I pulled out the key Uncle Paul had promised to leave for me when I'd told him I would arrive late.

Movement caught my eye, and my head pivoted, followed by the swing of my flashlight, and I glimpsed a ragged orange tabby cat hopping into the dumpster. The skin on the back of my neck prickled, and I peered out into the alleyway, on hyperalert for any other movement.

The moon slid behind the clouds again, and the alley dipped into shadow. Gads, I was being ridiculous. Not normally timid, I mentally kicked myself for standing there expecting to play a starring role in a B-rated horror flick. I cringed and swung around to face my new home. At least for the next few weeks, this was home. What had I gotten myself into? I straightened my spine. I knew exactly what I'd gotten into. Or rather, out of. Ignoring the inky blackness of the alley at my back, I slid the key into the door's lock, turned it, and eased the door open.

I stepped softly through the doorway, relieved when the floors didn't squeak. I hadn't seen Uncle Paul in years, and I didn't want our reunion to be the result of my noisy arrival in the middle of the night. Especially after he'd requested I be quiet if I came in this late.

According to his email, the second door to the right was a guest bedroom, and I used my flashlight to guide my way, pointing it at the floor to keep from accidentally shining it into Uncle Paul's room. Tiptoeing, I moved across the hardwood floor and eased the bedroom door shut before flipping a wall switch and turning to survey my new digs.

A made-up bed with clean sheets stood against one wall beside a nightstand supporting a bedside lamp. Across the room, a couple of bottles of water, an apple, and a bag of chips lay on a long, ornate dresser. I smiled at this thoughtful provision of a late-night snack. After I gobbled it down, exhaustion set in, and I shimmied out of my jeans and slipped off my bra, draping them over a comfy-looking chair in the corner, and crawled into the bed.

The next morning I opened my eyes to a still-dark room, surprised to find it after eight AM when I looked at my phone. After flicking on the bedside lamp, I realized there were no windows, a detail I'd overlooked in my exhausted state the night before. Guess I wouldn't be waking up to sunshine and birds singing, and I wouldn't be opening a window to let fresh air in on a balmy morning or evening. After where I'd spent the last three months . . .

Determined not to find fault with the only option I had for a home, and one that had been so graciously offered, I searched for a plus to having no windows. I'd have a nice, dark room if I needed to sleep in every once in a while. And I wouldn't have to worry about Peeping Toms either. Okay, so I was reaching a bit.

Following a call of nature and a desire to shower, I opened the two extra doors in the room, finding a closet and a small bathroom, which also exited back into the main part of the apartment. With both bathroom doors locked, I grabbed a quick shower and returned to my room to dress and unpack the rest of my small duffle. Later I'd bring in a few more things from the car.

Clean, dressed in jeans and a lightweight red sweater, and with my wavy blonde hair clipped up into a messy bun, I opened my bedroom door to bright light flooding the open floor plan through tall windows set in the far end of the apartment. This was more like it. A kitchen stood across from me, with a long island and bar-stools. An eight-foot dining table filled an area farther down the home, with a large L-shaped couch, coffee table, and large flat-screen TV hanging over a gas fireplace taking up the remaining space. In the far front corner, a closed door led to a built-out room, too small to be a bedroom or office but possibly a storage closet or coat closet.

"Uncle Paul?" I stepped into the gleaming kitchen and sniffed. Nope, no coffee yet. I crept along the back counter, locating the coffeepot but no filters or coffee. Two doors stood to the side of the kitchen. One led to a laundry room, the other to a pantry, where I struck pay dirt.

As the coffee burbled down into the pot, I located drinkware, finally relaxing once I had a mug of the steaming brew in my hands. With my treasure, I moved around the apartment. A door farther down the right wall stood open, and I peeked into a larger bedroom, which must be Uncle Paul's room, as he'd said it was a two-bedroom apartment. I ducked back out, not wanting to intrude on his private space, and continued my perusal of the home.

"Uncle Paul?" Still no answer.

I stepped to one of the floor-to-ceiling windows and peered out into the quaint street below. Old-fashioned storefronts bordered a cobblestone street with wide, clean sidewalks running down each side. Wrought-iron benches and dwarf maple trees dotted the walkways, adding an inviting feel. As many of the stores hadn't yet opened, few pedestrians moved along the walkways.

Closing my eyes and inhaling the fortifying aroma of the steaming coffee, I let excitement and hope take the place of more recent, darker emotions. I had a new direction, a new life ahead of me. My eyes popped open, and I strode back across to my new room, where, with my free hand, I grabbed my now-empty duffle. Might as well store it and give myself a feeling of actually living here.

I smiled as I walked across to the storage closet area, hoping I could find a small nook to stash my unneeded bag. As I approached the closet door, I slowed. A deadbolt was set into the door, as well as a knob lock. What the hell did Uncle Paul have that needed both a deadbolt that locked from inside the closet and a knob lock that locked from inside the apartment? I tossed my duffle at the couch, wincing when it missed and landed on the floor, and turned back to the puzzle of the doubly lockable door. Gads, now I sounded like Nancy Drew.

Rolling my eyes at myself, I reached to turn the knob. Unlocked. As was the deadbolt. Intense curiosity overriding good manners—my mother would be horrified—I slowly and silently turned the knob and eased the door open just enough to peek through. A surprised "Oh!" escaped my lips, and I swung the door wider.

A polished-wood landing fronted a spiral staircase leading down into—what? Maybe the bookstore my uncle owned below? I started down the stairs, curious to see where I'd be helping out for the next few weeks and hoping to find my absent uncle. A few steps down, I could see to the bottom, and I froze, the coffee cup slipping from my fingers to tumble down the stairs, splattering coffee on the treads and handrail as it went.

My heart crashed, and my breath rushed out in a scream. I caught the railing as my knees buckled, and I sank down onto a step.

At the bottom lay Uncle Paul. The angle of his limbs and head told me all I needed to know.

Chapter Two

The blue and red police lights sent out happy rays of color as they twirled, belying the grim nature of what lay inside my uncle's bookstore. I sat in the back of an ambulance, a blanket wrapped around my shoulders, as shudders racked my body.

A warm hand came to rest on my arm. "Would you like some water?" The EMT held out a bottle.

Words wouldn't push past the tightness in my chest and lump in my throat, so I mutely shook my head.

"The police want to ask you a few questions. I told them I'd see if you were up to it." She placed another blanket around my shoulders.

As if the day couldn't get any worse. My eyes closed, and I took a deep breath. "Tell them I'm ready." Tears stung the backs of my lids, and I blinked them away before the police could see them.

The EMT slid a tissue into my hand, and I blew my nose as she waved two men in suits over to where I sat.

"Ma'am, I'm Detective Frank Sutter," said a rotund man in a brown polyester suit that looked like it had seen far better days. "This is my partner, Detective Keith Logan. We'd like to ask you a few questions, if that's okay."

"I'm not sure what I can tell you." I sniffed and huddled deeper into the blankets, glad to have the shield of faux wool between me and the detectives.

"First, can you tell us your name?" Detective Logan spoke softly, his warm chocolate eyes both soothing and alluring. Taller than his partner, Logan seemed fit and firm under his well-cut, albeit not overtly expensive, charcoal suit. Dark, wavy hair lay back from his face and brushed the back of his collar, and his skin tones and the set of his cheekbones gave the impression he was from the Pacific Islands.

My mouth opened, and only a squeak came out, although I wasn't sure if it was from the stress or because Keith Logan was one of the hottest men I'd ever seen. Good Lord, what was wrong with me? It had to be the shock. I cleared my throat and tried again. "I'm Jenna Quinn. I'm Paul Baxter's niece."

"I understand you're the person who found Mr. Baxter." Detective Sutter pulled a pad and pen from his breast pocket and flipped it open in his meaty hands, making a quick note.

My throat closed, leaving me only able to nod again. Dear God, he was dead. Dead. What was I going to do now? Where would I go? Guilt crashed through me as I realized my fear about my predicament had supplanted my grief over the loss of my uncle.

"Can you walk us through what happened, please?" Detective Logan's kind gaze caught mine, and he gave a tiny nod of encouragement.

Another ragged breath shoved its way through me. "I arrived just before two AM this morning and used the key Uncle Paul had told me about. When I got up this morning, I went looking for him to let him know I'd arrived safely. I found him at the bottom of the stairs." A lone tear slid down my cheek.

Sutter grunted. "And you had never been here before?"

"No, I hadn't seen my uncle in almost ten years, and even then, it was when he and my aunt came to visit our family in Charlotte." Damn it. I winced, wishing I could take back the word *Charlotte*, but it was too late now. I prayed he wouldn't decide to dig too deeply into where I was from.

Another grunt as Sutter made notes. "Why were you here now? Was this a planned visit?"

Now came the sticky part. I chose my words carefully. "Uncle Paul had heard I was between jobs"—not a lie . . . technically— "and he wrote and asked me to come stay here for a while. We hadn't seen each other for so long, and he wanted to have the chance to reconnect." And now it would never happen. The sweet, funny uncle I remembered from all those years ago was gone, and I had no way to tell him I was sorry for never finding time to come visit. Grief finally outweighed my own struggles, and the tears flowed freely.

The EMT pressed another tissue into my hand, and I sopped at my eyes and cheeks and blew my nose.

"Can anyone verify when you left to come here so we can verify when you arrived?" Sutter looked at me, eyes narrowed and speculative.

"I live alone." Technically not another lie. I had lived alone, at least in the crappy rattrap motel I'd ended up in for the last two weeks. "No one can verify when I left."

More grunting. I wondered if he even realized he was doing it.

"We have your number from the nine-one-one call. We'll call you if we have any further questions." Sutter snapped the pad closed and slid it into his pocket.

Logan held out a business card. "Please let us know if you think of anything that might solve this."

His words registered as he walked away.

"Wait, what? Solve? It wasn't an accident?" Horror sliced through me.

Logan turned back to me. "Right now, we honestly aren't sure."

My mind reeled. What did he mean, *not sure*? Not sure as in "not sure exactly what happened," or not sure as in "we think he may have been murdered"? I swallowed back the scream of frustration and desperation that shoved against my throat. Having them think I had lost it wasn't a good idea.

I stopped an officer and confirmed I couldn't stay in the apartment until it was released as a possible crime scene, although I did manage to gain permission to gather my things, fully escorted and supervised, from the guest room and bathroom. As I numbly shoved my duffle into the back seat of my car, I shoved grief and fear to the back of my mind, almost losing that battle when the coroner's van pulled into the alleyway. I turned my head away, forcing myself not to think about the black zippered bag they would soon roll out.

I slid into my car and leaned my forehead on the steering wheel. My bank account had less than two hundred dollars in it, which wouldn't last long if I had to find a motel, especially when I added food costs on top.

Not wanting to witness the removal of the body, I turned the key in the ignition and put the car in gear, slamming on my brakes when Sutter tapped on my driver's side window.

"Going somewhere, Ms. Quinn?"

"You implied I was free to leave when you said you'd call if you had more questions." I kept the car in gear, ready to scoot away the moment Sutter moved out of my way.

Sutter grunted again. "I think it would be better if you rode with us."

The air left my lungs, and bile flooded to the back of my throat. I swallowed deeply to keep from vomiting on my steering wheel. "With you?" My voice came out in a trembling whisper.

Sutter's eyes narrowed and he pursed his lips, apparently assessing my onset of panic. "Yes. We have a few more questions we'd like to ask you down at the station." His cold eyes bored through me as if he already knew all my secrets.

My hands clutched the steering wheel, knuckles white. "I'd be happy to answer your questions, Detective. I'll follow you in my car."

Detective Logan approached and whispered something in Sutter's ear.

Sutter straightened, narrowing his eyes at me again and nodding before striding off to an unmarked sedan and sliding into the passenger seat. Logan got behind the wheel, and as the sedan pulled away from the parking lot, I followed.

Chapter Three

Sitting in a cramped, cell-like room, I leaned my elbows on the table, attempting to look calm. A large mirror dominated the opposite wall, and I knew they were watching me through one-way glass.

The door swung open, and I jumped.

Sutter and Logan entered and sat in the two empty seats across from me.

Sutter opened a folder he'd brought with him and slid a mug shot across the table at me. "Tell me about Charlotte." His voice slithered across my skin.

An icy chill froze me in place as I looked into my own eyes in the picture.

When I didn't speak, Sutter continued. "Embezzlement and murder. These are interesting charges, considering this morning's events."

I raised my gaze to meet his squarely, my jaw firm, and I hoped I didn't look like the trembling bag of Jell-O I felt like. "I was acquitted of all charges."

Another grunt. "So you were. But you haven't been acquitted for the murder this morning."

The room spun. "Why do you feel my uncle's death was murder?"

"We're not completely sure yet." Logan shot a glare at Sutter. Good cop, bad cop. Now I knew who played each part.

Grunt.

Did Sutter have a throat condition of some sort that caused him to continually grunt? The noise grated on my already frayed nerves.

"They never solved the Charlotte crimes, Ms. Quinn. I find that interesting." Sutter reached out and slid the mug shot back across the table to place it in his folder. "Your acquittal could simply mean you had a good lawyer and the police didn't have enough evidence. Yet."

"Or it could mean I am actually innocent. What happened in Charlotte is in the past. It has no bearing on what happened today." I straightened in my chair, refusing to be intimidated any longer. "Am I under arrest?"

Grunt. "Not at this time." *Grunt.* Sutter leaned forward, his glare menacing. "But don't plan on leaving town."

I nodded and rose. No reason to blurt out that I knew the whole "don't leave town" thing was blowing smoke. I wasn't under arrest, and I could legally go wherever I wanted. However, I also knew leaving town would add to his reasons to think I had killed my uncle. And it wasn't like I had anywhere to actually go.

As I walked from the station to my car, I pulled up local hotels and motels on my phone, hunting the lowest possible price. I located Hokes Folly Budget Inn, a private inn named after the town rather than a chain. I drove to the outskirts of town and pulled into the parking lot.

Door chimes jingled when I entered the lobby, and an elderly man popped out from the back room.

"Welcome to Hokes Folly, miss. Would you like a room?"

I looked around a lobby full of worn but clean furniture, windows that sparkled, and healthy plants and figured the place had to be better than the last motel I'd stayed in. We spoke briefly, and after exchanging money for a key, I had a place to sleep for the night that didn't eat up all of my remaining funds.

My stomach rumbled, and I realized I'd never gotten the chance to eat breakfast. The clock on the nightstand read 3:23. If I played it right, I could get by on one meal today, saving more money for later. I headed out the door in search of a McDonald's and their famous value menu.

Two cheeseburgers later, I was full and exhausted from the day's emotional roller coaster, and I crumpled into an exhausted heap on the bed. Covers over my head, I fell into a restless sleep, tossing and turning for most of the night.

Around six AM, I rose and grabbed a shower. When I was dry and dressed, I reached for my phone—my one splurge on my dwindling budget—and placed a call, pacing the floor while I talked.

After a few rings, a low, soothing voice answered. "Quinn residence."

"Dad?" A lump rose in my throat as the overwhelming need to run home and hide plowed over me.

"Jenna. It's great to hear from you. How was your trip?"

I could almost hear a smile in his voice. "The trip was fine. Is Mom around?" Uncle Paul had been married to Mom's older sister until Aunt Irene lost a battle with cancer nearly a decade ago.

"Your mom is a little . . . under the weather right now. She's napping upstairs. Is everything okay?"

I sighed deeply. There was no easy way to do this. "Dad, Uncle Paul is dead."

"What?" my father gasped out. "How?"

"The police don't know yet. He was dead when I got here, but I didn't know it until yesterday morning. I'm sorry I didn't call sooner, but I didn't know how to tell you . . ." I let my voice trail off, at a loss for anything else to say. I refused to add that the police thought I might have killed him. That would crush them after all that had happened. I didn't want to worry them unless it was unavoidable.

Dad cleared his throat and sniffed loudly a few times, and it was all I could do not to bawl like a baby as I listened to him fight his own tears.

"I'll tell your mother when she wakes up." His voice trembled, and he cleared his throat again. "Will you be coming home?"

"Not yet." What reason could I give for staying without spilling the beans about the police? "I want to stay for the funeral. Will you be coming up?"

"I'm sure we'll try, but your mother just isn't feeling well right now." Dad sniffed one last time. "I'll let you know."

"Okay. Tell Mom I hope she feels better soon."

"Jenna?"

I swallowed hard. "Yes?"

"I love you. This isn't your fault either."

I barely managed the "I love you too" around the ever-growing lump in my throat.

After we hung up, I pictured him letting his grief flow. At least I hoped he wasn't bottling it up. I knew he'd stifle it at some point to be strong for Mom.

I flopped onto the bed, tucking my bare feet under the blanket, and reached for the TV remote, hoping to find something to watch to distract my mind. When I turned the TV on, the news was just starting.

"Thank you for joining me, Connie Dunne—"

"And me, Jonathan Greer," piped in her co-anchor.

"—here on Channel Five Morning News for weather updates and the news to start your day," the anchorwoman continued. "The top story this half hour is the death of Hokes Folly business owner Paul Baxter."

I grabbed the remote and turned up the volume.

The bottle blonde droned on in that newsy tone so many anchors used. "Yesterday morning, the body of Paul Baxter was discovered lying at the bottom of a set of spiral stairs leading from his business, Baxter's Book Emporium, to his apartment above. His niece, who allegedly arrived just before two AM, claims to have been looking for him in the apartment and found him dead."

An outraged gasp left me as my mug shot from Charlotte flashed on the screen.

The camera panned to Jonathan Greer. "Ms. Quinn, recently acquitted of murder and embezzlement in Charlotte, remains a person of interest in Baxter's death. At this time, it is not confirmed whether she is or is not a beneficiary of Baxter's will. However, sources report the law firm involved is the long-standing firm of Grimes and Waterford. The police are still investigating, and sources state they have strong reason to believe Baxter's death was not accidental. More on this story tonight at six."

A commercial for teeth whitener took over the screen, and I turned the TV off. Who were Grimes and Waterford? And what if I *was* in Uncle Paul's will? If I was, it meant two things. First, I might not be destitute anymore. Second, I now really did seem to have had a motive for killing my uncle.

I grabbed my phone, googled Grimes and Waterford in Hokes Folly, and called the phone number on their website to set an appointment. I had to get to the bottom of all of this before I ended up arrested for murder. Again.

Chapter Four

I'd been there two hours. The first hour of sitting in the waiting room of Grimes and Waterford hadn't been too bad. After two? I was bored. Frustrated. A little sleepy, since it was a bit on the warm side. I looked over at the receptionist, where she sat wrapped in a sweater behind her big desk. Maybe she was one of those people who was perpetually cold. I, however, was not. At twenty-six, I was too young to have started in on hot flashes, but I preferred to be able to feel a difference between outside and inside temperatures in the late summer.

I looked back at my lap and turned another page of *Car and Driver*. The article didn't hold my interest, nor did the magazine, to be honest, but I'd read everything else in the room, including old newspaper clippings hung on the walls, which talked about the partners' accomplishments. Anything to keep from thinking about my uncle's death and my current predicament.

With my eyes closed, I ran through memories of my long-ago visits with Aunt Irene and Uncle Paul. Though there had been the occasional Christmas card or brief email, it had been years since we'd seen each other. Uncle Paul's recent emails, in which he'd invited me to stay with him a while, had taken me by surprise, but I'd been at a point where I couldn't turn down such an offer without a darned good reason.

It would have been nice to see them again. Of course, it would have been impossible to see Aunt Irene. She'd passed away almost nine years ago, which was when Uncle Paul stopped visiting for several years, since Mom, Aunt Irene's younger sister, looked so much like her, and it caused him a lot of pain. When he'd finally started to visit again, I'd already gone off to college, so I'd missed out on that time. After college, I'd been too busy when he'd invited me. I'd always thought I'd have time later. Now there would never be a later.

When one of the inner doors of the office finally opened, I jumped, startled out of my walk down memory lane as an elderly woman swept into the waiting area, a tall, well-dressed African-American man right behind her.

"Are you Jenna Quinn?" the man asked.

I nodded, and he offered a well-manicured hand in greeting.

"I'm so glad you could wait. I'm Horace Grimes, and this is one of our town's treasures, Miss Olivia Hokes."

The tiny woman's silvering head rose a fraction, as if in regal approval of the compliment.

"She and her sister, Ophelia, are the only living members of the Hokes clan still left in Hokes Folly today." Mr. Grimes smiled at his diminutive client.

"Left living at all," corrected the woman, her chin lifting another fraction.

"Yes, of course." He bowed his head in agreement.

Dear God, I'd come to Mayberry. Although Mayberry might not be so bad after . . . I took a deep breath to clear my head. "It's nice to meet you." I smiled as sweetly as I could.

Sharp, blue eyes stared at me, full of shrewdness and a bit of bitterness, which clashed with the woman's frail and dainty outward appearance. "Of course it is."

Wow. Okay. Not knowing how to respond to the rude retort, I simply kept the sweet smile plastered to my face and hoped it looked believable.

Abruptly, Miss Hokes turned to the attorney, thumping the cane of her parasol—its lace exactly matched to her antique dress—on the hardwood floor. "Is this her?"

Olivia Hokes apparently didn't watch the morning news, or she'd have known exactly who I was. I'd spent the last two hours trying to ignore the receptionist's odd glances, as if she thought I might brandish a weapon at any moment.

"Yes. Yes, it is." Mr. Grimes's head nodded again, and I had to stifle a giggle when my exhausted and overloaded brain conjured up an image of a bobblehead dashboard doll with his face on it.

Miss Hokes looked me up and down. "She's tall." She sniffed in disapproval.

At a healthy five foot ten, I towered over the tiny woman, and I fought the urge to hunch my shoulders. Her gaze locked with mine, as if she were trying to burrow into my brain, and just as quickly, she shifted her gaze to my blonde hair and frowned. When I realized I had subconsciously put a hand up to check that my shoulder-length tresses weren't sticking out in some odd fashion, I snatched it back down, refusing to let this woman get to me.

Next, the woman placed a pair of antique spectacles on her nose and reached out to rub the material of my dress between her fingers. "Good workmanship, if a bit dowdy."

Excuse me? My eyebrows shot up. To be honest, I'd brought it with me to Uncle Paul's because it was comfortable, not because it would ever grace the cover of a fashion magazine. No, it didn't highlight my slim figure but hung loosely to my calves. Yet with its cap sleeves, scooped neckline, and soft, butter-yellow material with the hint of an intricate lacelike pattern in the right light, I'd hardly have considered it dowdy. However, it had been the dressiest thing I'd had in my suitcase and therefore won the "what shall I wear to the lawyer's office" contest.

Before I could speak, Mr. Grimes rescued me from further inspection, gently ushering the tiny woman toward the outer door, opening it, and nudging her through. "You have a nice day, Livie. And give Phillie my best."

With a final, arrogantly dismissive bow of her head, Olivia Hokes turned on her heel and marched away.

The lawyer heaved a deep sigh and leaned on the now-closed door. After a brief moment, he straightened and extended a welcoming hand. His open and friendly voice soothed some of my irritation. "I'm terribly sorry about the delay. Miss Hokes had a few matters that needed immediate attention, and her appointment ran longer than I anticipated. I hope you weren't too badly inconvenienced."

My southern upbringing took charge, and I smiled and again shook his hand, wondering if he even remembered offering it previously. "No, it's fine." Instinctively, I liked him. Maybe there was a "trust me" vibe lawyers were trained to give off, but somehow I didn't think he was faking it.

His earnest expression melted into a warm smile as he held open his office door so I could enter first. Masculine furniture, heavy and dark, dominated the large room. Floor-to-ceiling windows graced one wall, and a cool breeze wafted in through an open section, causing the filmy, burgundy drapery to billow inward. An adjoining wall surrounded a large fireplace, which I assumed was more than decoration but would be well used in the coming chilly autumn evenings in the mountains.

I took a seat in one of the large wingback chairs opposite the mahogany desk, opened my purse, and extracted my driver's license, handing it across the imposing desk. "You asked to see this to verify my identity, although I'm not really sure why."

"Thank you." He took the license and ran his gaze across it, glancing up to see that the picture matched the woman in his office. "Please get me a copy of your birth certificate as soon as you can so I can include it in the records."

"Birth certificate?"

"Yes, just as a legal requirement to prove you're the correct heir." He laid the license aside and shuffled through a stack of papers on his desk, seeming to compare the two before turning to a small printer-copier on the shelf behind him to make a copy. "Now." He handed me my license and pushed a new stack of papers across the desk to me. "I need your signature on each of these documents. This will allow me to change the names on the deeds to reflect new ownership."

"Deeds?" I hated to sit there probably looking like an idiot, but my mind drew a complete blank.

"Yes, the deeds to the apartment and the business." He must have caught my confused look, because he put the papers down, rested his arms on the desk, and leaned forward. "You have no idea what I'm talking about, do you?"

I shook my head. My stomach tightened. I wasn't overly fond of being blindsided by things anymore. "Did Uncle Paul leave me something in his will?"

Another warm smile spread across his face. "Jenna, you were the primary beneficiary."

My mind searched for the downside to what he was saying. Oh, wait, the fact that inheriting anything of value gave me a really great motive for murder. I could see Sutter's delighted look already.

"I'm surprised he never mentioned these things to you. But then again, Paul was a private man when it came to finances, so you likely wouldn't have been aware of his assets." Mr. Grimes leaned back and smiled. "Paul moved into the historic district before it was a town hot spot. He purchased his store location and his apartment for a song. These are now yours, along with the apartment's furniture and the bookstore's assets."

My breath left in a gasp, my chest squeezing tightly, and I could barely draw another. He'd left me everything. I'd figured on a few pieces of furniture or some sentimental items. But all of it? When I'd made the appointment, I hadn't really considered all the implications. I'd simply been grateful to have any wisp of hope, even if it only bought me a few weeks or months before I was once again completely broke. At least that would have given me time to look for some sort of job and life.

I shuddered, inwardly cringing at how greedy and money grabbing I seemed, even to myself, as if hoping somehow to gain from the death of my uncle. But even Uncle Paul had understood the situation I was in when he offered to have me come stay.

Mr. Grimes referred to a paper on his desk. "That's on top of six hundred forty-six thousand two hundred eighty-three dollars and twenty-nine cents in a savings account for his retirement and three thousand nine hundred forty-two dollars and thirty-five cents in the checking account, from which my fee has already been removed. Finally, there is the three hundred fifty thousand in life insurance policies, although this might take a few days to settle. Insurance companies don't generally pay out too quickly." He leaned over and touched my hand, looking me in the eyes as he smiled softly. "You, dear lady, are now a millionaire."

I swallowed hard. "Are you sure?" My mind spun. Things weren't as desperate as they'd been only this morning, but at what cost? "I mean, are you sure someone else wasn't supposed to inherit? I hadn't seen Uncle Paul since I was a teenager, and he was only my uncle by marriage. We'd only kept in touch through infrequent emails and a few Christmas cards."

"Jenna." His mellow voice soothed my jangled nerves once more. "As he was an only child himself, Paul had no siblings to whom to leave his estate. And in the event he had no children, either through birth or through adoption, everything not specified for someone else was to be divided evenly between any living children of Rose Quinn, Irene's younger sister. I've already made arrangements to disburse a couple of smaller bequests, but as Rose Quinn's only child, he definitely intended for you to inherit the bulk of his estate."

My head still couldn't, wouldn't, wrap around the fact that Uncle Paul had tried to help me out, even in death. Tears stung the backs of my eyes, and I blinked rapidly to wipe them away. "What about probate? I remember when my grandmother passed away a few years ago, it took months for everything to get settled."

Horace dipped his silvered head. "A good question. Paul set everything up in what's called a revocable living trust. This means all of his possessions were in a trust. He could use these things during his lifetime, but upon his death, the trust is disbursed to the beneficiaries. That would be any possible children, of which there were none, and you. It's immediate, no probate necessary." He tapped the papers lying in front of me. "If you'll sign here, here, and here"—he indicated the appropriate spaces—"I can complete the deed transfers from the trust to you."

With shaking fingers, I reached for the offered pen, staring at it in my hand for a moment, my mind a complete blank. I shook my head to clear my thoughts and signed the papers, grateful my signatures were legible.

"At least I can pay for a nice funeral for Uncle Paul now." While not technically a bonus, since he'd had to die for me to pay for his funeral, at least it wasn't one more instance where I would let him down.

Mr. Grimes pulled out another paper from his file. "No need. Paul carried a burial policy, which will pay for all funeral expenses. He'd already purchased a plot next to your aunt."

I shook my head again. "He thought of everything." That ache in my heart was becoming all too familiar. "What steps do I need to take?"

"None." He slid the paper back into the folder. "Your uncle wanted a quiet ceremony at the grave site. I've already notified the few he wanted to attend, including your parents and now you. However, your mother told me about her recent back surgery and that she's not able to travel this far yet."

What? Mom hadn't said anything to me about back surgery. Now a new guilt slammed through my head with the realization that she'd tried not to give me anything else to stress over. I knew she had a disk that was going bad in her lower back. It must have finally gotten to the point she needed it fixed, and she must've decided I didn't need to worry about what she considered a minor thing in the face of all my unavoidable drama. Wait, Dad had said she was under the weather. He must have been helping her hide her surgery from me. My mind warred between loving them and being mad at them. However, Mr. Grimes didn't need to know all my family laundry, so I nodded as if I had already been aware.

"In their absence," he continued, "it will be you and a few close friends. Everything is ready as soon as they release the body. I'll keep you posted."

"Thanks," I mumbled, still processing both my uncle's foresight and my mother's sacrifice.

23

Mr. Grimes neatly tucked the signed papers into a manila folder and stood. "I've spoken with Frank Sutter, and while we cannot get into the business or apartment today, they should finish up by tomorrow afternoon and will release the scene. If you'd like, I can meet you there around three PM."

I nodded mutely and garbled out a somewhat coherent good-bye, numbly walking out of his office to my car.

Chapter Five

After a restless second night at the Hokes Folly Budget Inn, I'd spent the day processing my new circumstances and the loss of my uncle. My brain had ridden a carousel of thought, circling round and round until I thought I'd scream. Mom had had surgery and hadn't told me, I was now a millionaire and business owner, Uncle Paul might have been murdered, and I could be a suspect. *But why would he have been murdered? And by whom?*

As three PM approached, I grabbed at the chance to stop my circuitous thoughts, snatched up my purse, and left the motel. When I arrived in the parking lot at the end of the street to the historic district, I stepped out of my car into a light drizzle and rushed down the alleyway to the back of Uncle Paul's—my—store. Horace Grimes must have seen me coming, as he held open the door and ushered me inside. The smell of fresh coffee met me, and the attorney handed me a cup of the steaming liquid.

For the first few minutes, Mr. Grimes kept up a running chatter. I took a deep breath, forcing my brain to focus on what the attorney said, and I picked up enough to get a feel for the town. Since Hokes Folly had only five thousand residents, give or take, the city council wanted to make sure it kept its historic feel. It seemed that, in an effort to draw vendors and customers alike, the council had rezoned an area of downtown as a historic district. The old warehouses, which had long ago been converted into stores with apartments above, had been given facelifts and facades to add turn-of-the-nineteenth-century charm. The town had blocked off both ends of the section of Center Street that ran from one end of the district to the other, allowing only foot traffic access along the cobblestone street to the storefronts. This had provided a quaint feel that appealed to customers, both locals and tourists. The moment vendors discovered the number of new customers, they had flooded into the area, snatching up empty units and even buying out existing businesses in order to obtain space. Some businesses, like Uncle Paul's bookstore, had been there long before it was a popular place to be.

As Mr. Grimes wrapped up his monologue, I took in the back room. Good Lord, it was a disaster, and I couldn't stop a groan from escaping. Books sat haphazardly on wooden and metal shelves, lay packed in cardboard boxes, and stood in tall piles on the floor. In a tiny corner kitchen area, heaps of books filled the double sink.

Apparently catching my startled look, Mr. Grimes answered the question I'd been afraid to ask. "It was always like this. No one tossed the room. Paul rarely got around to pricing the books back here and putting them out on the shelves. Every once in a while he'd find a rare book worth a lot of money in one of the lots he purchased from estate sales. He spent his time back here assessing and preparing them for auction. He generally procrastinated about the rest until it was so crammed he had no choice but to price them and put them out in the showroom."

"Oh." Taking a deep breath, I took in the rest of the back room, which ran the width of the store. An old rolltop desk sat in a corner, with a green-shaded brass lamp waiting to offer light after hours. Bookshelves surrounded the desk, stuffed, as was the rest of the back room, with random books in stacks and piles. I could almost see Uncle Paul hunched over the desk. I squeezed my eyes shut against the image and waited a moment to regain control.

Horace placed a warm and gentle hand on my shoulder, almost my undoing. "We don't have to go into the front room today if you'd prefer not to."

I stiffened my shoulders and shot him a tight smile. "No, it's okay." I took a deep breath. "I'd rather not do this alone, if that's okay."

He nodded and squeezed my shoulder softly before dropping his hand. "Whenever you're ready."

I waited a moment longer, steeling my resolve, and stepped through the curtain to the front area to get my first real look at the place. The only other time I'd seen it, I'd been too wrapped up in police lights, ambulances, coroners, and dealing with having found my dead uncle. Though I was prepared, a deep sadness enveloped me at the thought that I'd never see Uncle Paul here, never banter with him as we worked. My throat squeezed. I could almost see him among the shelves. My eyes closed against the sting of tears, and I took a slow breath before turning to let my gaze sweep across the other side of the large room.

As in the back, books sat willy-nilly on every surface available. My fingertips skimmed book spines as I wandered up and down aisles made narrow by stacks of books balanced precariously on the floor, occasionally pulling a book off a shelf when one caught my eye. I couldn't see any order to the way they were arranged. Paperback romances with hero and heroine draped across each other in a steamy embrace sat next to last year's low-carb cookbooks and antique poetry books with brass bindings and gold-edged pages.

"After Irene died, Paul spent most of his time here." Horace led me into another aisle. "If the store was open, he was here. If the store wasn't open, he was still often here, pricing and researching." He swept an arm down the aisle at the overflowing shelves of books. "These became his life, because books never die."

I pulled another book from the shelf and smiled softly. *Alice in Wonderland.* Uncle Paul had given me a copy of this book on my sixth birthday and I'd dragged it everywhere I went, forcing anyone I met to read sections of it to me again and again until I all but wore it out. I had been especially enthralled with the Cheshire Cat and the Mad Hatter's tea party. With another lump in my throat, I let my gaze wander down the rows of books. What other treasures would I find here?

Clutching the book to my chest, I skirted standing piles of books scattered down the aisle I was in and picked my way to the front counter. At last something organized. Sort of. A beautiful antique cash register sat on the long counter, and I stepped behind the counter to run my fingers over the keys, shaking my head at the incongruity of the oversized modern calculator next to it. A large cardboard box full of used plastic shopping bags hid under the counter, and a chest-high shelf with books on hold for customers and a few well-used reference books ran along the wall behind the counter, short enough to allow a view through the windows above.

As hard as I'd tried to ignore it, my brain finally zeroed in on the spiral staircase to one side of the front counter. In a last attempt to pretend things were normal, I focused on the nook under the steps, which contained a small folding table with a phone, a couple of phone books, and a coffeepot with a stack of Styrofoam cups. Well, that was one way to keep customers from running away when they started down those horrible aisles. They'd at least stay long enough to finish a cup of coffee, and maybe they'd luck into finding something to buy.

Involuntarily, my gaze swung to the stairs. My heart skipped and my stomach dropped at the white tape outlines at the bottom. An image of my uncle sprawled there, arms and legs at odd angles, clawed its way out of the recesses I'd stuffed it into, and I mentally shoved and stomped it back into place, determined not to break down.

"I'm so sorry," said Mr. Grimes from behind me. "I thought they'd sent out Elmer Peabody. He's our only crime scene cleanup man. He must be down with his gout again. I'll make sure he's here tomorrow, or I'll call in someone from another township."

I sucked in a breath and didn't look away from the awful white lines. "You said they'd released the store and apartment. Did they tell you what happened?" I tried not to remember the image of my uncle inside those lines.

"No, but my granddaughter works for the police, and she told me," the attorney replied gently. "He apparently fell down the stairs after taking some kind of sleeping medication."

"So it was an accident?" A deep sigh left my body. What a lonely place to die.

"From what I hear, the police aren't absolutely certain yet. My granddaughter wasn't quite sure why, though." Mr. Grimes took my elbow and turned me away from the white-taped floor. "She only heard there are a few unexplained details concerning his death that simply don't add up."

"Oh." I paused, wishing I hadn't always been too busy to visit when Uncle Paul had invited me here on my college breaks or the Christmas after I graduated. If only I could see the sweet man I remembered one last time . . . the sweet man someone might have murdered. A chill crept up my spine. I took a deep breath, pushing away the guilty feeling, as if I'd let him down somehow by never visiting, and now I was assessing his business—my business only now that it was too late to change things.

"Well." I cleared my throat, chasing away the tremble in my voice and sweeping my gaze across the room in any direction but toward the stairs. "It certainly is a bookstore." I'd definitely have my work cut out for me getting this place whipped into shape to sell. Or who knew? Maybe I'd keep it. It wasn't like I had any other job prospects. At least, if I owned my own business, no one could accuse me of embezzling and fire me.

Mr. Grimes chuckled again. "Yes, it is that. Paul was definitely not the most organized person in town. He did have someone working for him for a short time, but it didn't work out. Would you like me to go with you to the apartment above?"

I blinked, and my brain jerked to catch up to his abrupt subject change. "No, that's okay. I've already been up there."

"Of course." He nodded. "If you're sure . . ."

I assured him I was, and we carefully wove our way back through the stacks of books to the back door. "However, I'm not sure I'm staying in Hokes Folly. Is there anyone in town I could speak to about the possibility of selling?"

Horace's gaze softened, and he reached out to squeeze my shoulder gently. "I understand. It's a lot to take in all at once."

I nodded. "It's just that . . . I found him . . . he died here . . ." I took a shuddering breath.

"I know Paul would only want you to stay if you wanted to be here. I'll arrange for you to meet with an appraiser. Just do me one favor." He waited for me to raise my gaze to meet his. "Don't make any rushed decisions. Give it a little time. Sure, see what your options are, but make sure you know what you want before you act."

I thanked him for his advice and promised not to choose too quickly.

Before he exited, he pulled a set of keys to the store and the apartment out of his pocket. "You'll need both the store key and the house key for the door at the top of the stairs. The store key locks the deadbolt and the house key locks the knob. This is the only set of keys, so you might want to make a spare set, in case the police need them back."

"Need them back?" I looked at the key ring he gripped.

"They were on the coffee table in the apartment. The police found them during their search after you found the body. Since they were the only set, they were taken to secure the premises after they were done."

"Why two keys?" I held out my hand.

"Not every store owner lives in the apartment above. Some rent the apartments out. Having the two locks means the store owner can't enter the apartment, and the apartment owner can't use the stairs down into the store." Horace laid the keys in my palm.

At least now I knew why the deadbolt locked from the other side. "Got it."

"Be sure to lock up, whether you're staying here or not." His fingers kept a grip on the keys until I nodded. "If you need me, call."

I locked the door behind him and returned to the front room, stopping just past the curtain and closing my eyes. The quiet of the room settled into me, and I let the tears flow as my brain conjured images of Uncle Paul bustling up and down the aisles, helping customers, and using the antique cash register to ring them up. My chest expanded in a deep breath, and I opened my eyes and moved through the store.

The white lines glared at me from the bottom two stair treads and the floor below. My stomach churned, and I didn't think I could possibly touch any of it. I said a silent prayer that Elmer Peabody would be healthy enough to show up tomorrow. Until then, I'd have to use the outside stairs I'd used when I first arrived. I placed *Alice in Wonderland* on the counter. I'd clutched it like a shield since I'd pulled it from the shelf, but I didn't want it damaged in the rain on my way up to the apartment.

Guilt washed through me as my regrets over not seeing my uncle once more battled with my relief at now having a place to live. I'd had only a few more days' worth of funds. Uncle Paul's generosity had given me a fresh start, but it was only mine because he might have been murdered. Detective Sutter was so convinced I was the killer, I doubted he was even looking for someone else. I clenched my jaw and squared my shoulders, resolve settling in my core. If the police weren't going to find out about my uncle's death, then I would. I owed Uncle Paul that much. I'd stay in town long enough to at least accomplish that, even if it wasn't for the reason Horace Grimes had suggested I wait.

I turned and moved toward the back door, jumping when a loud knocking on the front glass shattered the silence.

Chapter Six

A woman huddled under the cover of a raincoat pulled over her head as she motioned for me to let her in. Not wanting to leave her standing out in the rain, which had begun to fall from the sky in buckets, I scooted to the door and turned the deadbolt. Bells jingled overhead as the door swished open, and the woman stepped in, letting the dripping raincoat fall away from her head. I relocked the door and turned to face her.

Bright red waves frizzed with damp hung to her shoulders, and she brushed a stray strand from her face. "I'm glad I caught you. I'm so sorry about your uncle." She grabbed me in a bear hug.

Somehow comforted by this stranger's hug, I felt the all-too-familiar sting of tears and took a deep breath to clear my head.

She squeezed once more and stepped back. "I'm sorry, I didn't even introduce myself. I'm Rita Wallace. I live over the store next door. I was friends with Paul."

I cleared my throat to push away the lump and smiled. "I'm Jenna Quinn, his niece."

"I know. He told me you were coming." Rita let her gaze sweep across the store, and a wistful smile tugged at the corners of her mouth. "It seems odd not to see him in here bustling around. He always seemed so busy, but it never got any less messy." As her gaze reached the spiral stairs, she gasped. "Is that . . . ?"

I nodded. "Someone named Elmer Peabody seems to be sick, so it hasn't been cleaned yet."

Her gaze flew back to my face, eyes glittering with unshed tears. She sniffed once and hooked her arm through mine. "We'll go up to my place. Do you have a raincoat?"

"No, but I did spot an umbrella in the back room earlier."

"Perfect." Rita tugged me toward the back door.

I grabbed the umbrella, and we stepped out into the rainy alley, running to the closest end of the stairs and up to the covered walk on the second floor. Her door was before mine, and she stopped me as I moved toward Uncle Paul's—my—front door.

"I was serious about you coming in. I'd really like to chat, if you're up to it." She opened her door and held it wide.

"Are you sure?" I took a tentative step forward. "I don't want to be an inconvenience."

"I'm sure." She nodded and walked through her door, leaving it open.

I stepped through the door into a replica of the apartment that was now mine. The furniture and knickknacks were different, but the layout was exactly the same.

"Sit." Rita gestured at padded bar stools beside the kitchen island bar. "I'm just putting on a pot of tea."

My upbringing kicked in. "Is there anything I can do to help?"

"Sure." Rita gestured toward a nearby cabinet. "Pick what tea you want."

I opened the cabinet door to an array of boxes and tins. Herbal teas, black teas, and green teas sat neatly arranged on the shelves. "Wow. That's a lot of tea." I scanned the boxes for something that looked familiar, but no Lipton or Red Diamond tea sat among the many boxes.

Rita chuckled and stepped up beside me. "Sorry. I forget sometimes that not everyone drinks tea." She reached past me to grab a box of jasmine green tea. "You'll like this one."

She flipped open the box and pulled out a couple of tea bags, dropping them into lavender mugs before pouring boiling water over them. Once the tea was steeping, we moved to the couch.

"I'm sorry about your uncle. He was a good man." Rita picked up her mug and dunked her tea bag a few times.

"Thanks. I hadn't seen him in a long time." I blew across the top of my mug. "Uncle Paul was married to my mother's older sister. We visited a few times when I was little, but they usually came to our house in Charlotte for holidays before Aunt Irene died."

"What do you do in Charlotte?" Rita propped her feet on the coffee table and crossed her ankles.

My stomach tightened, and I clenched my fists around the steaming mug, oblivious to the heat. I took a deep breath and internally counted to ten, forcing my voice into a polite tone. She must not have seen the news. "Nothing right now. I worked for a marketing company in the finance department until recently."

Rita grimaced. "I saw the news story."

There went that theory. "Oh." I dunked my tea bag, giving my hands something to do while I tried to come up with a polite response.

"Did you do it?" Her soft question didn't hold the accusatory tone I had become accustomed to hearing.

I looked up into green eyes that held compassion and openness. "No. I didn't. Not in Charlotte, and not here."

She held me in her intense gaze for a few moments, then nodded once. "Good enough for me."

My chest squeezed. Other than my parents, this was the first person who had seemed to completely believe me, and she was a veritable stranger. "It's that simple?"

A wide grin crossed her face. "It's that simple. I have a good instinct for people, and my gut tells me you're one of the good ones."

Tears filled my eyes, and she held out the tissue box. Frustrated that I was becoming a regular waterworks, I set my mug down and gratefully took one, wiping my eyes and blowing my nose before wadding the tissue into my hand and picking up my mug.

"When you're ready to talk about it, I'll be here. I've been told I'm a good listener." She smiled at me again.

"Thanks." I nodded. "Right now, I don't want to discuss it. Maybe one day."

Rita stood. "Then you shouldn't have to. I'm going to get another mug of tea. Want one?"

I hadn't even sipped the one I had, as it hadn't yet cooled enough to drink. She must have sucked down the boiling-hot liquid while I stared moodily into my own mug.

"No thanks. I'm still good."

When she returned, she plopped down on the couch and again propped her feet on the coffee table. "Maybe you could try your hand at selling books. Paul's store, messy as it is, has always been successful."

"I'm considering it." I swallowed the lump that had risen in the back of my throat and returned the smile, hoping it looked more genuine than it felt. "But I'm not sure how well I'd do, considering I've now been painted as a murderess who came here to kill my uncle."

Rita chuckled. "Honestly, I think the people here might surprise you. Give them time. It'll be a lot easier once they figure out what happened and, if he was murdered, catch the person who did it."

"Maybe." I glanced around the neat apartment and changed the subject, heading off any more discussion about my notoriety. "Did these apartments come furnished? It looks a lot like what Uncle Paul has—had—in his apartment."

A trill of laughter echoed in the large space. "What you see here is my lack of decorating creativity. I saw what Irene had done, and I copied the style. I've always liked retro, although it wasn't retro when Irene picked theirs out." Rita took her tea bag out and placed it on a small saucer. "She had an incredible eye. When she passed, Paul never changed anything. I don't think she meant for it to all stay the same, but Paul always had excuses. Time, money, or simply that he just liked it and didn't feel like changing."

"Sort of a memorial to her, I guess." I sipped my tea and scorched my tongue. How had she already finished off a mug this hot? I blew on it more, letting the repetitive breathing settle my nerves.

"Exactly." Rita put down her mug. "He really loved her. He did date some, but he never remarried. Although I think he might have, if he had found someone who could measure up to what he and Irene had together."

A soft smile tugged at the corners of my mouth. "I remember them. Aunt Irene was really kooky sometimes, but she was also very sweet. She and Uncle Paul were always hugging or kissing or holding hands. It seemed really sappy." I blew across the tea again.

Rita tucked her feet under her. "How old were you when your aunt passed away?"

"Seventeen. It was the summer before my senior year in high school."

"And you didn't see Paul after that?"

37

"No. He needed to get past the pain of losing Aunt Irene, and seeing Mom, who looked so much like her, was too much. It took a couple of years before he visited again. By that time, I was in college and was too busy to come home regularly. After college, life got in the way. I kept putting off making time to come see him. Now it's too late." I stared into my tea mug, lost in regret.

"I'm sure it meant a lot to him that you came to see him now."

I shook my head. "I never got to see him." That familiar lump rose in my throat again, and I took another scorching swig of tea to push it down.

"What happened?" Rita blew her nose and tossed the tissue into the wastebasket under the end table.

"After everything in Charlotte, I had nowhere to go." I leaned forward, planting my elbows on my knees and ducking my head. "Uncle Paul emailed me a few days ago and offered for me to come stay with him for a while. He even joked that I couldn't use being busy at work as an excuse this time."

Rita laughed loudly. "Yep, that sounds like Paul. So, what happened?"

I shrugged. "He'd told me where the key was, and when I got into town around two AM, I let myself in and went to bed. I found him the next morning."

A low whistle left her lips. "That's rough."

"Yeah." I shuddered at the memory of the distorted body at the bottom of the spiral stairs. "I never got to fully reconnect with him. Now I'll never get to."

Rita leaned over and touched my shoulder. "It seems that didn't matter to him after all. You were still obviously important to him."

"Yes," I agreed softly. "I guess you're right." I drew a ragged breath. "He left me everything in some sort of trust, and I can't even say thank-you."

Rita scooted closer and put her arm around my shoulders for a quick side squeeze, and I realized that hug was the best hug I'd had in a long time. Maybe the only hug I'd had for months. It was heavenly.

Before the maudlin-mixed-with-grateful thoughts could bring the frustrating lump back to my throat, I sucked down more tea, scorching myself again. At this rate, I wouldn't have much of a throat left.

"It's nice you can remember them, though. I only knew Irene through Paul's stories." Rita scooted back to her end of the couch, picked up her mug, and sipped her tea with a faraway look. She must be one of those people who could pour coffee straight out of a pot and guzzle it. Ouch!

"You sound like you knew Uncle Paul pretty well," I ventured.

"Yes, Paul and I dated for a bit about four years ago." Rita finished off her tea and set the mug on the table. "We got along wonderfully when we weren't dating. But after we started to go out, it became apparent to us both that we didn't suit each other."

"Why not?" I ignored my mother's voice in my head admonishing me for prying. I figured I was allowed to pry a bit in order to gain information about Uncle Paul and his possible murder. At least I tried to convince myself that was my reason.

"First, he was much older than I was. I know age shouldn't matter, but I was forty-six, and he was sixty. When you get older, you start to slow down a bit, and Paul wanted to be a lot slower than I did. I wanted to go and do and see, and Paul wanted to sit and talk and play games and work puzzles. Second, Paul wanted a homebody like his Irene. I'm simply not that person. I love to travel and learn new things, and I only garden and do housework when absolutely necessary."

I laughed. "We'll definitely get along. I hate housework too, much to my mother's disappointment. I think she secretly channels Martha Stewart."

My tea had finally cooled enough to drink comfortably, and I swallowed the last of it, got up, put my mug in the kitchen sink, and returned to the living room. "I should probably leave. I need to take care of a few things next door." I didn't really. I just dreaded walking into Uncle Paul's space, knowing he would never greet me there. But I didn't want to overstay my welcome at my new neighbor's house.

Rita followed me to the front door. "Where are you staying?"

I tilted my head in the direction of the other unit. "Right next door. It makes better sense to stay there than in a hotel, since I own it now."

Rita opened her door. "Well, good to know. I would've worried, seeing a stranger going in and out without knowing you were supposed to be there."

I stepped out the door. "Now you won't have to call nine-one-one." I plastered what I hoped looked like a relaxed smile on my face as she closed the door. No need to make her worry about my state of mind.

The rain had stopped during our visit, and I took the chance to grab my bags from the car. The trek to the parking lot gave me a few minutes to gather my emotions over entering Uncle Paul's loft. I had avoidance down to an art form these days.

Knowing I would be given the keys to the business and loft when I met with Horace Grimes, I had checked out of the motel and loaded everything into my car. It didn't make sense to waste money on an uncomfortable motel bed when I now owned a home. I slung both bags over my shoulders, grabbed my jacket from the back seat, and draped my favorite blanket over my arm. Taking a deep, steadying breath, I locked the car, turned, and marched toward the apartment, determined not to chicken out and head back to the motel.

Tamping down the feelings of grief, I strode into the apartment and stopped. I looked toward Uncle Paul's room. A lump rose in my throat again. I gritted my teeth. This was what Uncle Paul wanted for me. I wasn't an interloper, thief, bottom-feeder, or any of the other derogatory names my stressed-out brain tried to paint on my back. I swallowed the lump and walked to the spare bedroom. It was just too soon to take over the master.

My bags dropped onto the bed, and I unzipped them, ready to unpack and at least attempt to feel like I belonged here. Without allowing any time to second-guess myself, I strode to the dresser and pulled out a drawer. Empty. A relieved sigh pushed from my chest. I tucked my "delicates," as my mother would call them, into one drawer and a couple of sweaters into another. I'd already spied hangers in the closet for my jeans and shirts. As I checked the rest of the drawers to assess space, I discovered a cache of old photo albums. Unable to resist, I pulled several out and moved to the bed. Sitting cross-legged, I laid the first one across my lap and gently opened it, careful with the aging book.

Pictures of my mother and Aunt Irene, obviously much younger, covered the page. Dad, not a gray hair on his head, smiled in several, and Uncle Paul made a few appearances, his arms always linked with or encircling Aunt Irene. Toward the end of the album, an infant showed up on the glossy squares, and I chuckled to realize the baby was me. I closed the album and chose another.

Aunt Irene stood serenely in a long white dress, a veil draping down her back. Their wedding. My grandparents stood with them, and Mom, about thirteen years younger than Irene, stood holding her flower-girl basket as if it made her a queen. Other pictures were filled with people I didn't know. Through every photo, Aunt Irene's adoring looks and Uncle Paul's need to constantly touch her, hold her hand, hug her, made it blatantly obvious how besotted they were with each other. I smiled a sappy smile at the happy couple in the photos.

Album after album held more pictures of Uncle Paul and Aunt Irene's life together. Trips, vacations, family gatherings with Mom, Dad, and me. Everything was chronicled, eventually to be hidden away in a drawer as if too precious to get rid of but too painful to display.

I opened the cover of a slightly newer album and gasped. Memorialized were moments from my own life. Tears began to flow unchecked as I flipped through pages that held my high school graduation announcement, a copy of a photo I'd sent Mom from the beach I'd taken while on my senior trip after graduation, birthday pictures Mom must have sent him, a photo of me with my first car, my college graduation announcement, and a photo of me holding my degree while still dressed in cap and gown. Toward the back, I found clippings of my arrest and the subsequent news stories that had followed my recent struggles. I closed the book, deeply touched that Uncle Paul would keep pictures of my life. My heart broke that there were none of him and me together.

I went to the bathroom, wiped my eyes on a tissue, and blew my nose before returning to pick up the last album.

This album was the newest of them all. Inside, I discovered pictures of Rita and Paul together at various functions interspersed with impromptu photos, some printed on regular paper, as if from a mobile phone.

So, Rita and Uncle Paul really used to be an item. If she knew him so well, maybe Rita knew more about Uncle Paul's death than she had revealed. What if she'd been the one who . . . I shook my head. I had to start trusting someone at some point. She'd been incredibly gracious to me, and I couldn't live the rest of my life looking for reasons to push people away.

My stomach rumbled, pulling my attention away from the past into the very immediate future. I hadn't considered cooking when I thought up my plan to live in the apartment. I walked out of the bedroom, startled to see how dark it was. I hadn't realized just how long I'd been in there looking at photos.

In the kitchen, I assessed the pantry and cupboards, locating appropriate cookware and dishes. While I had enough to eat for tonight, it didn't seem Uncle Paul had been much of a foodie. A few cans of Campbell's soup sat with cereal, coffee, chips, and bread. A trip to the grocery store was definitely in order.

As I spooned down bites of chicken noodle soup, I made a list of things I'd need over the next couple of weeks while I looked into Uncle Paul's murder.

Chapter Seven

I awoke the next morning, pulled out of a sweet dream of playing with the Cheshire Cat while drinking scorching tea out of lavender mugs. As my brain registered the ringing was actually a phone and not a signal that the Red Queen was coming, I fumbled on my nightstand for the offending instrument. "Hello?"

"Good morning," came Horace Grimes's cheerful tones through the line. "I hope I didn't wake you."

I looked at the time on my phone. Eight thirty. I sat up, realizing I'd slept a lot later than I'd intended. Darn this windowless room. But then again, what did I have to get up early for? "No, I'm awake. What's up?" I ran my fingers through tangled waves of hair, brushing it away from my face.

"I took the liberty of setting up an appointment for you to meet with someone from Jergins and Associates to go over the property. By reputation, they are the best appraisers in the area, and they're also a realty company. They've been in Hokes Folly for years and might know of a few possible buyers. Someone will meet with you this afternoon at one. I hope that's convenient."

I mentally checked my schedule. Nope, I was free. "That would be fine. I don't have too much planned for this afternoon."

"Fantastic. They'll help you figure out what the store and loft are truly worth and might be able to advise you on ways to fix it up and increase the value if you choose to have them list it for you."

"Kind of a one-stop-shopping thing, is it?" I chuckled.

"I guess you could put it that way. I did ask them to meet you in the loft, to make it more convenient for you." The sound of shuffling papers came over the line. "I also suggest you take time today to go by the power, water, gas, and cable companies to move the accounts into your name. I've already paved the way for you. I took the liberty to provide each of them with a copy of Paul's death certificate and proof you're the new owner. All you need to do is show up, show ID, and sign the paperwork."

After thanking him profusely and saying goodbye, I showered, dressed, and fixed a meager breakfast. While the coffee hit the spot, Uncle Paul's taste in cereal and mine were not the same. However, with enough sugar spooned into it, I could get through a bowl of plain Wheaties. At least I'd be more regular.

While I crunched, interspersed with sips of fresh coffee to fortify the workings of my frazzled brain, I made a grocery list. If I remembered correctly, I'd seen a small grocery store near the historic district, and once I'd cleaned up my breakfast dishes, I headed in that direction as fast as I could legally drive. I preferred not to give the local police another reason to hassle me yet.

I found the remembered store a few blocks away, and as I got out of my car, I noticed a group of people with clipboards milling around near the entrance. A blonde woman, her rather ample bust crammed into a too-small pink sweater, detached herself from the group and made a beeline for me. I rushed, almost breaking into a run in an attempt to get into the store, but it was useless.

"Sign the petition to get a new indoor shopping mall built in town?" The woman looked as if she couldn't imagine anyone saying no to her.

"I don't think so. I'm only visiting." I tried to sidestep the woman, practicing my best powder-puff football moves I'd used in high school.

"That doesn't matter." The woman was definitely fast on her feet, in spite of the pencil-thin high heels she wore below calf-length, black stretch pants, and she countered my dodge with one of her own, shoving the clipboard into my face again as she did so. "We don't care if you're from here or not. We need a bunch of signatures. You'll sign, won't you?" Her bright-red mouth stretched open to reveal perfectly whitened and straightened teeth.

I shook my head. "I'm sorry. I don't really know all the issues at stake. I would simply like to get a few groceries, if you don't mind." I made another play to skirt around the woman.

When she tried to shove the clipboard at me again, a man marched out through the doorway to my rescue. "You guys better get back. You know the law. City ordinance says fifteen feet from the door. You don't stay out of the way, I'll call the sheriff!" He grabbed my arm and pulled me past the frustrated petition taker and her friends, letting go once he had me safely inside.

"I'm sorry about that. They've been running off my customers all day. I'm about fed up." The man stood, arms crossed, staring daggers at the group gathered on the other side of the glass doors.

"Thanks for the rescue. Sorry to say, but I was about to give up and find another store myself. The only problem is, I don't know where any other grocery stores are." When he turned, I grinned at him.

He seemed to relax a bit and smiled. "You take your time. I'll help you past them when you're ready to go."

I thanked him, grabbed a cart, and started down the first aisle. At least I'd managed not to pick one with a squeaky wheel. If I was going to be here for any length of time, I might have to find another store with more variety, but for my immediate needs, this one seemed to have pretty much all I could want.

Loud voices interrupted my comparison of two pasta sauces, and I peeked around the end of the aisle and looked toward the checkout counter.

"I told you, Stan, I'm not interested." The grocer's hands rested on his hips, and his red face glared at the other man.

"I should have known better than to approach you." The newcomer pounded his fist on the counter. "After all, you were one of Paul Baxter's main supporters when he killed my deal last year."

My ears perked up. The newcomer's voice held a nasty tone when he said my uncle's name. I leaned out a bit, hoping to get a better look at him without making it obvious I was eavesdropping. Mentally I swatted away my Mom-conscience again.

"Yes, I was, and I still think the same way." The grocer looked ready to bodily throw the other man out the door.

"I figured, what with Paul dead and out of the way, you'd finally come to your senses and see the good things this project has to offer this backward little town." The man huffily hitched up his pants and turned to go. "I can see I was wrong. So long, Benny." He stormed out the door and into the crowd of petition takers, who had heeded Benny's warning to stay away from the door.

I ducked back down the aisle, hoping I hadn't been seen, and continued shopping, giving Benny time to cool off. I rounded the last aisle, relieved to see Benny smiling at me from behind the checkout counter. My determination to get justice for Uncle Paul and save my own skin once again overrode my mother's training. Slowly I placed my items on the belt and listened to the soft beeping as the register rang up the items Benny slid past the scanner. As my buggy emptied, I knew I had to get over my reluctance to be forward with my questions, or I might end up in jail for a murder I didn't commit.

"Does he always barge in here and yell at you like that?" I gestured over my shoulder toward the leader of the group of petitioners on the other side of the glass doors.

Benny shrugged. "He's just the pushy sort. He wants what he wants, and what anyone else wants doesn't matter to him."

"So, what's this about a project you squashed?" I dug in my purse for a little of the cash I still had left.

Benny cocked his head and narrowed his eyes, apparently reluctant to answer what was indeed a rather nosy question from someone he didn't know at all.

"I'm sorry." I chuckled and tried to look sheepish. "My mom says I'm nosy. It's just that I'm thinking of moving here, and I want to make sure it's a safe place to live. That guy sounded like he was about to take your head off. Kind of scared me." I smiled and hoped he bought that load of crap.

Benny stared at me another long moment then nodded once. "Fair enough. Stan's harmless, I suppose, unless you're a part of the Hokes Folly Merchants Association. He had a project he wanted to move forward. The Merchants Association disagreed. One of our members spearheaded the efforts to stop the project. That member is now dead, and Stan thinks we should all now jump on his bandwagon."

"I take it that's not going to happen?" I zipped my purse and loaded a couple of my bags into the buggy.

"Not even close." Benny crossed his arms. "Especially if he runs around treating us all like mindless idiots that only disagreed with his project because Paul Baxter told us to."

I finished loading my bags into the buggy. "Sounds like a great guy." I chuckled, trying to lighten the mood.

Benny shrugged once more. "As I said, he's pretty much harmless. Just don't get in his way."

I nodded and headed for the door. The petition takers seemed engrossed in a group pep talk, and I crossed my fingers they'd stay that way until I could get to my car. I managed to avoid the buxom blonde, but I almost had to break into a run to do it, finally glad I'd developed at least one skill while learning to dodge persistent reporters.

When I got home, I lugged my purchases inside. After the third trip out to the parking lot, I had a slight idea why Uncle Paul hadn't stocked more in his pantry. I'd have to keep an eye on things and forestall another large trip.

When I'd put everything away, I fixed a quick lunch and was out the door on the way down to the store as soon as I'd cleaned up. As I walked out into the front room, I let the familiar sense of loss and sorrow wash over me. Giving myself these few minutes before the appraiser arrived would allow me time to gather my thoughts and rein in my galloping emotions before I ended up crying all over some poor agent.

Deep, calming breaths stilled my churning stomach as I approached the spiral stairs. The white lines still glared at me. Damn it. I had hoped they'd be gone already, not just for my own sanity but also to keep the appraiser from focusing on the fact that a man had been murdered in the store. I supposed it didn't matter, though. It wasn't like a real estate agent could keep from disclosing that little tidbit to any prospective buyers.

I glanced at my arm, where my watch face showed it was ten minutes to one. I snagged *Alice in Wonderland* off the counter where I'd left it the night before and tucked it under my arm for the trip back upstairs.

Promptly at one, a solid knock sounded on the door, and I credited it to my mother's training in how to be a proper southern hostess that I managed to keep my jaw from dropping at who stood on the walkway outside.

Chapter Eight

N ot only did the buxom petition taker from the grocery store stand there with an expectant smile on her face, but Stan, the man with whom Benny the grocer had argued with about my uncle, stood there as well. Had they followed me home? Man, these people must be desperate for signatures.

"I'm sorry, I'm still not interested in signing your petition." I stepped back to close the door.

A brown leather loafer stuck itself in my door before it could close. "I'm Stan Jergins. I own Jergins and Associates. I'm here to appraise the business and home for the purpose of a possible sale." He stuck a business card through the opening.

I took it and read it as I reopened the door, checking to make sure the face before me matched the picture on the business card. His graying, light-brown hair ruffled in the slight breeze, and his dress shirt sleeves, rolled up, exposed a tan that had the telltale hue of a spray-on. A large gold bracelet glinted in the sunshine. However, the slightly worn toes of his loafers, which peeked out from under his slacks, contradicted the well-off broker look he seemed to be pushing. Maybe he wasn't doing as well as Mr. Grimes suspected.

Behind him, the shapely blonde woman with whom I had played chase all but bounced on her toes in what seemed to be childish excitement. Surely he wasn't training her to be a professional appraiser or real estate agent.

This should prove to be an interesting couple of hours.

Warily, I looked for a clipboard, mentally preparing another no in case they tried again to get me to sign that petition. Thank God the woman didn't have it handy, and she seemed to be taking a back seat to Stan.

Holding out my hand, I stepped closer, speaking as his hand engulfed mine. "I'm Jenna Quinn. Mr. Grimes said you would be by. I'm sorry about the misunderstanding." What I hoped was a naïve and trustworthy smile crossed my face. I wanted Stan comfortable enough for me to get information from him without seeming like I was digging.

"I'm Stan, and this is Barbie. She wanted to come see the apartment. I hope you don't mind."

A chuckle burbled up, and I barely managed to choke it back as our hands dropped. *Barbie, indeed.* It fit. The fluffed-up blonde hair, the obviously artificially enhanced figure, the skintight clothing, and the incredibly high heels. She looked like the dolls I'd had as a child.

Barbie peeked out from behind Stan with a hopeful look on her artfully painted face.

I really didn't want the annoying woman in what was now my home, even if only for a short time, but I couldn't think of a polite way to refuse without risking irritating Stan. While I'd probably failed Mom recently with my prying into the grocer's conversation, not to mention Rita's past with Uncle Paul, at least she might be proud of how I handled this. Okay, maybe not the subterfuge, but definitely the manners. I kept the smile plastered to my face and nodded. "Of course I don't mind. Shall we get started?" I motioned them inside.

While mostly uneventful, the trip through the loft tested my willpower to obey Mom's etiquette training. More than once I had to resist an overwhelming urge to smack Barbie's hand away from tiny knickknacks on shelves and family photos tucked away in corners. It was all I could do not to order her out of my house after she made yet another derogatory comment about how disappointed she was that it wasn't bigger or that there weren't windows in the guest bedroom. I might also wish there were more windows, but it wasn't her place to voice it. She needed to keep her bright-red mouth shut.

Rather than start a catfight, I concentrated on my business with Stan, hoping to finish it before I gave in to the impulse to strangle Barbie. They received the full tour, and Stan seemed to be quite thorough with his assessments. He looked in each closet, took measurements, tapped on woodwork, snapped pictures of furniture—which would be sold with the loft, as I couldn't think of anything else to do with it—and checked the flow of water from each tap.

While he worked, I tried to come up with a reasonable way to bring up the argument I'd overheard at the grocery store. So much for willpower. I finally got my chance when Stan insisted we go down the spiral stairs to the store.

"Is that . . . ?" At last Barbie was at a loss for words, and she blanched at the sight of the body outline.

While the white lines still sent a chill up my spine, I was grateful it gave me the opportunity to find out why Stan Jergins hadn't liked my uncle. *Thank you, Elmer Peabody.* "Yes, that's where I found Uncle Paul's body." I did my best to avoid the lines as I hopped over the last few steps to the floor.

"I'm sorry for your loss." Stan's sad eyes and pitiful puppy look seemed about as sincere as his clipped words. But I had to hand it to him for the attempt. Obviously he wanted the sale, and if it meant offering condolences for a man he hated, he'd suck it up.

I mentally asked Uncle Paul's forgiveness for what I was about to say, especially since I was standing next to the spot where he died. "Thanks. I'm okay, really. I hadn't seen him in almost a decade. But it seemed everyone in town loved him." Crossing my fingers behind my back, I plastered what I hoped was an innocent expression on my face.

Stan gritted his teeth behind his attempt at a friendly smile. "Yes. Many loved him, although not all."

Bingo! "And you, Mr. Jergins? Did you love him, or were you on the 'not all' side?"

Stan shifted back and forth a couple of times, and he looked at his notepad and cleared his throat. His nostrils flared as he took a deep breath, and when he looked back up, his eyes held a fire that hadn't been there before. "Unfortunately, I must count myself in the 'not all' contingency."

I raised my eyebrows, trying to maintain the innocent look. "Why didn't you like him?"

"About a year ago, I put together a really sweet deal to build a shopping mall out by the interstate on the edge of town. It would've had ninety-five stores, complete with three huge department stores, a food court, and a parking garage. Your Uncle Paul and his friends managed to gather enough petition signatures from Hokes Folly residents to stop the whole deal dead in its tracks." His eyes held a manic expression, and his fists gripped his notepad so tightly they bent the cardboard backing.

I ignored the uneasy feeling roiling in my gut. I hoped he wasn't about to lose it completely while we were alone in the store, where no one could hear me scream, and I doubted Barbie would help me, but I couldn't stop now. I needed answers. "Why would he do that?"

"They whined about loss of property values in the neighborhood and loss of peace and quiet. And he got everyone from here in the historic district to sign too, because they thought it might take a few sales away from them." He faced me squarely now, as if he expected me to argue with him and was bracing for a possible fight. "He and everyone else should've thought about all those jobs in the stores, and there would've been security people, janitors, parking attendants." He ticked them off on his fingers. "All that new opportunity for employment might've really boosted the economy in this little town. But no." Stan's eyes hardened to flint. "Mr. High-and-Mighty Paul Baxter had to stop it before it could even get started."

I resisted the urge to step back while I wiped a bit of spittle off my arm that had flown out of his mouth during his tirade. "Is that what your current petition is about?"

"It is." He cracked his first big smile, but there was something a bit off about it. "I was already wining and dining my way into this deal with a new group of backers when Paul . . . met with his unfortunate end." Stan had the grace to attempt another solemn look.

Barbie chose this moment to rejoin the conversation, seeming to forget the white outline while grinning hugely at Stan. "Without Paul around to organize another petition to stop progress, Stan's big, beautiful mall is practically a done deal. Right, baby?"

Stan's grin was almost predatory. "That's right. With your uncle gone, I'm already getting more support for the venture." He pulled Barbie to him and gave her a side squeeze.

Sure, Stan creeped me out with his freakish rant, but I could understand his point. I could also see the point of the townsfolk. A mall like the one Stan proposed really would take away from the quaint charm I'd seen in Hokes Folly.

55

Would it bring more jobs? Absolutely. It might even help the town grow. But it would also bring more crime, as was always the case when a town grew too quickly. As for the sales in the historic district, those would suffer too. Rainy days would be spent at the new mall rather than in the historic district. New shops would abound, running out the tiny stores that had been there for decades. It was a matter of choosing what was more important: growth and modernization or staying true to the historic significance and turn-of-the-century styling.

Hoping to end the conversation without another unsettling lecture, I smacked on another fake smile. "I'm sure things will work out as they should." Then I changed subjects. "Shall we check out the rest of the store? As with the furniture upstairs, the fixtures and books will sell with the store, but a few decor items and all personal papers will go with me."

We walked through the store, cataloging things to stay and checking off things that might need repair before the sale. But my mind wasn't fully on the task. How much had Stan really hated Uncle Paul? I shuddered, pushing away disturbing thoughts while still stuck with the man. Finish up, usher them out, lock the doors. That was the new plan.

I breathed an inward sigh of relief when we finally moved to the front door. Stan added a few suggestions to increase curb appeal and promised to send me a copy of his list.

I thanked him, sagging against the door gratefully as they walked away. I stood there for a bit, needing a few moments to calm myself. Mr. Grimes believed the police were considering murder instead of an accidental death. At this point I was heavily leaning in that direction too, and I needed to find out who had killed Uncle Paul before I ended up with another murder hung around my neck. I assessed my conversation with Stan in the store and wondered how badly he had wanted Uncle Paul out of the way. Enough to kill? I shook my head.

With a list of service providers to visit, I jumped Uncle Paul's outline again and went upstairs to grab my purse and keys to head toward the first address on my list.

After two hours, I'd visited all the companies and signed all the paperwork. I then took an extra hour to explore the town. I found two larger grocery stores, although Benny's place was still more convenient, and located the library, post office, and a couple of dry cleaners.

By the time I got home, the sun was setting, and my stomach was rumbling. I pulled out a couple of cans of stew and set them on the stove to heat. My second supper here. Alone. I winced, remembering my promise to myself to start trusting more. When the stew was ready, I marched out the door and strode purposefully toward my neighbor's home, trying to remember if it was an olive branch of peace I should bring. Or maybe it was the pineapple of hospitality. Whatever. She was getting the stew of I'm-sick-of-eating-alone. I took a deep breath and rapped on her door.

Rita opened the door and smiled. "Come on in, neighbor."

I held my ground, my stomach churning as if I were asking someone out on a hot date. Gads, I needed to get out more. "I came to see if you wanted to join me for supper. I heated up vegetable stew, and I'd prefer not to eat alone." There. I'd thrown out the offer. Sadly, I realized it was true. I really didn't want to eat alone. I'd spent so many days and nights alone, hiding from reporters or worse, and I was sick and tired of always being by myself. "I'm not the best cook, but there's plenty."

"Sure." Rita smiled. "Let me grab something."

In a few moments she appeared, carrying a bottle of white wine, and followed me to my apartment and the waiting meal.

Once inside, she pulled out two wine goblets and a corkscrew, demonstrating her familiarity with Uncle Paul's kitchen as well as the fact that Uncle Paul never changed anything around. She poured the wine, I set the table, and we both sat.

I ladled stew into my bowl. "So, I met Stan Jergins today."

Rita shook her head and reached for the ladle. "That must have been fun." Sarcasm laced her voice.

I needed to bounce my ideas off someone who knew the people in town. I was too new to judge any of this. Rita wiped the edge of her bowl where she'd spilled a bit of stew on it, and I thought of her compassionate acceptance of me in spite of the evidence. If I was going to trust someone, it would definitely be her.

"I decided to do a bit of investigating of my own into Uncle Paul's death. The news said the police have a strong reason to think it's murder, and they implied as much when they interviewed me after I found his body." I spooned a bit of stew into my mouth.

"And you're worried because they implied you're a suspect?"

"You bet your backside I am." I took a deep breath. "After all I went through in Charlotte, I just can't assume the police will get it right. They're already determined to find a way to pin it on me."

Rita set her spoon down and reached for my hand, giving my fingers a gentle squeeze. "The police here tend to eventually get it right, for the most part, but I can understand where you're coming from. I'm in. How can I help?"

I released the tension in my shoulders, tension I hadn't even realized was there until Rita once again jumped to my defense, this time offering to help without me having to ask.

"To start, you can help me understand a couple of conversations I had today."

Over dinner, I filled her in on the argument I'd overheard at the grocery store and about my chat with Stan while he and Barbie were here. "He really seems to have hated Uncle Paul."

Rita inched her empty bowl away and leaned her arms on the table. "There's more to that story than meets the eye."

"Such as?" I was almost afraid to ask, but I'd already come this far. I had to know.

"There was bad blood between the two of them long before the mall deal came up. Years ago, Stan tried to woo Irene away from Paul." Rita sipped her wine.

"Are you serious?" No way would Aunt Irene cheat on Uncle Paul, especially with a slick jerk like Stan Jergins. From what I could remember and what I'd been told, Aunt Irene and Uncle Paul had been crazy about each other. "What happened?"

"Irene worked for Stan at the real estate office for a while when she and Paul first moved here. She wanted to make extra money to keep the bookstore business going until it could stand on its own. Since she always looked and acted much younger than she was, Stan flirted with her outrageously. He took her out to lunch, brought her flowers from his garden for doing 'such a good job,' and gave her bonuses he didn't give to other employees. He even baked her a cake for her birthday. Irene naïvely chalked it up to Stan being nice."

"Mom always said Irene only wanted to see the best in everyone." I knew firsthand how badly this could turn out. My gullible days were over. I hoped.

Rita sipped her wine again, swirling the remainder in the glass as she shared the story. "Well, one day Stan told Irene he needed her to work late at the office to help him close a big deal. After everyone else had gone, he trapped her in the copy room and tried to kiss her. He groped her a bit too. Irene managed to sock him one in the jaw. She hit him so hard, it cracked a tooth."

"Oh my God!" Laughter bubbled up. A vision of a young and cocky Stan nursing a broken tooth given by an irate older woman popped into my head. After all I'd been through with the man today, I rather liked that mental picture. Too bad I hadn't been there to see it in person.

"Old Stan had to get his tooth capped. Cost him a bundle. And Irene quit working for him. Paul finally got out of her what had happened, and he went to see Stan. He told Stan to stay away from his wife or he'd kill him. The two men came to actual blows over the incident."

"Who won?" I thought of the man who should have stood up for me against everyone in Charlotte. Seeing some butt kicking definitely held appeal, but he'd never been the physical type. Turned out he wasn't the "stand-up" type in any fashion. I pulled myself back to the present as Rita answered my question.

"Paul whipped him good, and Stan, who was twenty-nine at the time, couldn't get over being beaten by a man in his late forties. And that was after he'd had a tooth cracked by a woman fourteen years older than he was. It was too much for poor Stan's overinflated ego. He never forgave the two of them for what he considered a grave injustice, and when the mall thing came up, he couldn't get past the idea that Paul only went against him on the issue to be spiteful."

"Wow. I still can't believe it." I shook my head. "But at least I understand the hate and bitterness now."

"Oh, Stan hated him all right. Probably still does, and probably always will."

"The question is, did Stan hate Uncle Paul enough to kill him?" I'd been chewing on that for hours.

"I don't know. Maybe. If he was provoked enough. Stan's got quite a temper. If he thought Paul was in his way again, he actually might have."

Chapter Nine

I took deep, slow breaths to keep the anger at bay. Sitting on my couch, I gripped my hands tightly in my lap to stop myself from jumping to my feet and waving my arms around like a maniac in frustration. Police presence in my home had disrupted the early hours of my morning. I hadn't even had time to get dressed, so I sat in my old knit pajamas and a fuzzy robe, the only night garments I'd kept after tossing out all the sexy silk things my ex had insisted I buy. It was hard to be dignified with fuzzy Cookie Monster slippers on your feet, but I would be damned if Sutter would sit in my living room and treat me like a criminal.

"And you're sure you don't know who might have broken into the store in the night." Sarcasm dripped from the seemingly affirming statement.

"As you already know, Detective Sutter, I've only been in town for four and a half days. How could I possibly know who'd want to break into a store I'd never seen before then?" Inhale. Exhale. Inhale. Exhale.

Rita, who had rushed over the moment she noticed a police car outside, walked over from the kitchen area with a fresh pot of coffee and four mugs. "Do you think it's connected with Paul's death?"

"We're not at liberty to say." Detective Frank Sutter referred to his tiny notebook, turning the pages with fleshy fingers.

"Well, it's a good thing Gladys Washburn comes in at six AM to clean, or the front door would have stood open for several more hours before Jenna found out." Rita placed a steaming mug on the coffee table in front of me, giving me an odd look.

I smiled weakly at her, shoving aside my anger at feeling railroaded again. Inhale. Exhale. I turned back to the detective. "Since you wouldn't let me into the store, I have to ask, did anything seem damaged?"

Detective Logan spoke, his gentle tone calming my nerves. "As you know, Mrs. Washburn walked through the store with us. Since she's been cleaning it for so many years, she probably has a better idea than anybody what's in there. She didn't see anything missing, only thrown around, as if someone was searching for something. Do you know what that might be?"

I gratefully wrapped my fingers around the warm mug, racking my brain over every little thing I knew about Uncle Paul. "No, I honestly have no idea."

Detective Sutter glared at me, and I shuddered. His calculating gaze sent a chill down my spine.

After a brief silence, he changed his line of questioning. "Had you had any recent contact with Mr. Baxter before arriving in town?"

"I hadn't seen him since I was a teenager." I shifted, trying to find a more relaxed pose. "We did exchange rare emails, and he had recently emailed an invitation for me to come stay with him for a few weeks while I got my feet back under me."

Grunt. His eyes narrowed. "Did he send you anything in the mail lately?"

"No, he did not." I locked eyes with him, determined not to let him think I was intimidated. Two could play the shock game. "Does this have anything to do with Uncle Paul's murder?"

Sutter's graying, bushy eyebrows went up a notch, and he shot a quick glance at his partner before answering. "So, you're admitting it was murder now?"

"Frank Sutter, have you always been a jackwagon, or did you study it in police school?" Rita plopped a mug of coffee down in front of him, sloshing a bit over the sides. "Jenna's the victim here, so stop treating her like she's the one who committed a crime."

I shot Rita a quick glance, catching the tiny wink she shot me. This woman who barely knew me had stood up for me. It was all I could do to stifle the smile.

Sutter glared, this time at Rita, picked up his mug, and took a swig of coffee.

I held back a smirk when Sutter grimaced as if he'd burned his tongue. This was my home now, and the morning's events had nothing to do with what had happened in Charlotte. If anyone was going to be digging for information, it would be me. "I'd like to know exactly why you think it was murder."

Detective Logan answered. "According to the coroner, Paul died around seven PM, and we found a sleeping medication in his bloodstream—"

"Paul would never have taken sleeping pills." Rita handed Detective Logan a mug of coffee. "He was too much of a health nut. He hated over-the-counter drugs and felt prescriptions were overprescribed. There's no way he willingly took sleeping medications."

"Yes, ma'am. We think that too. Several people have the same opinion as you do. But we need more to go on than opinion."

Detective Logan's open honesty was refreshing after the subtle jabs his partner had thrown.

Sutter gave him an "I'm in charge" glare over the rim of his coffee mug.

Logan clenched his jaw and closed his eyes. The fire in them had died down when he opened them again.

"It was what we didn't find that made us consider he may have been given the medications without his knowledge: a pill bottle," said Sutter.

"See." Rita interrupted for the second time. "I told you. Paul was a night owl. He loved staying up late. He would never have tried to go to bed that early."

I nodded. "His email said he was usually up until midnight and if I came in later to use the hidden key and not wake him." The thought washed through my brain that I'd spent the night in a house with a dead body in the store below. I shuddered.

"That strengthens our case." Logan made a note in his own little book.

"Against me?" I stared directly at Sutter, mentally pinning him to his seat. Might as well get it out in the open.

A slow, menacing smile spread across Sutter's round face. "Care to share your sleeping pill prescription number with us? It would save us a lot of time."

I matched his slow smile, which seemed to unnerve him, as his own slipped from his face at my answer. "I do not now have, nor have I ever had, a sleeping pill prescription. Are you basing everything on the medications in his bloodstream?" Surely they had more to go on than that. But then, what did I know? I'd seen how the police sometimes jumped to the easy solution and didn't look further. It didn't always happen like it did on TV.

"Not completely." Logan snapped his book shut. "We have other loose ends to tie up, but we aren't at liberty to divulge that information at this time."

I looked over at Rita, who rolled her eyes. Were all cops taught this phrase in police training as a polite way to say "none of your business"?

The two detectives looked at each other for a few seconds before Sutter spoke. "We'd like to discuss an argument the cleaning lady overheard on the day of Mr. Baxter's death."

"Oh?" What could I add to an eyewitness account of an incident that happened before I came to town?

"Yes. She says she heard Mr. Baxter arguing with a man who had come to see him that morning before the store opened." Sutter again consulted his little notebook. "According to her account, Baxter let the man in and they went into the back room while she was there cleaning the store. She says she couldn't hear what they argued about, but she could tell they were pretty fired up about something. Do you have any idea who the man your uncle argued with might be?" The detective leaned forward, his pencil poised to take notes.

"No, sir. I don't. The argument happened before I arrived, and since Uncle Paul was already dead by then, he couldn't tell me either." I looked to Rita. "Can you think of anyone?"

Rita's brow wrinkled, and she shook her head. "I can't think of anyone off the top of my head . . . unless . . . well . . . Stan Jergins has had a long-term beef with Paul."

"Stan Jergins?" Logan flipped to a new page in his book and made a note.

"Yes," Rita explained. "Stan's a real estate agent who constantly battled with Paul over the possible building of a large shopping mall. Stan wanted to set up the deal, and Paul kept organizing the townsfolk to squash it. Stan was getting ready to rev up his building proposals again, and it seems mighty handy that Paul is conveniently out of the way now."

"Thank you, Miss Wallace. We appreciate the information." Sutter glanced at his notebook once more. "If there's nothing further either of you might add . . ."

I tried to think of anything else I could pry out of them and came up empty. Ready to have the conversation over, I stated, "No, not anything we can think of." I looked at Rita, who shook her head.

Sutter continued to regard his notebook. "Interesting." He leaned back, reached into his inside jacket pocket, and withdrew a folded paper. Slowly he unfolded it. A small green square was stapled to the upper corner. "We found this letter in Baxter's email."

I reached for it, but Sutter moved it to his other hand and began to read.

"'Jenna, I know we haven't been in contact much over the last few years, but I've heard you might need a place to land for a while until you get your feet under you again. I would love to have you stay with me. You would be welcome here for as long as you needed. I have plenty of room, so you would have your privacy. While you're here, you can help me with a little mystery I've run across. It's quite exciting and will be major news if it turns out the way I think it will. I could use your help to work through it all. I hope to hear from you soon. Love, Uncle Paul.'" Sutter extended the page toward me. "Care to explain what little mystery he was talking about?"

As I accepted the page, tears threatened to overwhelm me. I sucked in a breath, determined to retain at least some semblance of composure. "Detective, this is the email he sent, offering me a place to stay. However, we never had the opportunity to discuss what mystery he meant."

"Oh?" Sutter grunted and crossed his arms. "I think you might have come, found out what the big mystery was, and decided your uncle was in the way."

"Oh for God's sake, Frank. Enough." Rita slapped her hand down on the arm of the couch and stood. "She's told you she doesn't know. You have nothing to prove she ever had a conversation with Paul about his mystery, whatever it was, and you have nothing showing she came earlier that evening and killed him, or you'd have arrested her by now. You're not going to sit here and browbeat her about the whole mess."

Detective Logan rose, gesturing to his partner, who hefted himself to his feet. "You're absolutely correct, Ms. Wallace." He turned and nodded at me.

I rose, anger and sadness still warring in my heart. "I'm more than happy to help in any way I can. I'd like to see justice for my uncle."

"If you think of anything else, please call me at this number, day or night." Detective Logan handed Rita and me each a business card with his contact information. "And thanks to both of you for all your help."

I took a step forward, wrapping my robe more snugly closed and tightening its belt, since I didn't even have a bra on yet and wasn't exactly under-blessed. "Detective Logan." What was I doing? They were leaving. *Don't call them back.*

"Yes?" He turned and looked at me.

"Aren't you forgetting something?" At his questioning look, I continued. "My store? The one that was broken into?"

"Oh yes." He cleared his throat. "We'll keep you informed of our progress to apprehend the perpetrator or perpetrators of this crime. In the meantime, we've taken down all we need to downstairs, and you're free to enter the premises. And once again, thank you for your help on this matter."

After the men left, Rita wrapped an arm around my shoulders and gave me a quick squeeze. "Don't let Frank get to you. He treats everyone that way. I think his motto is 'Guilty until proven innocent,' even when he has no idea what someone might be guilty of. In his book, everyone is guilty of something."

A shudder washed over me, and my knees threatened to buckle as fear replaced the angry bravado. "I think a lot of cops have that attitude." I opened my eyes and caught Rita's questioning look. "If we don't figure out what really happened to Uncle Paul, history could repeat itself, and I could end up in jail again."

Rita nodded, and we gathered the coffee things and took them to the kitchen. Silently Rita returned the half-full coffeepot to its base while I rinsed the cups and placed them in the dishwasher.

Finally, I had to ask. "Rita, why didn't you bring up the Aunt Irene angle of Stan's vendetta with Uncle Paul?"

She turned and leaned on the counter. "Honey, if Stan killed Paul, it was over that real estate deal. I thought about our talk for a long time last night before bed. I really think he could've done it."

"The police will probably check to see if Stan had a prescription for sleeping medications or if he had access to them. Maybe they'll put him in a lineup for the cleaning lady to see if she recognizes him. He could be the man she saw Uncle Paul let into the store that day." I washed the last dish and set it in the dish rack, pulling the sink plug with my other hand and visualizing my stress rushing down the drain with the dirty water. It didn't help.

"As many ads as he splashes around town, I can't believe she wouldn't know his face," Rita said.

Drying my hands on a dish towel, I turned to face Rita. "Thank you for not dragging Aunt Irene's and Uncle Paul's memories through the mud." I hopped up to sit on the kitchen counter, letting my legs swing.

"I would never do that. Without them here to defend themselves, there's no telling what the gossips would do. Everyone loved Paul and Irene, but you never know what folks will say to get attention." Rita flashed a playful grin. "Besides, I wouldn't want to make the new neighbor mad at me after knowing her less than two days."

I chuckled, trying to let go of the tension still knotted in my stomach. "Well, it seems I've got a lot to do today, so I guess I'd better get going." I hopped off the counter and walked to the bedroom to get my keys.

Rita followed. "It's early yet. What's on your agenda for the rest of the day?"

"First, I need to go check the store. If there's damage, I need to get someone out to repair things. Then I'll start wading through some of the mess." I wasn't looking forward to all the work, but it would be a wonderful distraction for a while. And I was eager to get everything in place so the store would look its best. Whether I sold it or kept it, it had to be done.

"Want some company?"

"If you have the time, I'd love some." I smiled, happy not to face the mess alone.

"I have the day off, and I might as well accomplish something. Besides, it might be fun. You never know what we might find in all those piles. Maybe even something worth killing for."

Chapter Ten

Once properly dressed, I met Rita downstairs, and we walked through the disarray. My heart sank at the mess. The store hadn't been neat and tidy to begin with, but now it looked like a tornado had swept through it. Books had been pulled off the shelves, items had been scattered behind the counter, and even the plastic bags had been tossed across the floor. On top of that, the front door, counter, cash register, and coffee station were covered in black fingerprint dust. And Elmer Peabody still hadn't come to remove the white lines.

I called a locksmith to come fix the broken front-door lock, grateful that whoever broke in hadn't smashed the glass. Next, I used the phone number I'd gotten from Horace Grimes and called Gladys Washburn, asking her to come help clean up and offering to pay overtime if needed.

When she arrived, the three of us went to work, cleaning, wiping down, vacuuming, and, thanks to Gladys, removing the white tape from the stairs and scouring the floor and stairs in the general area where the body had been found. She would definitely get a nice Christmas bonus this year.

I was thrilled when the cleaning portion of the day was completed before ten AM and Gladys was able to go to her next client's home, after we'd hugged and cried together a moment and I'd promised her she would still come clean for me once a week. We walked out with her as she left, and I took the opportunity to step back and look at the store from the front for the first time, getting a customer's view of my new, albeit possibly short-lived, business. Plus, it was a handy excuse to avoid the even bigger job of straightening and organizing the store after many of the books had been tossed around willy-nilly.

A plain sign proudly hung over the door bearing the words Baxter's Book Emporium in bold, black lettering. *Way to be creative, Uncle Paul.* I shook my head. A name change was definitely in order. If I stayed.

The phone jangled from inside, and we hurried back inside to the sound of tinkling bells over the door. I rushed to answer the call, hoping it would be my first real customer. Remembering the sign outside, I answered cheerfully, "Baxter's Book Emporium."

"Are you happy with your sales? Would you like to increase your daily profit? Well, we at Book Distributors of America would like to offer you—"

A telemarketer? Really? I interrupted the salesman before he could get too far into his spiel. "I'm sorry, but I'm not interested right now." Over the top of his second attempt at stating his case, I hung up and let my gaze scan the room, once again taking in the utter chaos. "Any idea where to start?"

"I don't think it'll make any difference." Rita chuckled. "But as my grandmother used to say, 'Rita Sue, there won't be no gettin' to the end if you don't make no beginnin'.'"

"Rita Sue?"

"Don't knock it. It's my name." Rita grinned.

"Seriously?" At her pursed lips and narrowed eyes, I sobered. "Well, it fit perfectly with that southern accent you were faking."

"Who says the accent was fake?"

Good Lord, now I was insulting her. "You don't have a southern accent now."

"Honey, let me tell you somethin' about myself." Rita slipped back into her southern drawl. "I grew up in a li'l ol' town in Georgia. My whole family speaks with this here accent."

"Why did you learn not to use it?" As I asked, I moved to the coffee station and opened the cabinet beneath it, hoping to find coffee-making supplies. Maybe if I had coffee in my mouth, I wouldn't put my foot in it so much.

Rita's accent disappeared. "After I graduated from cosmetology school—" She held up her hand to forestall my interruption. "I know, I know, a very stereotypical thing for a southern girl from a small country town to do."

"I wasn't going to say that." Under her glare, I winced. *Okay, so maybe I was.* I pulled out a stack of filters and fitted one into the coffeemaker, but there had been no coffee with them. "I was going to say it was interesting that you found your vocation so young in life." A weak claim, but it would have to do. "Come on, I need coffee. Let's look in the back to see if we can find some."

"Mm-hmm." Rita shot me a look that said she didn't believe me, but she followed me down an aisle to the jumbled back room.

"So, what came next?" I looked into cabinets and under counters. There had to be coffee somewhere!

"As I was saying, after I graduated, I went out to Hollywood, determined to make a name for myself and a fortune to boot. One of the first things I learned was the country bumpkin thing didn't go over well out there. So, I sort of remade myself. I gave myself a makeover, saved my pennies and replaced my wardrobe, and managed to get an interview with a Hollywood makeup artist. I got the job, and the rest is history."

"Just like that?" I turned to stare at her. "You make it sound so easy to up and change your whole way of life." I didn't think I'd ever feel like I'd changed enough to get past what had happened in Charlotte.

She chuckled. "Oh honey, let me tell you, it was anything but easy. I made a lot of mistakes, but eventually I got my foot in the door with a couple of well-known professionals."

"Did you stay with the same artist the whole time?" I returned to my search for coffee.

"Yes, but eventually the glamour wore off, and the stress of Hollywood got old." Rita riffled through the desk drawers. "A few years ago, when I heard about a job at the Hokes Bluff Inn, I jumped at it. And here I am." She raised a can of Folgers in her hand like it was the World Cup. "Found it!"

"Thank God." I followed her this time as we headed back to the coffeemaker. "What does a makeup artist do at a hotel?"

"Haven't you heard about the Hokes Bluff Inn?" Rita glanced over her shoulder at me.

"No. What's so special about it?" So it was a fancy hotel. It couldn't be that big a deal.

"And you a native of the lovely state of North Carolina. Shame on you for not knowing about your own historical landmarks." Rita turned and shook her finger in mock sternness.

"Oh, and you can tell me all of the historical landmarks in Georgia?" I gave her what I hoped was a withering look. I apparently failed.

Rita saucily waved aside her own shortcoming. "No, but that's beside the point. If you've not heard of the Hokes Bluff Inn, you're in for a treat. This is definitely history with some personality. It's also the reason for the town's name. You'll love this."

Armed with fresh coffee, we began sorting stacks of books, separating them by category, while Rita told the colorful story of the town of Hokes Folly.

Chapter Eleven

B efore I let her start her story, I created a store section plan for each type of book, so we wouldn't start out by simply moving books from one random pile to the other. We moved to the front corner, armed with a few empty cardboard boxes I'd found and labeled with things like Cookbooks, Romance, and Self-Help, and sat amid the clutter.

"Are you familiar with the Vanderbilt family?" Rita asked.

I searched my memory. "As in Vanderbilt University in Tennessee?"

"Yep, that's the one. In the late 1800s, Cornelius Vanderbilt donated a million dollars, and they renamed the college after him."

"What does Vanderbilt University have to do with your inn?" I sipped my coffee and hoped this story would make the time pass more quickly while we pawed through scattered piles of books.

"Cornelius had a son, George Washington Vanderbilt. The Vanderbilt family built several large, expensively gorgeous estates. One of those estates, the one George built, is here in North Carolina."

"I know. I've always wanted to visit Biltmore in Asheville, but I've never managed to find the time." And once I'd had the time, fun vacation junkets had no longer been an option. "I've heard it's absolutely fantastic."

"Make time. It's worth it. Biltmore had every possible amenity for the times. And then some. George wanted to build a completely self-sustaining estate like the ones in Europe, and he succeeded."

"Cool." I added a trip to Biltmore to my checklist of things to do. "But what does this have to do with Hokes Folly?"

Rita grabbed a small pile of books from the floor and separated them into the boxes, but her eyes sparkled as if she was truly enjoying telling her story. "I've always loved the history of Hokes Folly, and I'm tickled to have a captive audience."

"It's not like I have anywhere else to be right now." I grinned and moved to the next pile of books.

"Very true." Rita handed me a cookbook to stick into the box next to me. "John Jacob Hokes inherited a large sum of money in the spring of 1895 at the age of thirty-one. An uncle, whose only son had died as a child from a bad case of strep throat, passed away and left it all to dear John as his brother's oldest son. Good old Uncle Barton Hokes had made his fortune the same way the Vanderbilt family had—in shipping and railroading."

"Wait, Hokes. As in Olivia Hokes?" I cringed at the memory of the rude woman.

Rita chuckled. "I take it you've met one of our 'town treasures.'"

I nodded. "Not a memory I relish."

She handed me another cookbook. "John was their great-great-great-uncle. And he'd inherited scads of cash. This was wonderful, except for one thing. He had no head for handling money. All of his life, whenever he'd gotten ahold of some, he squandered it on poor investments or gambling. So, when he inherited this fortune, he decided to hire a financial adviser and a solicitor."

"Things were great for a while. John was invited to some of the best parties and was on the guest list for certain balls where eligible daughters were trotted out by mothers hoping to rebuild family finances through marriage to money, in spite of the fact that it was, after all, only inherited business money. But there were still some things John wasn't considered 'good enough' for. As a result, he went through life with a chip on his shoulder, always expecting the worst from society."

I jumped in, wanting to know how the hotel played in. "And he moved here, and they named the town after him?"

"Stop rushing my story. I don't get to tell this very often. Let me enjoy it."

"Okay, okay." I held up my hands in mock surrender before grabbing another handful of books to sort. At least the story was keeping me from thinking about my own issues for a while.

"When George Vanderbilt opened Biltmore on Christmas Eve, 1895, he threw a ritzy party for his family and friends, and John Hokes didn't get an invitation. Feeling left out again, John set out to prove he was as good and as smart as any of them. It wasn't until years later that it came out that John had been on the invitation list but his was unfortunately lost in the mail."

"Too bad our dear old postal service hasn't improved much over the years," I grumbled under my breath.

"So very true." Rita shook her head. "Well, due to this particular error, John decided to one-up Vanderbilt. He planned an estate to rival Biltmore. He went about sixty miles from what is now Asheville and made sure his elevation was a bit higher than Vanderbilt's. He chose an architect and a landscaper who could create a style to outshine Biltmore's, and by late 1896, the work had begun. John's house would have all that his perceived rival's had, and then some. It would have three hundred rooms instead of only two hundred fifty, two indoor swimming pools instead of only one—one for ladies and one for men so anyone could swim at any hour—a larger staff to better serve the guests, larger gardens, a larger conservatory with plants even more exotic . . . well, you get the picture."

"Yep." I sang a few bars of "Anything You Can Do, I Can Do Better."

"Exactly." Rita shifted down the row, working only on the books piled in the floor space for now. "The construction went well. The house took shape, one slow piece at a time. Until 1901, when John's financial adviser made some very bad investments and lost John's fortune in a matter of months. The house was only about eighty percent built. The grounds were still a mess, since the landscaping was supposed to be finished in the last year of construction."

"How awful for him." I knew exactly how it felt to have every hope and dream snatched away in an instant.

"It was, in more ways than one. He'd insisted they complete the gardener's cottage so he could live on the estate during the actual building process." She handed me yet another cookbook, which topped off the cookbook box.

As I took the box to the proposed cookbook area and emptied it, I raised my voice to answer. "At least he had a place to stay and wasn't out on the street with nowhere to go." I thought of my own recent past and shuddered.

"Yes, but there was the problem. It also allowed him to spend long hours looking through his windows at the great hulking monstrosity of unfinished work that was supposed to have been his shining achievement."

"What a waste of a lifetime." I strode back down the aisle and sat again.

"Oh, it gets better. The town that had sprung up on the estate with folks there to build and maintain the house and grounds continued to prosper. The estate was originally named Hokes Bluff, and the town was called Hokes Bluff Village. However, when the lord of the manor went financially belly-up, the town renamed itself Hokes Folly."

When Rita held out three more cookbooks, I simply handed her the cookbook box for her to fill. "You mean the town is named after someone's failure?" That was wrong on so many levels.

"You got it, babe." Rita shifted down the aisle.

"That's horrible." I shook my head. "What happened to him?"

Rita settled herself by another stack of books and began sorting. "The locals got used to seeing him mumble to himself as he walked the streets, running his errands. He babbled to everyone about how he would one day reclaim his fortune and finish the building of the estate. They all figured he'd become delusional or just plain senile. They made fun of him, played jokes and pranks on him, and it was said some parents even used him as an example to their kids of what would happen if they didn't eat their veggies, go to bed, get good grades, or do what their parents said."

"You've got to be kidding." I thought about the frustrated old man desperately clinging to his lifelong dream, and I found myself rooting for him.

"Sadly, I'm dead-level serious. As the Great Depression took hold of the town, the young and able left to find work, and the town began to die. In 1934, at the age of seventy, John Hokes finally passed away, never having achieved his dream of finishing Hokes Bluff. Upon his death, the government seized the unfinished manor and land in payment for back taxes."

"There was nothing left for an inheritance of any kind so someone else could try to finish his work?"

"Nothing at all. Although there was John's nephew, Olivia and Ophelia Hokes's great-grandfather."

"I haven't met Ophelia yet, but if she's anything like Olivia, I can wait." I had no desire to be scrutinized again.

"The Hokes sisters are definitely unique. Their great-grandfather petitioned the government about the manor and land. He wanted to retain ownership of the estate and proposed a way to pay off his uncle's debt, but the government refused. He was furious, but there was nothing he could do about it. That little tidbit of history has always stuck in Olivia Hokes's craw. If her great-grandfather had been able to gain control of the estate, she and her sister would probably be extremely rich women right now."

"I didn't get the impression they were financially struggling." The vintage dress Olivia had worn to the lawyer's office was worth a small fortune in the right market.

"They do have quite a nest egg." Rita leaned back against the shelves and took a sip of what had to be cold coffee by now. "But they don't have nearly what they might've if they'd been the ones in control of the estate."

"And where does the inn come in?" I stood, picked up a full box of mystery books, and emptied it two aisles over in the appropriate new section.

"In 1997, a major hotel conglomerate bought the estate and one thousand of the surrounding acres from the government for a song. They completed the manor, using its original plans and landscaping. This took two years. In the fall of '99, Hokes Bluff Inn opened its doors to the paying public. This boosted the economy as tourists poured dollars into the town, shopping in the historic downtown shops. Restaurants popped up almost overnight, as did bed-and-breakfasts and gas stations and a bunch of other service-oriented businesses. And now Hokes Folly is the booming metropolis you see today." Rita spread her hands as if to encompass the town as I walked back through the piles to where she sat.

"That's great, but you still haven't gotten around to explaining how being a makeup artist landed you a job at the hotel in the first place."

"Oh, yeah." Rita brushed dust off her hands and arched her back to stretch. "I almost forgot you asked. This is the best part. The Hokes Bluff Inn is a five-star facility. But there's a twist that makes it a must-do for the rich and famous. When you arrive, you have to park your vehicle in an enclosed and attended parking facility two miles from the manor house. You're then taken down a winding road through some really beautiful trees to the hotel in one of several horse-drawn carriages, which are exact replicas of designs from the 1890s.

"Once you're at the manor house, staff dressed in period costumes carry your bags and escort you to your assigned room. The atmosphere is like it would have been around 1900. Even the meals, games, and entertainment are all set up to be as authentic as possible."

"Kind of like a step back in time." I had remained standing, and I shifted down the aisle, working on upper shelves from which the books had not been tossed, while Rita continued to sit on the floor and work on random stacks.

"Exactly like a step back in time. Each guest is provided with either a lady's maid or a valet, depending on gender. Here's where I come in. Throughout the day, the women will dress for activities and meals just as they would have in 1900. On the estate grounds near the manor, there is a separate facility where the ladies go to have their hair done in turn-of-the-century styles, and period costumes are provided for both men and women. Basically, my staff and I get to take each woman and make her a turn-of-the-century work of art. And I'm quite good at it too." Rita added a flip of her red tresses and a flashy grin.

"It sounds like things are pretty realistic."

"That's how it's meant to be, and they've done a beautiful job of it."

"I'd love a behind-the-scenes tour sometime, if you can swing it."

"I think I can manage that."

I had finally reached the end of the row of bookshelves, and I glanced at my watch. Almost noon. No wonder I was hungry. "Hey, it's lunchtime." I stretched. "Want to stop to grab a bite to eat?"

"Sure. I know just the place." Rita stood and leaned over to pick up a full box of science fiction books and groaned. "I'm too old to be playing on the floor." She took the books to their new section.

We walked down Center Street to a small publike restaurant with dim lighting and a wooden floor. A long bar stretched along one wall, and a huge gilt-framed mirror hung behind it. Light filtered through the stained-glass windows and made softly colored patterns on every surface. Seated at a small, round table near the bar, I ran my fingers through the tiny rainbows that played across the tabletop while we waited for someone to take our order.

We had received our drinks and ordered lunch when the local noon news came on the television mounted on the wall behind the bar.

"Thank you for joining me, Connie Dunne—"

"And me, Jonathan Greer," piped in her co-anchor.

"—here on Channel Five Noon News for weather updates and highlights of our evening news," the anchorwoman continued. "The top story this half hour is the arrest of the man who allegedly murdered local bookstore owner Paul Baxter five days ago."

Chapter Twelve

I almost dropped my glass of sweet tea. As the newswoman gave a quick overview of the recent crime, I held my breath.

"Do you think they arrested Stan Jergins because of what I said?" whispered Rita, her face pale.

"I don't know. We'll find out in a minute." I shushed her with a wave of my hand. I didn't want to miss any of this. If they'd arrested someone else, wouldn't it stand to reason I was off the hook?

The newswoman droned on. "At around ten thirty this morning, police arrested twenty-year-old Mason Craig at his residence. Mr. Craig was overheard making threats of physical violence to Mr. Baxter nine months ago when Mr. Baxter fired him for allegedly stealing. Mr. Craig allegedly murdered Mr. Baxter over this grudge. Sources tell us that, although Mr. Craig had moved to another town after the alleged theft, he was in Hokes Folly on the day of the murder. More on this breaking story at six.

"And now, on to the weather." The newswoman turned the cameras to an overweight weatherman wearing out-of-date clothes, whose jolly face and happy demeanor probably did a lot to take the bite out of the more serious stories for many of the viewers.

I tuned out the rest of the news and leaned in toward Rita. "Who's Mason Craig?"

"He worked for Paul for about two months last year," replied Rita quietly. "The first few weeks were okay, but then Paul kept coming up short on a regular basis when he counted the drawer at night. He fired Mason, and the problem stopped."

"This kid threatened bodily harm over getting fired?" Had Uncle Paul been naïve enough to hire someone with violent tendencies?

"No. Mason didn't threaten him until he tried to get another job and no one would hire him. He assumed Paul had told them not to, which wasn't true. First, that would be illegal, and second, it wasn't Paul's style. The other store owners simply figured if Paul had fired him, there must be a darned good reason, so they chose to pass when he applied."

Our food had finally arrived, and Rita took a bite of her hoagie.

"Why didn't Uncle Paul have him arrested?" I winced, not truly wishing that on anyone.

"Because he couldn't really prove Mason was stealing. He never actually caught him in the act."

"So Mason left town?" I struggled to put events together in my mind. No matter how I looked at it, it didn't add up.

"It was either that or work at Burger King or McDonald's. He supposedly moved to be able to work at a higher-than-minimum-wage job, since he brags about his big job every chance he gets." Rita took a sip of her drink and nibbled at her hoagie again.

"I can't believe he came back after all this time to murder Uncle Paul. Why wait? And if it had been that long, why not let it go?" Something stank in Denmark. I wasn't quite sure what, but I knew this was wrong.

Rita swallowed another bite. "He wouldn't have come back simply to murder Paul."

"Did he have a girlfriend or boyfriend here?" I pushed my salad around on my plate with my fork. My appetite was gone.

If this kid was getting railroaded, I could definitely relate, and I didn't have the right to feel relieved I wasn't the one arrested. Did I?

"Nothing quite so romantic. His mother passed away a month or so before Mason went to work for Paul. He comes back every once in a while to tend to her grave site."

I finally forced myself to take a bite of my salad, but I was too unsettled to enjoy the flavors bursting from the mixed greens and homemade dressing.

"There's only one thing that confuses me," Rita said.

"What's that?" My stomach churned, and I gave up and pushed my salad away.

"Mason usually comes on a Wednesday, because his mother passed away on a Wednesday. Paul was killed on a Sunday," Rita stated, as if I'd know what that meant.

My eyebrows shot up. "You know when Mason usually comes to town?"

"Paul did. He'd met Mason in the cemetery when he went to visit Irene's grave site. That's how Mason came to work for Paul in the first place. The kid always took Wednesday afternoons off to tend his mother's grave site. After he fired Mason, Paul made sure he was never at the cemetery on Wednesdays. He changed his regular day to Sunday."

"Okay, but why is that so confusing?" I took a sip of sweet tea, hoping it would calm my stomach.

"If Mason had been coming here for so long on Wednesdays, why did he show up on a Sunday?" Rita propped her elbows on the table in front of her empty plate.

"Maybe he had something he had to do that Wednesday that he couldn't get out of." I shrugged. What did I know about why a kid would go to a cemetery on a specific day?

"Maybe. But if he'd never looked up Paul to have it out with him before now, then why that week?"

"Why not that week?" Okay, now I was arguing simply for the sake of arguing. A twinge of unease pinged at the back of my mind. Maybe I was arguing because I wanted someone, anyone, to be guilty so I wouldn't have to go through another ordeal like the one in Charlotte.

"No, I mean, if he hadn't had it out with Paul before now, he probably wouldn't have done it, period. So, if he ran into Paul, it would've been at the cemetery." Rita picked up her napkin and folded it several times.

"I see where you're going." The hamster finally started running in the wheel. "If he'd actually seen Uncle Paul at the cemetery, then Mason could've had it out with him right there."

"Exactly. And he wouldn't have gone to Paul's home to start up an old argument then kill him with sleeping pills, now would he?"

My mind raced. "And if he'd shown up at the house acting mad after having picked a fight at the cemetery, Uncle Paul would've had the good sense not to open the door." At least I hoped he would have. I hadn't seen him in a long time, so who knew?

"You're right about that." Rita wiped a bit of mayo off her finger with her napkin.

"If Mason didn't do it, who does that leave?" I had resumed pushing my food around my plate in the hope that I'd actually talk myself into eating some of it. Were the police so inept they would first hassle me as a suspect, then arrest someone else on such flimsy evidence?

"Stan?"

I shook my head. "Maybe not. If he'd been a possibility, wouldn't the police have arrested him instead of Mason?"

"You're probably right." Rita sipped her drink, seemingly lost in thought for a moment. "The police were going to question Gladys about who she saw come to the house to argue with Paul. If it was Mason, then they've pretty much wrapped up the case."

"But what if it wasn't Mason who Gladys saw? What if it *was* Stan? Maybe he's still a suspect." I choked down another tasteless bite. Maybe that crazy detective thought I was still a suspect too.

"The police must have something stronger to go on than the fact that Mason was in town on a Sunday. They can't go around arresting someone over a suspicion, can they? Don't they have to have hard evidence, or whatever it's called?"

I flinched. Boy did I know better. "You'd think so, but how many times have the police arrested someone, only to find out later they have the wrong person?"

Rita reached over and gave my hand a squeeze. Not a full hug, but from Rita, it felt the same. "I don't understand something, though."

"Oh?"

"Yeah. You said when you got here, you never went to the store, right?"

I nodded.

"But when the police arrived, the store was locked." She took another bite and chewed.

"Right." I nodded again, trying to figure out where she was going with this.

"Since Paul had the only set of keys, and his keys were on the coffee table upstairs, and the only way to lock the store from the outside is with the keys . . ." She sipped her drink, apparently waiting for me to catch up with her train of thought.

My frazzled brain finally put the pieces together, and the last vestiges of my already slim appetite fled. "Whoever killed him had to leave through the apartment."

"It's likely, in my opinion. After all, Paul did fall down the stairs, which implies he was upstairs with the killer to begin with." She brushed her hands off, laid her napkin across her empty plate, and finished the last of her tea. "Are you ready to head back to the store?"

I looked at my plate. "I guess I should ask for a to-go box."

Rita looked up from rummaging in her purse for her wallet. "Hey, you didn't eat much. Are you okay?"

"Yeah. I'm just worried. A murdered uncle isn't exactly the kind of thing that happens to me every day, especially when I'm the initial suspect. Now I'm also worried they're railroading some young kid who doesn't have the ability to fight back. It's killed my appetite and upset my stomach. I don't see how you managed to eat all of your huge sandwich."

"Honey, I learned a long time ago to never let anything come between me and a good meal."

I laughed, but it was more of a yeah-okay-sure kind of laugh than a funny-ha-ha laugh. "I wish I could say the same." I signaled a server to bring a to-go box. At least I'd have supper already prepared for tonight. With all the bending and getting up and down off the floor, I probably wouldn't feel much like cooking.

"Put all this mess out of your mind for now. There's nothing you can do anyway."

"You're right." I didn't voice the other thought circling through my brain. When I'd arrived, that skittish feeling I'd felt, those noises I'd heard, might have been a killer still searching the apartment. What if they'd still been inside? I took a deep breath, knowing I was being ridiculous, and reached for my wallet.

After paying, we headed back toward the bookstore to continue straightening out the mess Uncle Paul had left. When we got close, I blinked, trying to make sure I wasn't seeing things. A small figure peered in the front window, then raised its hand and pounded on the glass angrily.

What the hell?

Chapter Thirteen

The figure turned out to be none other than Olivia Hokes.
What could possibly have the woman so upset she felt the
need to beat on store windows?

I rushed forward before she could damage the glass. "May I
help you, Miss Hokes?" I smiled in what I hoped was a believable,
friendly-store-owner manner.

"Yes," came the clipped retort. "You can get my book." She
pursed her lips and gave a tilted nod, her hands now clasped in
front of another vintage dress.

"Excuse me?" I racked my brain, shoving the revelations from
moments ago to the back of my mind and mentally searching
through the books I'd seen on the shelf behind the counter, yet I
couldn't remember seeing anything with her name on it. But then
I hadn't exactly been looking either.

"My book." Olivia squinted at me, her hands now on her hips.
"The one Paul Baxter was supposed to order but kept saying had
never come in. I know it really did. It was very rare, and I wouldn't
put it past him if he kept it out of spite. I saw you in there today,
and I want my book. Now. If you don't give it to me immediately,
I'll call the police."

I shot a look at Rita, who raised her eyebrows and shrugged her shoulders.

Smile. Be sweet. Don't piss off customers. What was the old saying? The customer is always right, or something like that. "Miss Hokes, I'm sure if Uncle Paul told you he didn't have the book, then he really didn't have it yet."

"Well, I want that book," Olivia Hokes spat out. "You'd better find it, or else. It's a 1923 treatise on the history of Hokes Folly. Paul said he'd located a copy and promised to order it. I need it for my collection."

"Your collection?" I glanced again at Rita and received a second shrug.

"Yes." The woman seemed to puff up with smugness and self-importance. "I have the largest collection on Hokes Folly anywhere in the state. There are two libraries begging me to donate the books to them in my will."

"You do understand the book you want might not be here." I typed the information into the notes on my phone.

"If it's not, then you'd better look for it to come. I want it the moment it's here. I'll be watching you." She narrowed her eyes at me. "I'll know when your shipments come in."

"Yes, ma'am." I gritted my teeth, determined not to be rude to the woman. "The book might be held at the post office if it arrived after Uncle Paul's death."

"It's one more thing that old man messed up. He had to cause me trouble even after he's dead and gone." Olivia Hokes turned on her heel, stomped away to the shop next door, and went inside.

I brushed a stray hair out of my face and turned to Rita. "Do you have any idea what that was all about?"

"None whatsoever." Rita shook her head, her forehead wrinkled and an amused look in her eyes. "Let's go before your neighbor decides to really call the police and have us arrested for loitering or something."

"Neighbor?" Oh God, was I going to have to see her every day? I followed Rita into the store, letting the sweet tinkle of the bell over the door cheer me.

"Yep, she and her sister, Ophelia, run the antique clothing store next door under my apartment. So, you'd better try to patch things up with her by finding the book she wants."

We searched every logical place the book could be. An hour later, I plopped down on the floor in the back room by three stacks of books stuffed under the desk, while Rita perched on the kitchen counter she'd cleared of yet another stack.

"Didn't Uncle Paul keep records of any kind?" I tugged a bit of hair out of my face and tucked it behind my ear.

Rita laughed. "Oh, but that would be too easy. Paul thought modern computers were useless. They might crash, there might be a power outage, or someone might steal them, so he refused to own one. He felt it was all better kept up in his head, so no one could mess with it."

I shook my head. A new computer went on my list of things to buy for the store. With no place else to look, I finally called the post office and asked how to go about retrieving Uncle Paul's mail. As his legal heir, I figured I had a right to it. The lady at the post office said there was indeed a stack of mail, including packages, that had been held at the post office, since no one had come to pick them up. There would be forms to fill out, and she told me at which branch the mail would be held.

"Well, I guess I'm off to get the mail. Want to come?" I brushed as much dust off my jeans as I could and pulled my purse from under the counter.

She shook her head. "No sense in both of us going. I'll stay here and keep at the book piles."

* * *

Two long hours and many forms later, I lugged several heavy boxes of books and a stack of Uncle Paul's personal and business mail out to the car. I was itching to dig into the boxes, hoping to at least find Olivia's book and maybe discover something to answer the questions surrounding his death. However, I knew Rita would insist on helping, and I didn't want to have to go through it all twice.

"Hey," she called from the back of the store as I walked in with the first two boxes. "Need a hand?" She didn't wait for an answer before clapping her hands.

"Very funny." I heaved a box onto the front counter. "You'd better behave, or I'll have to look for another assistant to go through the goodies."

"Ouch." Rita walked to the front and reached for the other box, helping me lift it onto the counter. "Did you carry these all the way from the parking area?"

"No, I waved my magic wand, and they floated in the air beside me." I rolled my eyes as I headed toward the door. "Come on, there are more."

After we'd made three trips and brought in more than a dozen boxes, as well as the stack of mail, I plopped down onto the stool behind the counter. "I'll probably be sore tomorrow. I think I've used muscles today that haven't been used in way too long."

"You should exercise more." Rita pawed through the mail on the counter.

"Gee, thanks for the advice." I stood and stretched. Maybe I needed to start working out again. I'd stopped when I couldn't go to the gym without whispers behind hands or a surprise visit from a reporter looking for the latest angle. Gritting my teeth, I forced the memories away and stood.

The phone jangled and interrupted my morbid thoughts.

"Baxter's Book Emporium," I answered.

"Jenna, this is Horace Grimes. I wanted to let you know the autopsy has been completed and the body has come back to Hokes Folly and is now at the Haven of Rest Funeral Home. I've already spoken with the funeral director, and as Paul's wishes were on file with him, everything is taken care of. The funeral is set for Sunday at one PM."

I flopped into the chair I'd vacated. "Thanks for letting me know. Do I need to help notify anyone? Place an ad? Anything?"

"No," he responded in that calming voice I'd come to appreciate. "I'll handle everything so you don't have to. I'll see you on Sunday."

The line went dead, and I placed the phone back in its cradle.

"Are you okay?" Rita leaned on the counter in front of me.

"Yeah. It was only Mr. Grimes. Uncle Paul's funeral will be Sunday at one."

Rita walked around the counter, knelt beside me, and gave me a full-on hug. I melted into it, reveling in the sisterly warmth I drew from it.

After a moment, I disengaged and stood, determined not to get emotional and weepy there in the store, where a customer might, just might, walk in. I took a fortifying breath, mentally stepping off the emotional roller coaster I'd come to know too well. "We'd better get at it if we hope to make it through the mail and all of these books today."

She nodded and moved back to the other side of the counter. We quickly sorted the mail into piles of personal mail, bills, packages, and what looked like business correspondence.

I slid the bills to the side to go through and pay later then picked up a handful of the business letters and thumbed through them. "These are all out-of-date sales ads." I tossed the handful into the trash can.

Box cutter in hand, I opened the first of the packages that weren't book boxes. It contained new checks, and I stuck these under the counter. Too bad he'd ordered them, since I'd be changing the store's name and would have to replace them . . . if I stayed. I grabbed the second box. It and the next one held large reference volumes used to price other books.

"I hope it gets better than this." Rita sighed and reached for another package. "I'm not sure if I can stand much more excitement."

I gave her a withering look. "I'm sorry if business items aren't thrilling enough for you, but they're a necessary part of running a store." I waved a hand toward the aisles. "You could always go organize some more books if you're bored."

"Nah, we're finally getting to the good stuff." Rita grinned and cut open the first book box.

Several packages later, Rita whooped and did a fist pump. "I found it!"

"Thank God." I heaved a sigh of relief. I hadn't been looking forward to telling Olivia Hokes we couldn't find her book. I looked at the time on my phone. "How late is Olivia's store open?"

"Not sure, but I think they've already closed today. I saw Olivia walking toward the parking area a little while ago." Rita checked the coffeepot. "If we're going to be here a bit longer, want me to start another pot?"

"Sure." I reached for another book box. "I'd like to finish sorting through most of this tonight, if you don't mind."

After opening the remaining boxes and tossing out as much junk mail as we could find, we started opening the business letters to the store.

"Hey, Jenna, look at this." Rita flattened a letter on the counter.

"What is it?" I plopped my elbows on the counter and leaned in to see the letter.

Rita read out loud. "'Dear Mr. Baxter, as you know, I cannot confirm the validity of authorship, but I can confirm, based upon the single page you showed me, the authenticity of the ink and paper. I would have been able to do a more thorough job if you had left the book with me, but I can confirm that both the type and age of the ink and paper place them around the nineteen thirties. I hope this has been a help to you in your search. Sincerely, Linus Talbot, Director of Antique Books, Hokes Folly Community Library.'" She leaned back and slid the letter toward me.

I picked it up and skimmed through it again, trying to read between the lines and glean more information than was printed on the page. No luck. "What do you make of it?"

Rita poured herself a cup of coffee and took a sip. "I would guess Paul was researching some book he'd bought at auction."

"What do you mean?" I set the letter on the counter and accepted the steaming Styrofoam cup she offered me.

"When Paul went to estate sales, he bought books by the lot. He didn't get to pick through to look for the good ones. He either had to buy the whole box or set of boxes or leave it. That's pretty much standard policy at estate auctions. Most of the time he got decent stuff he could easily sell. Sometimes he got absolute junk he had to all but give away to get rid of, but every once in a while he discovered a true gem."

"And?" I blew gently across the cup, willing it to cool faster so I wouldn't scorch my tongue.

"If he found a book he thought might really be worth something, he looked up a friend at the library who had access to dating equipment for books. He wanted to make sure a book was the real deal before putting it up for auction."

"So this is no big deal then." Disappointed, I put the letter on the to-be-filed pile and reached for another envelope.

"Well, there is one odd thing," said Rita thoughtfully. "If he wanted a book authenticated, he would've wanted everything about it confirmed, not simply the age of the paper and ink. And he usually left the book at the library until it was fully authenticated."

"Why wouldn't he have done that this time?" I picked up the letter again and studied the signature at the bottom. "Do you think this has anything to do with the mystery he mentioned in his email?"

"There's only one way to know." Rita flopped down into the chair, stretched her legs out, and crossed her ankles. "Since whatever it is he wanted to authenticate legally belongs to you now, tomorrow we call good old Linus Talbot and ask what Paul showed him."

Chapter Fourteen

S aturday morning dawned bright and beautiful, but by the time I walked down to the store, dark clouds hung low overhead, and the morning's gentle breezes had picked up, whipping through the light sweater I'd worn as I swept the front walk. Rita had returned to her job at the inn, so I faced my store alone. *My store.* That would take some getting used to if I stayed, an idea that wormed its way deeper and deeper into my brain with each passing day.

Seeing Olivia's book on the counter where we'd left it, I decided to deliver it before the bottom fell out of those clouds. I didn't want to give the rain a chance to damage the book after all we'd gone through to find it. With the book gripped in my hand against the gusting winds, I walked down the sidewalk and entered the little shop next door to the sound of a soft, electronic ding, which I assumed would be echoed in the back room.

No one came to greet me right away, so I looked around the softly lit room. As with much of the town, it was like a step back in time. Velvet upholstery covered an antique fainting couch and settee; the furniture appeared well cared for and comfortable. Two reprints of *Godey's Lady's Book* lay displayed on a little antique reading table, and a Tiffany lamp gave enough light to see the pictures and read the captions.

Around the small sitting area stood beautifully displayed racks of well-kept clothing from other eras, and I browsed through the store, imagining myself wearing some of it. It seemed the store carried items dating back to at least the 1950s, but some were much older and appeared to be either replicas or possibly originals from as far back as the 1800s.

A soft footstep sounded, and I turned. The approaching woman looked a bit like Olivia, but instead of harsh bitterness, I saw gentleness and peace.

Laugh lines edged the woman's eyes, and her mouth turned up in a slightly timid smile. "May I help you?"

"Yes, I'm looking for Olivia Hokes. Is she in today?" I hoped I wasn't going to karmically pay for the crossed fingers behind my back and the fervent wish that I wouldn't have to talk to her.

"No, not yet. I'm her sister, Ophelia Hokes. May I help you in some way?"

While I couldn't be surprised at a familial relationship due to the basic physical resemblance, right down to the short, sideswept, dark-brown-but-graying hair, I still had a hard time swallowing that this mousy, sweet-looking woman was a sister of the volatile Olivia Hokes. "I'm Jenna Quinn from the bookstore." I gestured with my free hand toward the wall that joined our two stores.

"I've been expecting you," said Ophelia softly. "Livie said you'd be by today with a book for her."

I gritted my teeth and tamped down my irritation at Olivia's assumption that Uncle Paul had tried to cheat her. "Please tell your sister Uncle Paul had not yet received the book, but I did find it in a shipment that arrived at the post office after his death." I extended the book toward the tiny woman. "She can come by and pay for it when she gets in." Not that I really wanted to see her. I'd almost rather give her the book than have to politely put up with her snotty remarks again. Almost. However, the drive to sell something, anything, to be productive again, was too strong.

Ophelia took the book with trembling fingers, holding it in one palm and gently stroking it with her other hand. "Thank you." Her voice had dropped to an almost inaudible level, and she bowed her head, blinking rapidly.

I was a sucker for seeing someone else in tears, and her distress pulled at my heart. "Are you all right?" I gently laid my hand on the frail fingers that caressed the book's cover.

"Yes, I'm fine." Ophelia turned her hand over and gave mine a brief, tiny squeeze. "I can't seem to get over Paul's passing."

"Did you know Uncle Paul well?"

"Oh yes. He and I were quite close." The older woman blushed, and her eyes seemed to sparkle at the memory before filling with sadness again.

I barely kept my mouth from popping open into an O. *Uncle Paul and Ophelia Hokes?* It seemed odd that Uncle Paul would have a close relationship with a woman whose sister so obviously despised him. "Were you and Paul serious?"

"Yes, we were, until my sister got in the way." Ophelia moved to the sitting area and sank onto the settee, sighing deeply.

"What did Olivia do?" I took a seat on the delicate-looking fainting couch, hoping it was sturdier than it appeared.

"It's a bit of a story, and I'm sure you have more interesting ways to spend your time than to sit and listen to me ramble on."

"No. I'd love to hear about you and Uncle Paul. I was a teenager the last time I saw him, so I would really appreciate it if you could share your memories with me." Aiming at getting the older woman to open up, I was surprised to realize I really meant what I said. I crossed my legs and waited, almost holding my breath, hoping she wouldn't shut me out.

After a moment, Ophelia nodded her head once. "When Paul and Irene first came to town and Paul opened his store next door, I started having a little crush on him." She blushed again, and a small smile tugged at the corners of her mouth before she sobered. "Unfortunately, so did Livie."

"Uh-oh. A love triangle." I could imagine Olivia steamrolling over her more-timid sister to get what she wanted.

"A quadrangle, actually." Ophelia held up four fingers. "Don't forget Irene. Neither my sister nor I gave Paul any idea of our feelings, since he was so very obviously in love with his wife." Ophelia's eyes took on a wistful look. "It was beautiful to see. He treated her like a queen, like she was so precious to him. I think that's what made me like him so much."

"I remember them always hugging and holding hands. They seemed so happy." I wondered if my own eyes mirrored her wistful look. There had been a time not too long ago when I'd have given anything to be treated that way.

"Oh, they were. And after Irene died, God rest her soul, Paul mourned her for a long time. When he started dating again, Livie and I realized he was beginning to heal—which took nearly five years. He went out with Rita Wallace, the lady who lives upstairs"— she pointed at the ceiling of her store—"for a time. After they ended things, Livie announced she was going to make him fall in love with her."

"Make him?" I could hardly believe the woman's audacity, but it seemed to fit the overall picture I'd already formed of Olivia Hokes.

"Yes, it was presumptuous of her. But that's Livie's way. She never just lets anything happen to her. In her opinion, only she can make things happen in her life. It's a bit hard to live with at times, but you do get used to her after a while." Ophelia pursed her lips and straightened her spine.

I laughed and patted the woman's arm. "I understand completely."

"Oh, do you have an older sister too?"

"No." I grinned. "But I've met yours twice now."

Ophelia laughed loudly at this, and I was glad to see it brought more color to her pale cheeks.

"What happened when Olivia tried to make Uncle Paul fall for her?" Good Lord, that must have been amusing to watch. After what Rita had said about dating Uncle Paul, I couldn't see him being attracted to Olivia. Ophelia maybe. But definitely not Olivia.

"Well." Ophelia leaned in and whispered conspiratorially. "Paul was having none of it. He definitely didn't want to date someone as stubborn and demanding as Livie, someone the exact opposite of his late wife."

Impression confirmed. "He totally brushed her off?"

"Not really. He couldn't manage to find an excuse every time she gave an invitation to tea or asked him to drive her somewhere. He and I had a bit of time together too, since Livie felt it would be better for her reputation to have a chaperone. Although I still don't understand what a sixty-two-year-old woman needed with a chaperone, I went along willingly, because it gave me an excuse to be around Paul." She blushed and ducked her head again.

"You really had a thing for him, didn't you?"

This sweet, gentle woman brought out in me the instinct to protect her, and I tucked my hands between my knees, suppressing the urge to hug her, since I didn't want her to think I was one of those crazy people who hugged complete strangers on a whim. Which I was. But she didn't know that. Yet.

"Yes," came the whispered reply. "I did then and still do, I guess. But I couldn't let Paul know, because Livie had already called dibs on him."

My heart broke for Ophelia. "You could've gone against her."

"Oh no." She held up her hands as if to block something. "You don't cross Livie unless you absolutely have to."

"I can see that." I shot her a conspiratorial grin, glad to see it mirrored on Ophelia's face. I could only imagine what Olivia would do when crossed, especially by her usually submissive sister.

Ophelia dropped her hands to her lap and shook her head. "It didn't matter anyway. Paul asked me out. I was thrilled, but Livie was furious. She decided she couldn't stand him anymore and did everything she could to make both Paul and me completely miserable."

"Uncle Paul chose you over her?" *Good for him!* Uncle Paul went up a notch in my estimation. Too bad this settee didn't. It seemed the longer I sat here, the more uncomfortable it became. I shifted a bit, crossing my legs in the opposite direction.

"Yes, and it wasn't the first time she'd lost a man to another woman. It was only the most recent and the only time she lost one to me."

"Ohhhhhh." Now I was getting the bigger picture. In Olivia's mind, not only had Ophelia snagged a man out from under her, the ultimate sister betrayal, but it stomped all over past issues that had to still sting.

Ophelia sighed. "The first time was when she was left at the altar by her fiancé on her wedding day. There she stood, all gussied up, her flowers perfect." Ophelia's eyes looked back in time. "She refused to leave until almost midnight. She couldn't believe the man had actually dumped her. But it seems he'd found himself another woman. A Dear John letter waited for her at home."

"How awful." I hoped I sounded truly sympathetic, but I couldn't seem to picture any man wanting to marry the harsh and demanding Olivia.

"Yes, it was terrible for a while," agreed Ophelia. "She stayed in her room for three weeks. She refused to eat or get out of bed. I made all of her favorite foods and brought them to her on a beautiful tray, and she threw them at me. My sister screamed and yelled at anyone who came into the room. It was a nightmare. Not only had she been stood up, but the whole town knew about it."

"Then what happened?" This sounded more like the Olivia I had met.

"Our father had finally had enough. He went in and had a long talk with her. I never knew exactly what he said, but after that things got better."

"In what way?"

"She finally decided men weren't worth her trouble. She announced she was never going to let a man hurt her again and she would never marry. She devoted her time to keeping the house running, and after Mama died, she stayed on to keep house for Daddy." Ophelia heaved a heavy sigh and shook her head. "It's a shame too. Livie was such a pretty girl, and sweet to boot. It's too bad she let circumstances change her."

Sweet? Olivia? My eyebrows shot up with a will of their own, and I reached up to scratch my forehead to cover it. I hoped. But who would've guessed Olivia could be anything but brusque, at best? I could see why nobody would want to go out with Olivia as she was now, all bitter and angry, but they might have if she'd been nicer before. "You mean nobody else ever asked to marry her? Nobody ever tried to woo her into changing her mind?"

"She never let anyone get close enough to her to want to ask," came the simple answer. "If any man ever sent flowers or asked her out, Livie cut him off at the pockets. She refused gifts, hung up on phone calls, even slammed the door in one man's face. In short, she was incredibly rude to some very nice guys. It didn't take long for the flowers and phone calls to stop once word got around about her bad attitude."

"So, when she decided to go after Uncle Paul, it was a major step for her."

"Yes, it was." Ophelia nodded. "It was the first time in"—she paused, counting her fingertips with her thumb—"forty-four years that she'd decided a man was worth her time. And in the two and a half years since Paul rejected her, she's become more bitter and angry at men than ever before."

"What about you, Miss Hokes? Did you never get the chance to marry?" At this point, I was genuinely curious. I knew she still had her maiden name, but surely someone as sweet as she was had received offers.

"Call me Phillie. All my friends do. Miss Hokes reminds me I'm an old maid, and Ophelia sounds stuffy." She giggled.

"Okay, Phillie." I grinned back at her, shifting on the settee once more, wishing it was as comfortable as it was pretty.

"Now, to answer your question, no, I never found the right man to marry either, because Livie was determined to keep me from it." She stood, walked to the front counter, and leaned over its high edge to place Olivia's book beside the cash register.

"What do you mean?" My eyebrows shot up again as I followed her, my backside grateful for the reprieve. I could see Olivia running off her own boyfriends, but why Phillie's?

"Since Livie decided to hate men, she wanted me, her dear little sister, to hate them as well. Twice I almost married, but both times she ruined it for me." She sighed resignedly, as if she'd come to accept her lot in life but still wished things had been different.

"How?" I hated to pry too much, but the woman seemed to want to talk about her past, and for several reasons, I was genuinely interested in hearing her story. Once again I shoved my mother's admonishments about how a lady would never pry out of my mind. But then, I'd done a lot of things my mother wouldn't approve of in the last few months. Why stop now?

She turned and leaned back against the counter. "The first time, I was nineteen and had gotten engaged to a wonderful man named Robert Kelly. He was funny and gorgeous. He was also somewhat of a gambler, and unfortunately, he wasn't very good at his chosen hobby. One night he lost over fifty thousand dollars and came to Daddy to ask for a loan. Daddy refused. Livie apparently overheard the conversation. She had money from investments, since Daddy had given her the money he'd saved for her honeymoon. She offered to pay Robert's gambling debts if he'd never see me again. He was about to lose his house and his car, so what choice did he have? As a result, I lost a fiancé, and Livie had one more reason to hate weak men." Phillie shrugged. "Even if it was probably for the best, it still hurt."

At least she'd found out what a jerk the guy was before she married him. I knew from experience that, even though it hurt, it was always better to have dodged the bullet of marrying the wrong guy. "What about the second time?"

"Oh yes, the second time." Phillie straightened and walked around the counter, finally picking up a teacup. "There was another man who was also funny and gorgeous . . . isn't it amusing how we remember them all as 'funny and gorgeous'?" She chuckled.

"Yep." I only wished my last memory of a "funny and gorgeous" man wasn't so close to a nightmare.

Phillie pulled me back from my darker thoughts. "Would you like some tea?" She held up another cup.

I shook my head, glad for the momentary distraction. "No thank you. I've had my daily caffeine intake already. Tell me about this second funny and gorgeous guy."

She poured tea into her cup and held it to her lips to blow softly on the hot liquid. "This guy seemed more interested in my father's business than in me. He wanted to inherit what he thought would be a fortune. Livie convinced him Daddy was leaving the company to her, since she was the older sister, and I would have money in a trust he wouldn't be able to touch. He dumped me for her, and she promptly kicked him to the curb."

"I'm so sorry." I couldn't imagine being humiliated in such a manner by a sister, of all people. But then, I'd never had a sister, so who was I to say?

"It hurt for a while, but I realized it would've been terrible, since the man obviously didn't love me at all. I was glad I found out before I actually married him. It would've been awful being married to someone who only saw me as a way to increase his net worth."

"Did you never want to marry after that?"

"Oh, I wanted to, all right. But I figured, after ruining two possible matches for me, Livie wouldn't give anyone else a chance either. So I gave up." She shrugged her shoulders. "I know that's not a very courageous thing to do, but Livie and I have had a good life together. It hasn't been so bad."

I leaned in and rested my forearms on the counter. "Until Uncle Paul." I could now see the strong appeal my uncle had held for Phillie. He was the kind of man the guys from her past hadn't been: sweet, loving, attentive, and above all, genuine.

Phillie nodded stiffly. "Yes. Until your Uncle Paul. Livie thought I was paying her back for ruining my chances to marry by stealing Paul out from under her. Rather than let me be happy, she set out to ruin that one too."

My ears perked up. Now we were getting somewhere. "What did she do to ruin your relationship with Uncle Paul?"

"When she realized she couldn't make Paul want to spend time with her, she insisted he shouldn't spend time with me either." Phillie paused and wrinkled her brow. "I think she didn't want to be alone at her age. I can understand, but I wish . . ." Her eyes misted over.

Not wanting her to fall too deeply into her grief over a past that never got to happen, I gently changed the direction of—if I was being honest with myself—what had now become a subtle interrogation. "How did she manage to separate the two of you?"

Phillie sniffed and pulled a tissue from the box behind the tall counter to blot her eyes. "She kept after him and kept after him. She tried acting sweet and submissive and tender in a last-ditch effort."

"I'll bet Uncle Paul saw through that one." The man I was growing to know so much better through the women who cared for him wouldn't have been that gullible.

"He did. And when it didn't work, she tried to bribe him. Then she threatened him. She was snotty to him in every way."

"And Paul finally had a bellyful and stopped seeing you?" I was surprised he'd given up so easily.

"Oh no. Paul would've put up with her if I'd wanted him to. But she hadn't been kind to me either. She'd threatened to throw me out of our home, even though it's half mine. She threatened to toss me out of this business, even though this is half mine too. She told me Paul had buried one wife and asked if I wanted to be the next. She reminded me over and over of how the men in my life had always let me down. She screamed and yelled and pitched fits at everything I said or did. I finally had enough. I told Paul he deserved better. He said we could manage in spite of her and actually asked me to marry him." Phillie choked up and pulled another tissue from the box behind the counter.

Wow. What a witch. I shook my head. I was almost glad I didn't have a sister at this point. "Why didn't you marry him? It would have moved you away from your sister."

"Not really. I wouldn't have lived in the same house with her, but I would still have owned part of this business. I love this store and didn't want to give it up. And Paul's store and apartment are right next door. Even if I'd quit working here and sold my half to Livie, we would've seen her every day. Paul deserved better. He deserved a wife without so much baggage."

"So you broke it off with him?" Phillie was stronger than I'd given her credit for, and it made me like her even more.

"Yes, and he said he understood. I know it hurt him, but he was very much a gentleman about the whole thing. He even said if I ever changed my mind to come and see him. The offer would stand." Phillie dabbed at her eyes with the tissue.

"That's so sweet." I sighed. It was almost like reading a romance novel . . . except for the murder at the end.

"Yes, it was. Paul was an incredibly sweet man. I wish Livie could've seen that."

We stood in silence for a few moments, lost in our own thoughts: Phillie perhaps thinking of happy memories with Uncle Paul, me thinking how hard it must have been for her to work next door to and watch the man she deeply loved, knowing she could never have him for herself.

After a minute, Phillie reached over and patted my hand. "We stayed friends, though, and snuck off for lunch together once a week, and sometimes I would make excuses to come in to the shop early so I could go up and have morning coffee with him. He talked about you and the things you told him in your emails." She paused, and her brow furrowed. "He also told me about your troubles. He never stopped believing in you."

I looked for censure in her eyes, any flicker that said she thought I had been guilty. There was none. "Can I ask you something?"

"Of course, dear. Anything."

"If your sister hated him, hated the thought of you two together so badly, might she have done something to make sure you never changed your mind and accepted his proposal?" I had kept my voice soft and reassuring, hoping she wouldn't draw back.

I watched as an array of emotions played across Phillie's face, and she once again dabbed at her eyes with the tissue and ducked her head.

She cleared her throat and squared her shoulders. "To be honest"—she took a deep breath—"I've wondered the same thing." She looked up into my eyes. "But I don't see it. I can't picture Livie resorting to physical violence."

I considered the woman I'd discovered pounding on my windows the day before, although that wasn't the same as murdering someone. "You did say she threw things around when she was angry at being dumped. Has she been violent otherwise?"

Phillie shook her head. "Not in the least. She'd never hurt anything or anyone physically. Her weapons are words. Yes, she resented Paul. No, she didn't want me to marry him. Yes, I fully believe she would have followed through on trying to make Paul and me miserable if we had married against her objections. But she simply does not have it in her to do anything worse than be verbally mean and cutting and abusive."

"I hope you're not upset that I asked." I really did like the older woman, and something in me wanted to protect her.

She reached out and patted my hand again. "I know you want answers, that you want to find out what happened to Paul. So do I.

But I promise, Livie isn't the answer." She shrugged. "I heard Frank Sutter thinks you had motive. Honestly, I can't believe that idiot considered you as a suspect in Paul's death. He always was a moron, even when he was a little boy. How he got that high up in a job that requires critical thinking is beyond me."

I couldn't contain the grin. Maybe Rita was right and the people here wouldn't judge me based on that stupid news story. "Thanks. I appreciate the vote of confidence."

Phillie returned my grin. "It's nothing, dear. I knew you through Paul's stories, and if he believed in you, I can do no less." She straightened and pursed her lips. "Now, I've taken up enough of your time. You've been sweet to listen to me drag up old memories, but you've got a bookstore to get cleaned up and reopened."

As if I needed to be reminded about the mess next door. I sighed. "You're right. I guess I'd better get everlastingly at it."

"You'll do fine. And if you need anything, give us a ring. That's what neighbors are for." Phillie walked with me to the door.

As I walked back to my own store, I thought about her offer. Would Livie be as willing to help out her newest neighbor? Or would she transfer the extreme grudge she'd had against Uncle Paul over to me?

Chapter Fifteen

I wondered if Linus Talbot would be on the job at the library on a Saturday. Hoping for the best, I pulled the letter from the envelope and called the number in the signature line as soon as I got back to the bookstore. Thrilled when the receptionist said he was there, I waited, not quite patiently, listening to poorly written Muzak while she connected me to his extension.

"Linus Talbot here," came a clipped but cultured voice after a few moments.

"Mr. Talbot, my name is Jenna Quinn. I'm Paul Baxter's niece. I inherited Baxter's Book Emporium after his recent death."

"We heard about your uncle. I'm so sorry for your loss, Miss Quinn." Mr. Talbot's voice warmed up a bit. "Paul was indeed a unique individual and will be greatly missed in the antique book world. Is there anything specific I can help you with?" His compassionate tones made me more comfortable asking questions.

"Yes, there is." I smoothed the creases from the letter. "You wrote to Uncle Paul about a book he'd recently brought to you for authentication. Can you tell me about it?" I crossed my fingers, hoping he'd actually be able to fill in a few gaps. Somebody had to have some answers, and I would keep asking questions until I found out who.

"I don't know much." He spoke slowly, as if searching his memory for the answer. "I was only allowed to look at one page. It was handwritten and in very good shape. Paul wanted to know if it was written in the early to mid-1930s. I do believe I confirmed that for him."

"Were you not able to tell him that at the time he brought you the book?" I settled onto the stool behind the counter.

"Yes, I was, but Paul wanted it in writing. I told him I would get to it as soon as I could. I think it was a week later when I finally found time to write and send the letter for him."

"Had Uncle Paul ever kept you from looking through a book for full authentication before?" I already knew the answer, but it never hurt to ask.

"No. As a matter of fact, he hadn't. I wondered about that myself."

Now came the big question. "Can you think of any reason why he would?"

"No. I tried to figure that one out too. Whatever it was, Paul obviously wanted to keep its contents secret. He said one day soon he'd bring it back for full authentication. Sadly, that day didn't come."

Oh, come on. He had to know *some*thing. "Did he tell you who wrote it?"

"No, I'm afraid he didn't. When I asked the author's name, he stated he'd rather not say. I'm sorry I can't be of more help, but your uncle simply didn't give me any more information about the book in question. Is there anything else I can do to help you, Miss Quinn?"

I didn't want to take up too much of his time and make him unwilling to help me if I needed him later. "No, there isn't. And thank you again. I appreciate you taking the time to speak with me." I slumped, only then realizing I'd been leaning forward in anticipation.

After he hung up, I resisted the temptation to bang the phone on the counter in frustration. All I'd learned was that Uncle Paul had kept an old book a secret. No answers. Only more questions.

My stomach rumbled as I started a pot of coffee. I'd forgotten to take my leftover salad from yesterday upstairs, so I retrieved it from the fridge in the back room and dug in, letting my gaze wander across the piles upon piles of books scattered up and down the aisles. This job would take over a week if I had to do this by myself.

The bells over the entrance door tinkled to announce an arrival. I quickly stuck my salad under the counter and wiped my mouth on a paper towel before turning to greet my first customer who wasn't trying to break my windows or threatening me with calling the police. Then I caught sight of who stood in my doorway. *Oh my God!* Maybe I was the one who should call the police now.

"Hi, I'm Mason Craig," began the well-dressed young man. "I used to work for Paul. I'm looking for the new owner."

Recognizing the name and his face from the newscast announcing his arrest for Uncle Paul's murder, I resisted the urge to lie. For all I knew, he recognized my name and face from that same news channel and was worried about me too. "I'm Jenna Quinn. I own the store now. What can I do for you, Mr. Craig?" I hoped he couldn't see the wariness in my eyes.

"I wondered if I could talk to you for a few minutes." He shifted from one foot to the other.

"I suppose so." I moved closer to the front windows to make sure I was visible to passersby. It never hurt to take precautions.

"I guess you've seen my picture on the local news, since you look like you'd love to do anything but talk to me." His shoulders sagged forward.

"Yes, I have seen your picture. They say you killed my uncle." Of course, they'd also accused me of the same thing. Nevertheless, I held myself tensed and ready to run while using my peripheral vision to scan for something I could use to defend myself if I needed it. Sadly, all I could come up with were clunky reference books. Not much help there.

Mason sat heavily on the chair at the end of the counter and raked a hand through his sandy hair. "I swear to you on my life, I never did anything to Paul Baxter." His piercing gaze met mine.

"Give me one reason why I should believe you had nothing to do with Uncle Paul's death after you told everyone you'd get revenge one day." I watched him intently, hoping to see some sign that I hadn't invited a murderer to sit and chat.

"I don't know. I guess nobody else does, so why should you?" Mason leaned forward and propped his elbows on his knees. "But I'd sure like to explain if I could."

"I'm listening." I stayed standing. No reason to tempt fate. While I of all people knew how easy it was to be charged for something you didn't do, that didn't mean everyone was innocent.

Mason took a deep breath. "Some time ago, I worked for Paul. We met shortly after my mother's funeral a little over a year ago, and I needed some extra cash to help pay for funeral expenses. Paul agreed to hire me full-time. He really didn't need anyone to work here, but it gave him more free time to research his old books. It worked out well for both of us."

"And then you stole." I crossed my arms over my chest, tilted my head, and glared at him, daring him to deny the fact.

"Yes, I stole." Mason ducked his head. "Paul could never prove it, and I denied it, of course, but he was right," he mumbled at his shoes. "After Mom died, I started hanging out with a bunch of druggies. Dope helped dull the pain. I stole from Paul to pay my dealer."

I narrowed my eyes at him, trying to see through the story and emotion to get at the truth. "I still haven't heard anything to keep me from thinking you had something to do with his death."

"There's more. When Paul fired me, he also blackballed me at all of the other businesses around here. I couldn't get a decent job."

"I'm still not hearing anything that says 'I'm innocent.'" Logic dictated I throw him out, but something made me wait and listen. I wasn't sure why, but after the way I'd been railroaded, it seemed only fair to at least hear him out.

"When Paul ruined my chances here, I moved, and it was the best thing that could've happened to me. I got away from that stupid bunch of guys I'd been hanging with and got straight for the first time since my mom died. I wasn't angry at Paul. He did me a favor, even if he didn't realize it, but somehow I think he did. I had no reason to hurt him, much less kill him." Mason shifted in his seat and sighed deeply.

I watched him carefully as he spoke, and the tension he radiated was incredible. However, the desperate lilt of his voice was one I recognized from my own past, and I could tell he was close to tears, although he made a macho attempt to mask it by jiggling his leg and clenching his fists in his lap.

Maybe it was female intuition, or maybe I was gullible, but in my opinion this kid was no more a killer than I was. "So why did the police arrest you?"

"They found out I'd been in town the day Paul was killed. Actually, I had hoped to catch Paul at the cemetery. I wanted to explain to him what I just told you. I must've just missed him. I was going to try again next week, but then, well, he died."

"The only thing they had was that you were in town that day?" I filled a coffee cup and handed it to Mason.

"Not really." He wrapped his hands around the Styrofoam cup and stared into its depths. "My mother used to use the same kind of sleeping pills found in Paul's bloodstream. They figured I kept some, which is stupid, because I took those to get to sleep for the first couple of weeks after she died. They're what started me into drugs. Once they were gone, which was before I even started working for Paul, I looked for something else to knock the edge off the pain. It went downhill from there. But since the sleeping pills started it all, I obviously don't still have them, although they're trying to prove I could've gotten more."

"Either way, I don't think that would be enough evidence to hold you." I poured myself a cup of coffee, which I needed right about now, and took a sip as I let his words sink in, still looking for holes in his story in case my desire to champion those wrongly accused had won out over common sense.

"I don't either. Nobody saw me here that day, and my fingerprints weren't here either. But they shouldn't be, since I haven't been here in over a year, and I've never been upstairs." He took a long swallow from his cup, and it seemed to fortify him a tad.

"Still not a very strong case."

"That's why bail was set so low." Mason sighed. "I barely managed to scrape up the cash as it was. And now they tell me not to leave town until this is all straightened out. I guess I'm going to lose my job over this too."

My heart broke for the boy, as I knew exactly how he felt. But this wasn't about me. I needed to set the record straight. "Uncle Paul didn't blackball you."

Mason's head whipped up. "He didn't?" Confused creases snaked across his brow.

"No, he didn't. He wouldn't have betrayed you like that. The other business owners decided if he'd fired you, they didn't want to hire you." I watched for his reaction to this information.

"But I thought . . ." He shook his head. "Wow. You know, I think he tried to tell me back then, but I wouldn't give him the chance." His shoulders slumped again. "Now he'll never know he actually helped me."

I quickly changed the subject before he could slip deeper into despair. "Where will you stay while you're here?"

"I've still got a few friends in town. One of them will put me up for a while." Mason caught my concerned gaze. "Don't worry, I don't mean any of the 'friends' I had back when I took drugs. Some friends from before."

"I guess that'll do for a place to stay. What about your job?" My mind whirled. I knew this kid was being railroaded like I had been. Something clicked inside me, and I was determined not to let him face it all alone.

"I hope they'll let me borrow on my time off. I have a few days of vacation time and sick leave available. After that I'll be on leave without pay." He looked like a lost little boy.

I took a deep breath, hoping I was right and not simply letting my own situation make me blind to someone who really was guilty. "I could use some help around here going through these books. I'm trying to organize them so customers can find what they want. Are you interested in the job? It'll only be for minimum wage. I can't offer any benefits, but at least you could pay some of your bills so you won't lose your apartment or have your car repossessed while you're here."

Mason looked at me, his eyes wide and brows high. "You'd trust me to work here again? After what I did to Paul?"

118

"I don't think I'll have that problem this time around, will I?" At least I hoped not. I tossed my now-empty Styrofoam cup into the trash, sat on the stool behind the counter, and crossed my arms.

"No, ma'am! I swear." Mason jumped up, sloshing his coffee a bit. He grabbed the paper napkins from my once-again-forgotten lunch and wiped up the spill. "You'll see. I'll be a lot of help to you. After a few days, you'll figure out you can't do without me."

"Well, then." I waved an arm around to encompass the whole front room. "Let's get cracking."

The rest of the day passed too quickly, but we managed to get about a quarter of the way through the stacks of books in the front room. Now, including what Rita and I had done the day before, half the stacks were sorted. Of course, they still needed to be alphabetized and reshelved.

When it was time to leave for the day, I locked up with a smile, realizing how much closer I was to completing this huge task, thanks to Mason's assistance. He really would be a big help in the coming days. My smile sagged. But he wouldn't be for too long unless we could find a way to prove his innocence . . . and mine.

Chapter Sixteen

Sunday morning I donned a conservative black dress Rita had loaned me and went to church with her. I figured a lot of folks had seen that awful news report almost a week ago, but it still surprised me how many people knew who I was, even before Rita introduced me to them. Oddly enough, her prediction that folks wouldn't be hateful still held true. Maybe because it was a church service, or maybe because small-town folks stuck together. I wasn't technically from Hokes Folly, but Uncle Paul had been such a major figure in town, everyone accepted me as one of the family. Go figure. By the time church was over, I was sure my shoulder would show a bruise by bedtime from all the pats on the back, and the muscles in my face were sore from smiling and saying "Thank you" to all the offered "I'm sorry for your loss" condolences.

Afterward, Rita and I ate lunch at a tiny café near the historic district, and I made a mental note of its location so I could broaden my lunchtime possibilities from driving to a local McDonald's and eating at the pub where we'd first heard of Mason's arrest.

I wasn't looking forward to the next event of the day. As I didn't know where the cemetery was, I rode with Rita. Without the distraction of driving, I had too much time to think about where we were going and why. Instead, I filled her in on my afternoon with Mason, starting with his story and ending with why I believed he was innocent.

On impulse, I'd invited Mason to the small gathering of close friends, since I figured he deserved one last chance to say goodbye to a man he had wanted to thank in person. When we pulled into the parking lot, he was in the far corner, standing beside his clunker. We took the space next to his. Rita stared him in the eyes for several long moments, and I had to hand it to the kid, he didn't flinch. She nodded, agreeing he might not have killed Uncle Paul, but she'd withhold final judgment until further evidence came in.

The three of us walked to the grave together and were met by Horace Grimes, Olivia and Ophelia Hokes, and a small handful of others I had yet to meet. The minister from Rita's church stepped forward and read from the Bible. As he spoke, my mind focused on the large mahogany casket hovering over the open hole in the ground. A bouquet of lavender bearded irises lay on top, and I remembered these had been my aunt's favorite flower.

A tear slipped down my cheek. Even in death, he honored her. I looked at the double headstone, which now bore the inscriptions of both Aunt Irene and Uncle Paul. "Together for eternity" was carved at the bottom. I looked over at the Hokes sisters. Phillie wept quietly into a delicate lace handkerchief, while Livie remained stoic. Or maybe that was resentment I read in her expression. I couldn't be sure.

After the brief service and a sweet prayer offered by Horace, who it seemed had been not only Uncle Paul's attorney but also his best friend, folks began to walk back toward the parked cars. Mason stepped forward and laid his hand on the casket, silently mouthing a few words to Paul. I waited, scanning the cemetery so I wouldn't accidentally intrude on his private moment of farewell.

Motion caught my eye, and I spied a man who looked a lot like Stan Jergins cresting the hill into another portion of the cemetery. I couldn't be sure, though, as his back was to me, and I really didn't know the man that well. Had he come to offer condolences? Was he simply here visiting another grave? Or had he come to gloat over his rival's death?

Mason shifted beside the casket, and I turned back to see him walking toward his parked car. Rita still waited for me. I moved forward and placed my hand on the warm wood of the casket for my last moments with a man I should have made more time for. Grief once again swamped me, and this time I let the tears run freely. I wept for the fun times, the laughter, the thoughtful gifts, the funny jokes, and all the moments we'd shared during my childhood. I wept for all the invitations to visit that I'd turned down in the last ten years. I wept for the not-quite-intimate emails we'd swapped, realizing we hadn't really communicated beyond acquaintance pleasantries since I'd started turning him down. I wept for the loss of a man who had offered a home and protection at a time when I so desperately needed both. I wept for the loss of possibility and promise of a rebuilt relationship. I wept from gratitude for his thoughtful provisions, even in death, which meant I would never again be destitute. I wept for the loss of the next few decades of laughter and funny jokes and fun times that would now never come, not even in the form of scattered emails.

A warm hand slid across my shoulders, and Rita hugged me from the side while pressing a tissue into my free hand. I gratefully accepted it, wiped it across my eyes, and blew my nose. I patted the casket one last time then removed several of the irises and placed them on Aunt Irene's grave before turning to leave.

Rita linked her arm through mine as we walked across the cemetery toward the mostly empty parking lot. "Are you okay?"

I nodded and sniffed. "It's just a lot to process."

She squeezed my arm with hers. "Shall we go home?"

"Yes." We'd arrived at her car, and I opened the passenger door and slid inside. "I'd rather be busy, though. I'll probably change clothes and go downstairs to the store to work on the books for a while."

Rita walked around the car and got in. "Care for some company?"

I smiled a still-watery smile and nodded, knowing Rita was processing her own grief as well. We rode the rest of the way home in silence, each of us lost in our own memories of Uncle Paul.

After Rita and I arrived at the store an hour later, Mason popped in unexpectedly, offering to help out. It seemed Rita and I weren't the only ones who needed to be busy after the somber start to the afternoon.

Time passed quickly with the three of us working steadily, and when Monday morning rolled around, the store looked more like a real bookstore and less like a dumping ground. We'd managed to sort the rest of the shop and had begun the process of alphabetizing and reshelving, and I could see the light at the end of the tunnel. Of course, there were still all the books in the back room, but I pushed those to the back of my mind. There would be time enough for them later.

I hummed as I made coffee for the morning, determined to honor Uncle Paul's memory by organizing the store and making it appealing to buyers . . . or making it easier to run myself. I still wasn't sure which direction I'd go with that. The smell of perking coffee lifted my mood, and I determinedly procrastinated making a decision. With a smile, I unlocked the front door for Mason before turning back to get my first cup after the last of it came gurgling down into the pot.

The bells tinkled over the door, announcing Mason's arrival. He was barely inside when the door slammed open so hard it almost tore the bells down from the wall above. Mason and I both jumped as a man barged into the store.

"Who's in charge here?" he demanded, hands on his hips.

What the hell? I stepped forward. "I'm Jenna Quinn. I own the store. We're closed today, but is there something I could help you with?" I hoped my voice sounded friendlier than I felt.

"The owner, huh?" The man sneered at me. "Not for long, babe. I'm here to claim my inheritance, and this is part of it."

"I'm sorry, but I think you have the wrong store." I glanced at Mason, read his lips as he mouthed *nine-one-one* and raised his eyebrows in question, and shook my head.

"Is this the store that belonged to Paul Baxter?" The man's voice held a challenge.

"It is. I'm his niece. I inherited this store, along with the rest of Uncle Paul's holdings, upon his death last week." Trying to give him the benefit of the doubt, I assumed he had mixed up the address he wanted and had stormed into my store by mistake.

"I'm definitely in the right place." His expression moved from sneering to leering. "I'm Paul Baxter's long-lost son. I've got the papers to prove it. Thanks for helping straighten out the place, Cousin. As cute as you are, I wouldn't mind if you came in every day to make the coffee, but the kid here has to go."

His slimy grin made my skin crawl, and I set my coffee cup down before I succumbed to the temptation to toss it in his face. "Mister . . . what did you say your name was?" I struggled to keep my voice calm.

"Childers. Norman Childers. But you can call me Norm. After all, we're family."

"Well, *Mr. Childers.*" I spit the words out. "I believe I hold the deed to this property, and until it's proven you have a legitimate claim, I'm the owner of this establishment. For now, I would like you to leave."

"Can do, babe. Right after I check out the inventory." He started down the aisle toward the back room.

I gestured to Mason, and we both made it down the side aisles and to the back-room entrance before Norman. We stood with our arms crossed, blocking his way.

"Mr. Childers, if and when you bring me proof you have any right to see the back room of *my* business, then you will be allowed access to *my* inventory. Until then, I really think you should leave before I call the police." I leveled a glare at him, determined he wouldn't see the way my hands shook.

Norman turned to Mason. "Can't you talk some sense into your boss? She needs to learn some manners."

Mason met Norman's glare with a glare of his own, his spine held stiff and his arms still crossed. "I believe she asked you to leave. Do I need to help you to the door, or do you think you can remember the way?"

Way to go, Mason! Maybe I needed to give this kid a raise.

Norman's jaw tightened, and he pointed his finger into Mason's face. "Look, boy, for now you and my cousin can have it your way. But you'll be hearing from my lawyer before the day is out. And when you do, you'd better watch your back." He turned and stomped out into the street, treating the door as roughly as he had upon entering.

Mason and I stared at each other in shocked silence, not even moving from where we still guarded the back room.

"What was that all about?" Mason asked finally, his eyes wide.

"I have no clue." Stunned, I looked toward the door, almost afraid the obnoxious man might storm back inside. "I never heard Uncle Paul talk about a son. Did you?"

"Not even a hint. But then, I didn't know Paul for long before . . ." Mason left his history with Paul unstated.

"I guess for now the best thing to do is call Mr. Grimes." I skipped past Mason's reference to the theft he'd committed in the past and stalked toward the front counter. "He'll get to the bottom of this."

After setting up an appointment through the lawyer's secretary, I turned back to Mason. "I'll be back soon. Keep the doors locked and try to get some more done on these stacks of books piled everywhere."

Mason squared his shoulders, a look of determination on his face. "You got it, boss. You won't recognize this place when you get back."

I gently laid a hand on his arm. "I do trust you, Mason. I wouldn't leave you here alone if I didn't."

"Yeah, okay. I just don't want anything to mess it up this time." He ducked his head. "Hokes Folly is home. I want to move back, but I can't unless I prove I'm worth hiring."

On impulse, I gave him a quick hug. Okay, so I *was* the crazy chick who hugged veritable strangers. "Somehow we'll work this out, okay? For now, I have to go, but you do a great job and I'll put in a good word with every business in town."

I walked out the door to the tune of his happy whistling.

* * *

My time with the lawyer proved the legal system should go back to simpler times when "Finders keepers, losers weepers" had been a hard-and-fast rule. Mr. Grimes confirmed he had indeed received papers from a law firm in Raleigh regarding the newly found, long-lost heir. I had inherited only because Uncle Paul had no children "either by birth or adoption" to whom to leave his estate.

The attorney admitted he hadn't had a chance to completely go through Norman Childers's papers, but according to the letter accompanying them, Uncle Paul had had an affair with Norman's mother roughly five years after he and Aunt Irene were married. I found this hard to accept, but until proof could be located to negate the claims, Mr. Grimes advised cooperation.

So, here we sat, back door to the alley open, waiting to let the man into Uncle Paul's store and home, or rather my store and home now. His tardiness irritated me to no end.

First, the man's claim was based on Uncle Paul being unfaithful to Aunt Irene. I simply couldn't swallow that.

Second, the man had made me miss good working hours, and since I wanted to keep Mason out of his sights, I'd let my new employee go home early for the day.

Third, he wanted to take away something that, in a very short time, had come to mean a great deal to me. Aside from the fact that without it I would have no way to support myself, it was mine, and he had no right to try to take it. And he wouldn't succeed. Not without a fight on his hands. I was done walking away without a fight.

Fourth, he was a downright jerk. Even his presence conjured up childhood memories of playground bullies, and I'd had enough of bullies in my recent past to last a lifetime.

Fifth . . .

My ranting mental list ended as a sleek, red Corvette pulled into the alleyway behind the store. As Norman Childers got out of his car, I took a few deep breaths then calmly stepped to the doorway and greeted him with as much civility as I could muster.

"Hey, Cousin, nice place." His voice reeked of sarcasm.

"Yes, it is." I took a deep breath and mentally counted to ten.

"Shall we proceed?" Mr. Grimes stepped between us and ushered Norman inside.

"Sure thing. I want to see if the back room is as much of a dump as the storefront." Norman's nose wrinkled as if he'd smelled something distasteful. "But this would make a nice site for a Starbucks, don't you think?" He pointedly looked around the attorney to make eye contact with me.

I gritted my teeth, swallowing the ugly retort that leapt to mind.

Horace Grimes again inserted himself. "The downtown historic district has rules on what can and cannot be placed here. Should you be confirmed as heir, we will discuss what is possible."

"And if you managed to get around that rule, there is no way the municipal association would let you build something so out of place here." I clutched my hands tightly behind my back to keep from shoving Norman's back out into the alley and slamming the door.

"There are ways around those little problems. Money solves everything. You only have to know whose palm to grease." He grinned and winked at me as he stepped past me.

During his first visit to the store, he'd blown through the place like a whirlwind, never stopping long enough to touch or even notice anything. Today was vastly different. Today he demonstrated an incredible lack of respect for the property. Repeatedly I had to request that he not destroy books by pulling at their bindings or tugging on the pages. He knocked on the walls, looked in the refrigerator drawers, and even stood on a chair to look above the ceiling tiles.

After we moved into the front room, he began pulling books off the shelves, creating more mess for me to clean up. Behind the counter, he looked in every nook and cranny, and he even pulled out the coffee supplies in the cabinets under the coffee station.

Norman's gaze settled on the spiral stairs that wound their way upward. "So this is where the old man bought it, huh?" His eyes skimmed over to the bottom of the stairs, but his voice wasn't as grieving as I thought it ought to be for a man who had lost a father, even if he hadn't known him personally.

"Yes. He fell down the stairs. I found him the next morning." I thought about Uncle Paul lying there alone for hours, no matter that he was dead. What had really happened before I arrived?

Norman interrupted my thoughts. "Well, his loss is our gain." He winked at me and grinned. "Well, mine anyway. But you're cute, and we're family, so I may let you stay on as a barista."

I mentally counted to ten, again stifling the urge to throw him out. I glanced at Horace, who had remained silent, catching his worried look and the shake of his head, as if he knew what was going on in my head.

Eager to get the ordeal over, I suggested we move upstairs for a brief look.

Norman's eyes sparkled in a way that made the hairs on the back of my neck stand up. "I thought we'd never get to this part." He turned and bounded up, and I heard his grunt of frustration when he rattled the doorknob but couldn't turn it.

"Do I really have to do this?" I spoke softly over my shoulder to Horace as we ascended the stairs.

"Legally, no. However, it's best to accommodate him so you don't seem like you're hiding anything."

The strained tone in Horace's voice let me know I wasn't the only one freaked out about Norman and his behavior.

As we moved through the apartment, I tried to ignore Norman's rudeness. He commented negatively on each piece of

furniture—"God, this is outdated"—each painting—"Could anyone have worse taste than this?"—each work of art—"That's just
got to go . . . to the dump." Did he ever shut up? He was even worse
than Barbie had been.

He then went through every kitchen cabinet and the pantry,
pulled at the drapes, lifted the couch cushions, and thumped on
the dining, coffee, and end tables, as if to test their solidity.

As we finished the tour of the main area of the apartment,
Norman stomped toward the bedrooms. Apparently catching my
startled look, Horace managed to get to Uncle Paul's doorway
before I could, successfully blocking Norman's way.

"Outa my way." Norman unsuccessfully attempted to sidestep
Horace. "I want to see the rest of the place. If that's the old man's
bedroom, isn't that where he would have kept anything valuable?"
Norman looked over Horace's shoulder, letting his eyes roam
greedily around Uncle Paul's bedroom.

"What sort of valuables did you have in mind?" I tried but was
unable to keep the irritable snip from my voice. "I haven't had time
to catalog anything in Uncle Paul's room yet, but I'm sure he may
still have a few costume pieces that belonged to my aunt."

"Not that kind of cheap junk." Norman slid sideways, trying
to push past Horace into the room. "I mean really valuable items."

Thank God for Horace, who shifted his own weight and stood
solidly in Norman's way. He might not be saying much, but his
presence was comforting, and I was thrilled I wasn't facing this
alone.

"What type of things, Mr. Childers?" I gritted my teeth to keep
from yelling. If I wasn't careful, I'd wear down my teeth to bare
roots before this was all over.

"Oh, I don't know, objects of valuable art, really rare books,
that sort of thing." He crossed his arms, glaring at Horace.

Seeming to give up on Uncle Paul's room, he now looked down the apartment toward my room.

Oh no, you don't! I skittered across the space, arriving in time to block Norman from my own doorway. "If you don't mind, Mr. Childers, I would appreciate it if you don't disturb my things." My gaze met his in a stare down. He blinked first, and I inwardly pumped my fist in victory. On the outside, however, I kept my face straight.

"They won't be your things for long, now will they, Cousin?" He smirked and winked at me, reaching out to run a few strands of my hair through his fingers. "But if you play your cards right, you might get to keep living here with me."

I smacked his hand away from my face but stood my ground. Now I understood how someone might be driven to murder. That thought sobered me, and I struggled to regain my inner composure. "I'm sure the disposition of my uncle's estate would be best handled by our attorneys. Now, if you're ready to go?" I gestured toward the front door.

"Not until I see the rest of the rooms here, babe." Norman crossed his arms and glared into my eyes.

I could stand no more of the man for one day. "Mr. Childers, I must decline." I was determined to stand firm on this one. "You see, I have made my home, although a possibly temporary one, in this apartment. Under no circumstances will I let you inside either bedroom to create the mess you've left me to straighten up here or downstairs in the store. Here I draw the line." I stared daggers at him, my back straight and my fists clenched at my sides.

Norman turned to the attorney. "Can she do that? Can she keep me out?"

Horace's head bobbed in a staccato nod. "Yes, as her home is there now, without a court order, you cannot force her to show you the premises. Frankly, as there has not yet been a court mandate, she let you in here only out of a spirit of cooperation." The attorney's tight voice and clenched jaw spoke volumes of his opinion of Norman Childers.

"I guess I can wait a few more days to see those. The papers should have cleared everything up with you lawyers by then." He turned to leave but called over his shoulder as he headed for the door, "Remember, anything, and I mean *anything*, you find must stay with the estate when I gain control. There will be no pilfering or stealing from Norman Childers."

How dare he? As if I would ever think of taking something that didn't belong to me. Wait a minute—who was the one trying to steal what didn't belong to him? And why? Norman obviously had no interest in the apartment, the business, or the town. He was, from all appearances, not in need of money. Massive lessons in manners, yes. But not money.

Norman Childers was looking for something else. My mind flashed to the book Uncle Paul had asked Linus Talbot to authenticate. Could this be the "valuable" item Norman wanted?

Chapter Seventeen

Tuesday proved difficult. All day I put up with Norman moving in and out of my store, *my* store. The angrier I got at Norman, the more the idea of staying and making a go of the store on my own appealed to me. Maybe it was that psychological thing where kids want to play with a toy only when another child desires it. Norman wanted what I had, and I was determined I would keep it. He spent the day peering over my shoulder, telling me what a great job I was doing for him and chatting with my few customers. He'd stood outside my door at one point for over an hour, announcing to everyone who passed that he now owned Baxter's Book Emporium. The final straw came in the early afternoon when I overheard a conversation with an elderly female customer who made the mistake of stopping to talk with him.

"What are your plans for the bookstore?" she sweetly asked.

"I'll probably get rid of all this old junk cluttering up the shelves and turn this place into a first-class adult video store. I may even add a couple of peep-show booths in the back."

The woman gasped and placed her hand at her throat. "What?" she asked weakly.

"Sure. It'll get more male customers into the downtown area. Good for everyone's businesses. It'll help change the profile of the typical customer around here. I'll bet it'll be the most popular store in town with the men." Norman elbowed the woman, continuing as she paled even further. "And I'll bet we'll have our share of women customers too. How about a discount coupon? Or you could come by and audition for a booth space. I'm sure there would be guys who'd want to see a more mature woman put on a show." He winked at her.

The lady finally managed to gain strength from her building indignation at such rude insinuations. "I would never stoop to darken the door of such a place. As a matter of fact"—she aimed this comment at me as I rushed to the door to try to stop Norman's outrageous claims—"I'll never come back to this store. I'll be sure to tell all of my friends not to come here either. And you, young lady, should be ashamed working in a place like this. What would your mother say?" With that, the woman stormed down the sidewalk, her back rigid and her nose in the air.

By the time I'd recovered from the shock enough to go after Norman, he'd walked beyond my reach, calling over his shoulder that he was going to grab a late lunch. I stood on the sidewalk watching the retreating figure move down the street, gritting my teeth each time he stopped to chat with folks and point at my bookstore. It was obvious he was repeating his story of an adult video store, as several people angrily pulled away from him and gave me scathing looks as they passed me, leaving me to fantasize about throttling my supposed cousin.

"That man is going to ruin any chance of this bookstore succeeding." I kicked a small stone lying on the sidewalk, watching it skitter into the street. "One of these days, someone is going to shut him up permanently, but by then it'll probably be too late for my poor store."

I jumped when I heard a voice behind me. "Problems?"

I turned and found myself face-to-face with none other than Olivia Hokes. Just what I needed. Although at this point I had to be nice to any neighbors still willing to talk to me. "Yes. I'm trying to figure out how not to lose every possible customer I could ever have." I hoped she hadn't heard my comment about someone permanently shutting Norman up. I looked back and burned another hole into his retreating figure with imaginary lasers from my eyes.

Following my gaze, Olivia's watched Norman's back as he distanced himself from my anger. "Is that nice man bothering you?"

"Nice?" I couldn't keep my voice from exploding out at the tiny woman, and when she flinched and took a step back, I quickly apologized. "I'm sorry, Miss Hokes, it's simply that he's ruining my business, and I have no way to stop him."

"How is he managing to ruin your business?" Olivia's concern seemed genuine.

Maybe I had misjudged her. Could be I'd previously caught her on a bad day. Both times. At least today didn't seem to be one of them. "Earlier he told me he'd turn this place into a Starbucks. Now he's telling everyone he owns the place now and is going to turn it into an adult video store with peep-show booths in back. He's alienating customers, and no one will want to shop here." My chest tightened, and my throat closed on the last words.

Olivia put her hand on her chest. "Oh my," she gasped. "I can see why you're mad. But how is he getting away with saying he owns the place? I thought Paul left it to you."

"He did." I pinched the bridge of my nose in an attempt to block the building headache I'd fought since Norman had shown up again first thing this morning. "The only problem is Norman says he's the rightful heir. He claims to be Uncle Paul's illegitimate son."

"Oh no." The hand remained at the tiny woman's chest. "That doesn't sound like the Paul Baxter I knew. What are you going to do?"

"There's apparently not much I can do right now." I expelled a frustrated breath. "I tried to reach my parents last night, but Mom's still kind of hazy on pain pills." At her odd look, I quickly added, "She had surgery on one of her spinal disks. Dad wasn't sure about things, and he asked me to wait a couple of days until she's a little more herself. I hope they can help fight Norman. As it is, though, I have to put up with him until Mom's a little more clearheaded."

The older woman patted my arm. "If there's any way we can help, call us."

"I will. Thanks."

Olivia disappeared back inside the antique clothing store. I shook my head at the odd conversation. What had made the woman stand up for Uncle Paul, a man she seemed to intensely dislike?

I shook my head once more and reentered the bookstore when Mason signaled I had a phone call. After crossing the room with quick strides, I picked up the receiver. "May I help you?" I hoped my voice came out sounding as cheerful as I meant it to be.

"Miss Quinn?" The voice on the other end sounded official.

"This is Jenna Quinn. May I help you?" I repeated my question.

"I'm with Hokes Folly Community Bank. We've had to freeze the accounts of the late Paul Baxter."

"On what grounds?" My stomach clenched, and I closed my eyes, knowing the answer.

"We've received an affidavit from a law firm in Raleigh stating that a Norman Childers is contesting the disbursement of Paul Baxter's trust. Mr. Childers claims to be the rightful beneficiary,

136

and if that's the case, we cannot release the funds to anyone but him. We have to wait to see how this all works out."

I gripped the phone tightly and swallowed back a snotty retort. After all, it wasn't this poor woman's fault. She was only the bearer of bad news. "Thank you so much for notifying me. I haven't written any checks against the account yet, so there should be no problems."

After saying goodbye, it was all I could do not to slam the phone down as hard as I could, but instead I placed the phone on the base with a gentleness I didn't feel. No sooner had I hung up than it rang again.

"Now what?" I reached for the receiver. "Baxter's Book Emporium." I tried to put on my cheerful bookseller voice once more. After all, I couldn't afford to lose a customer right now because I was rude to them on the phone.

"Miss Quinn?"

I couldn't quite place the familiar voice. "Yes?"

"This is Horace Grimes. May I talk to you for a moment?" His strained tones communicated his unease with the call.

"Sure. What's up?" I had a feeling I was going to regret asking.

He cleared his throat. "Norman Childers is officially contesting the trust disbursement. Since we have to wait until we have the correct beneficiary identified, we cannot allow one or the other of you to have access to the store without proper supervision. I'm sorry."

"Can he really do all of this with just a few old papers? Can't we do a DNA test or something?" My chest tightened, and I tried to calm my breathing.

"So far, Norman has not responded to a request for a test. I'm preparing legal papers to send to his attorney insisting on it.

However, even then it could take weeks to get it through the court and to get a test completed."

The room spun, and I squeezed my eyes shut to stop the tears that threatened to come. "I'll try to wrap things up here and have the keys to the store to you first thing in the morning. Will that be okay?"

"Yes. That's fine." Horace sounded relieved.

"If there's nothing more . . ."

"Actually, there is the little matter of the apartment. You might not own it either. You'll either have to move out by the end of the day tomorrow or you'll have to sign an agreement to pay rent into the trust."

My knees wobbled, and I sat on the phone table with a thump, causing its spindly legs to shift and creak. Fortunately, it didn't collapse, but it would've fit the situation if it had. Everything else seemed to be falling out from under me again. Why not this?

Mentally I assessed my dwindling finances, knowing it wouldn't take long to deplete what was left. My stomach plummeted. "I'll sign the agreement, Mr. Grimes. Norman Childers may be able to ruin my business and may try to steal my inheritance, but I'll be damned if he's going to put me out on the street as well." *Not when I finally have a home again!*

Ignoring the fact that Horace Grimes was no more responsible for any of this than the bank lady, I disconnected the call without saying goodbye, knowing I would burst into tears if I tried to utter another word. This was unfortunate, since the phone rang for the third time almost immediately.

"Baxter's Book Emporium." There was no hope of getting the cheerful tone I'd aimed for with the first two calls.

"Miss Quinn," said another slightly familiar voice.

"Yes?" I snapped, not caring if I pissed off a customer. Right now I only wanted to find a corner and cry.

"This is Stan Jergins. As we had discussed the possibility of representing you in the sale of Paul Baxter's store and apartment, I am letting you know that this has been indefinitely put on hold. Norman Childers informs me he's the rightful heir and will live in the apartment and will run the business after he straightens out the legalities."

"Oh?" Fury ripped through me, overriding the despair that had threatened to overwhelm me moments before. "Mr. Jergins, I'm sorry to hear you say that. I'm sure another real estate agent will be more than willing to handle the sale and earn a large commission after I prove Mr. Childers is a fraud. Will there be anything else?" I chose not to tell Stan that I might not sell either.

"No. I . . . no . . ." The stuttered reply sounded over the line.

"Good. Thank you for your call." Giving Stan no time to add anything, I disconnected, indulging myself with a tiny slam into the phone's cradle. How dare Norman Childers? Who did he think he was? He sure wasn't Uncle Paul's son as he claimed, so who was he really? And why was he so hot to get ahold of Uncle Paul's estate?

Norman didn't reappear at the store that afternoon, much to my relief. I would probably have hit him over the head with one of the large cookbooks on my shelves. If he'd tried this kind of thing before, it was a miracle someone hadn't killed him already.

Mason and I worked steadily all afternoon, determined to get as much done as we could before leaving. Who knew when we'd get to come back and finish? Or *if* we'd get to come back. We stayed later than usual and accomplished a lot. Not that it really mattered if Norman Childers managed to cheat me out of my inheritance and was serious about an adult store.

I tried not to get worked up again when I said goodbye to Mason as he walked toward his car. I turned and looked around the store once more. *My* bookstore. There had to be a way to put a stop to Norman Childers, and I'd find that way, no matter what it took.

Chapter Eighteen

Wednesday morning, I again sat in the waiting room of Grimes and Waterford. This time, however, I didn't bother to thumb through a magazine. Not only had I read them all during my first visit, but I wouldn't have been able to focus on the words anyway. Instead, I fumed, envisioning myself in a Perry Mason-esque courtroom scene, slamming my hand on the railing of the witness stand that held Norman Childers and cornering him into confessing he was a fraud and a thief.

Partway through the third version of these events, Mr. Grimes's door opened, and he ushered out his previous client, motioning me to enter. "I'm glad you could stop by, Jenna. I really hate to have to do this, but it's best to get it over with as soon as possible."

"Rip the Band Aid off quickly, is that it?" I slid past him into the room and sat rigidly in the leather wingback chair.

"I guess you could call it that." He sighed as he sank into his own chair behind the imposing desk and slid a stack of papers across it.

I held back my anger as I signed the papers, agreeing to pay rent into the trust, knowing no real way around it until I had proof Norman Childers was lying through his perfectly capped teeth. I had no clue where I'd come up with rent money, since my own funds were pitifully low, but the first payment wasn't for two weeks, which gave me time to find proof of Norman's fraud. With shaking hands, I reached into my purse and pulled out the keys to the store and slid them across the desk toward the attorney. Only my mother's voice in my head had kept me from making an extra key on the way over.

Mr. Grimes picked up the keys and held them out, offering them to me. "About ten minutes ago, I spoke with Mr. Childers concerning the store. He feels it'll serve no purpose to close it indefinitely, so he's agreed to allow you to keep the keys and continue to organize and run the business until further notice."

"He'll allow me?" I struggled not to scream like a banshee. "This guy has a lot of nerve. First he doesn't trust me to have the keys to *my* inheritance. Then I have to pay rent on *my* own home. Now he'll *allow* me to run *my* own business?" My voice had risen to a crescendo. I knew the attorney wasn't to blame for any of this, but I simply couldn't stop myself.

"Look on the bright side. At least you won't lose customers because the doors are closed." A hopeful smile followed the soothe-the-crazy-lady-ranting-in-my-office tone he used.

"No." I jumped to my feet and placed my palms on the desk, leaning toward the attorney. "We'll lose customers because of his loud mouth." I told the lawyer of Norman's stated intentions for the bookstore, plopping back into my seat in resignation after my—if I was being honest with myself—temper tantrum.

Mr. Grimes steepled his fingers and sat silent for a moment. "I don't think the historic area of town is zoned for that. I'll look into it for you, but I'm pretty sure it has to be a type of business that might have existed around the year 1900. Somehow I doubt an adult peep show, much less an adult video store, would qualify."

"Unfortunately, the damage will already be done." I sighed, remembering the scathing looks and irate customers. "Everyone is angry at the proposed change, and if he doesn't stop, no one will continue to come to the store, because every business and upstanding citizen in town will boycott us."

"Let's hope it doesn't come to that," said the lawyer evenly.

I tried to control my anger at Norman Childers as I finally asked the question that had been running circles in my brain for the last twenty-four hours. "Mr. Grimes, what exactly does Norman Childers have that started all of this?"

The attorney cleared his throat. "He has an affidavit from his mother, who recently passed away, and love letters from Paul to his mother dated back to the time of Norman's conception."

I clenched my fists. "Supposed conception, please."

"Very well, supposed conception." Mr. Grimes looked at me and blinked. "Jenna, I'm very sure the man was indeed conceived at the time he claims. The question is not whether or when he was conceived, but rather who was involved in the conceiving process."

I relaxed and chuckled sheepishly. "You're right." I sobered. "I don't like to see Uncle Paul's and Aunt Irene's names dragged through the mud. If he's actually Uncle Paul's son, why did he wait this long to come forward? Why not while Uncle Paul was still alive?"

Mr. Grimes consulted the stack of papers in front of him. "It seems Norman's mother never told him his father's identity. He found the signed affidavit among her papers after her death. She left it along with a letter telling him she wanted him to be able to find his father if he so chose. I have a copy of that letter here also." He selected a piece of paper from the stack on his desk and offered it to me.

I quickly scanned the letter then read it again while the lawyer waited patiently. "This doesn't say anything about the identity of

Norman's father. It only says he should read the papers included with it and do what he thought was right."

"It was found with the affidavit stating that Paul Warren Baxter of North Carolina was her son's father." Mr. Grimes produced another piece of paper for me to read.

I resisted the urge to reduce the paper to confetti. The lawyer probably didn't have the original anyway. If I shredded this copy, Norman would simply supply another.

"This doesn't say much either. Only Uncle Paul's name and what state he lived in." I looked at the paper once more, stopping at the notarized date. "I just realized something. Uncle Paul and Aunt Irene moved to North Carolina when I was nine. I remember they lived in Arizona before that. Mom made a big deal over them living closer to us and not having to drive so far to come see us. The date on this affidavit is from several years before they lived here. How can that be possible if it's legitimate?"

Mr. Grimes took the paper from my outstretched hand and scanned it. "I can't believe I missed this. It could help you out a lot in court. I'll get my investigators on it immediately."

"Good." It was about time we found something to fight with. Though not the type to revel in the downfall of another person, I couldn't help but feel a bit smug. "This'll help poke a few holes in Norman's story."

"We still have Paul's letters to Norman's mother." The lawyer laid a few pages on the desk in front of me.

I skimmed them and noticed the glaring problem instantly. "These letters are typed. Only the signatures are handwritten. And they could have been forged."

"That's true," he agreed. "We have handwriting experts looking at them now. On the surface, the signatures look genuine, but we aren't taking any chances. I've also filed the papers for the DNA test, but as I said before, it will be several weeks to get through the court system."

"At least you aren't swallowing all of this garbage hook, line, and sinker." I sat back with a frustrated huff. I closed my eyes and tried to relax my rock-hard shoulders, glad to have Horace Grimes on my side.

"No. We're taking every precaution to ensure the validity of these documents."

I changed the subject. "So, how did Norman supposedly track down his long-lost father after all these years?"

Mr. Grimes pulled another page out of the pile. "It seems, upon finding these papers among his mother's effects, Norman hired a private detective to locate your uncle, his supposed father. It took a bit over a week to finish the job, and by that time your uncle had already died. So Norman came to claim his 'rightful inheritance' from the interloper—specifically, you."

"Interloper?" My eyebrows shot up. "He actually called me an interloper? On what grounds?"

"He claimed you and your family knew about him and you accepted the inheritance without disclosing the fact of his birth." Mr. Grimes looked uncomfortable.

"Do you really believe that?" My back was ramrod straight, shoulders in tight knots again, and I bored into the attorney's eyes with my gaze.

"No. Of course not." His gaze remained steady. "We simply have no proof yet of its invalidity."

"*Yet* is the operative word here." I placed my palms on his desk and rose. "But we will, Mr. Grimes. You can bet your bottom dollar on that one."

* * *

Laura Gail Black

I'd spent most of the morning with Horace Grimes and came away more angry and confused than when I'd gone in. Throwing away the wrapper of the cardboard-flavored hamburger I'd just choked down at a small diner near the attorney's office, I stomped out to my car. It was too late to get the first morning traffic into my store, and since afternoons were usually pretty slow anyway, or they had been this last week, I decided to leave the store closed for the day. At the very least, it would keep Norman from using it as his base of operations.

Instead I walked up and down the historic downtown sidewalks, visiting with my new neighbors in business. A little PR wouldn't hurt. As I had already covered my bases with the Hokes sisters, I began elsewhere, starting up one side of the street and stopping in each store to introduce myself. I hoped to build up the bookstore's reputation and my own against the damage Norman Childers had inflicted. In each store, I first encountered slight hostility, especially with those who had seen the initial news report of my possible involvement in Uncle Paul's death. However, hostility turned to indignation when I explained the current business situation. All seemed to be supportive of my efforts and gave well wishes in my quest to stop Norman from gaining control of the store.

"He came in here," said one irate storekeeper, "running off my paying customers and wanting to know if he could leave discount coupons for his adult video store on our counter. I told him to get out and not come back."

I apologized profusely for the umpteenth time and promised to do my best to keep him away in the future. Continuing my mission, I entered store after store, only to hear similar remarks. By the time I had visited every business on the street, my feet and back ached from wearing shoes that were cute, yes, but not suited to walking so far. Sensing I had put things as right as they could be

146

under the circumstances and hoping I had gained the support of my neighbors, I headed back to the apartment, tired but more relaxed than I'd been since Norman Childers had steamrolled his way into town two days ago.

Realizing it was time to call Mom and Dad, I pulled out my phone and called them as I walked through my front door.

"Hello?" Joe Quinn's warm voice answered the telephone.

"Dad." I breathed a sigh of relief, happy to hear a familiar voice.

"Wait. Let me get your mom on the other line. Rose? It's Jenna."

His fatherly concern wrapped warmly around my heart as I unburdened myself on my parents.

Chapter Nineteen

Thursday morning a white-jacketed driver helped me into the carriage for the ride up to the Hokes Bluff Inn from the parking lot. I breathed deeply of the sweet mountain air as we rode through the forest. Near the end of the lane, the trees thinned, and I caught my first glimpse of the stately manor.

Beautiful landscaping wrapped the hotel in flowering shrubs, lush lawns, and stately trees, providing long stretches of shade in contrast to the late-morning sunshine. After the driver helped me exit the carriage, I crossed to the wide and inviting front steps. Once the uniformed attendant opened the doors to the interior of the hotel, I truly felt like I had stepped back in time.

My jaw dropped at the opulence in the lobby. What a breathtaking masterpiece John Hokes had planned. Early morning light streamed through glass sections of the vaulted ceilings, and live trees grew from holes in the marble floor.

While I waited for Rita to join me, I strolled around the room, looking at expensive paintings adorning silk-paneled walls. I wasn't an art expert by any stretch of the imagination, but many were replicas of originals by well-known artists, although Monet was the only one I could identify without standing on the ornate furniture to get a closer look at the signatures.

Huge pieces of furniture placed carefully around the large room, unmistakably expensive antiques, looked like they belonged in a museum. Exotically patterned Oriental carpets graced the hardwood floors. Above my head hung a chandelier that must have weighed several hundred pounds, and highly polished brass wall sconces held electric lights to supplement the magnificent light from above. Although my khaki slacks were crisply pressed and my heather-blue polo complemented my blue eyes, I felt dowdy compared to the sheer elegance of the room.

I jumped as Rita tapped me on the shoulder from behind. "Gee whiz! Don't scare me like that. You almost gave me a heart attack."

Rita's period costume was as elegant as the surroundings. The silvery blue of the day dress set off her upswept red hair. The high neckline, puffed upper sleeves, and tiny waistline gave way to a skirt that belled out below the knees like a morning glory, with a small train behind. "Sorry. I'm dying to know what you've managed to scrape up on that nasty Mr. Childers. He's not exactly our most appreciated patron. Quite a few of us would love to see his stupid story debunked. And I'm one of them."

"I can only imagine." I grinned.

We had discussed Norman over dinner the evening before, and I'd called to let her know I was coming today, armed with new information.

"I can't believe you didn't tell me last night about this secret dirt you've got on Norman." Rita tried unsuccessfully to pout, as a tickled grin kept her from pulling her mouth down into a frown.

"I only found out this morning when my dad called back. They needed to verify a few facts before I could talk about it. And I'm not telling you what it is until I can tell that weasel. I want to see the look on his face when I prove he's lying through his teeth." I'd savored the prospect of that very moment all morning. Okay, so it wasn't my Perry Mason moment, but it would still satisfy my growing need to finally stick it to someone who was screwing me over, this time Norman Childers.

"Then let's get at it." Rita practically dragged me across the elegant lobby in the direction of the bank of elevators at the far end.

"Elevators?" I looked around, surprised something so out of place would be here. "I thought this was supposed to be period-accurate to the turn of the twentieth century."

Rita shifted to tour-guide mode. "Elevators were first used in the early 1800s. By the early 1900s, they weren't that uncommon and had become electric rather than steam or hydraulic driven."

"Hey, you're good at this." I followed behind her, finally arriving at the elevators at the far end of the vast lobby.

She'd told the bellhop to hold one of the three elevators, explaining we had bad news for the patron in suite 412.

"I hope it's bad enough to send him packing," said the bellboy, who obviously didn't like Norman any more than anyone else who'd met him. "He's a lousy tipper, and he treats us bellboys like we're gunk to be scraped off the bottom of his shoe or something." The doors opened on the fourth floor, and as we stepped out, the bellboy added, "Good luck. I hope you get the sucker."

I almost bounced as I walked, internally doing the Snoopy happy dance as I followed Rita's silent footsteps, her elegant dress whispering as she walked. Finally at Norman's door, I took a deep breath and reveled in the moment one last time before banging loudly, a goofy grin plastered on my face.

"Norman, you jerk, I know you're in there!" I yelled through the door when it didn't open after the first few knocks. I pounded harder. "Come out and face me like a man, you weasel. I know the truth."

I almost jumped out of my shoes when the door was yanked open not by Norman but by Detective Frank Sutter. "I'm so sorry, we must have the wrong room," I stammered. "I was looking for suite four-twelve and Norman Childers." I grabbed Rita's arm and turned to go.

"You found the right room, Miss Quinn. But Norman can't come to the door right now."

I stopped in my tracks and turned, frustrated to be blocked by this irritating detective. This hadn't been part of my dream scenario. "Oh? And why not?"

"Because he's dead."

Chapter Twenty

M y breath left in a whoosh, and my knees would have buckled, taking me to a pile on the floor, if Rita hadn't held me up.

"Why don't you two lovely ladies come in?" Sutter gestured into the room, and too stunned to object, we obediently went where he pointed.

In the corner, near a lavish couch, lay a body-sized lump under a white sheet. Sutter's partner stood nearby, leaning in to speak to someone in a coroner's jacket.

Detective Logan saw us and came across the room. "Miss Quinn, what are you doing here?" His concern was noticeable, and his gaze locked on to me, his chocolate-brown eyes warm and compassionate.

It was all I could do to resist the temptation to brush a stray lock of wavy, dark hair off his forehead.

Sutter's eyes, however, gave me a nasty look. "Yes, exactly what did you have to discuss with our dearly departed guest over there?"

"I wanted to talk to him about some personal business." I wasn't sure how much to divulge. After all, now that Norman was dead, it didn't matter if he claimed to be Uncle Paul's son. Or did it?

"Personal business." *Grunt*. "I find it highly coincidental that you're connected to yet another dead body." His snarky tone inferred he found it anything but coincidental. "Look, Miss Quinn, let's be frank with one another. Why don't you tell me the truth?" He raised his eyebrows slightly and tilted his head, a look of sympathy on his face belied by the cold glint in his eyes.

I stifled a hysterical giggle and choked back the reflexive comment that he would be better at being Frank than I would.

Seeming to misunderstand my expression as a sudden onset of nerves, the detective led us to sit on a second couch across the room from the body. He angled me so I couldn't see Norman's remains. "I can help if you're honest with me from the start."

It hit me what Detective Sutter was getting at. He thought I'd killed Norman and had returned to the scene of the crime. My mouth dropped open, but no sound came out. Finally, I managed to push words out past the band tightening around my chest. "How dare you think that about me?"

"Excuse me?" Sutter narrowed his gaze.

"You think I did this too, don't you?" Indignation burned in my gut. I. Would. Not. Go. Through. This. Again.

"Jenna, he does not." Rita's voice had a soothing effect, as if she wanted to keep me from landing us in more hot water.

I was too incensed to care. "He does too. Look at him. His mind is all made up. And he doesn't even know why I'm here." Fury washed through me, and not simply at missing the opportunity to chew out Norman.

"We've had a rash of unusual crime for this area—murder, breaking and entering, now a second murder—and guess who the common denominator is." Sutter changed from the sympathetic ear to the hard-nosed cop. "I do think you might have killed Mr. Childers. I think the two of you may have already had an argument, possibly over whatever you were yelling about at the door a few minutes ago, possibly a falling-out among thieves. Maybe you two killed Baxter together. I think you attempted to kill Childers, then you left. I think you were coming back here to make sure you hadn't left anything of yours behind. But you messed up, because you did leave something behind."

"And what is that, Detective Sutter?" Thoroughly outraged by this time, I clutched at Rita's hand for support.

"A glove." Sutter motioned to Logan, who crossed the room to pick up a baggie.

As he approached, I saw a black glove in the bag. When he held it out toward me to show me, I saw it was made of fine silk and seemed to have been well cared for over many years.

"Hold out your hand," insisted Sutter, laying the bag flat in his palm.

Rita gripped my hand tighter. "You don't have to do this," she said softly in my ear. She looked at Sutter. "You do know, even if it does fit her, it doesn't prove a thing. Any female guest here could have worn that glove, and I'm sure we have more than one pair on hand exactly like it."

Sutter grinned a challenging grin. "Of course she doesn't have to, but then, if she doesn't, do we need to worry she's hiding something?"

The challenge had been thrown down, and I was tired of backing down like a timid mouse. "Fine. I will." I plopped my hand down into his on top of the glove, determined to prove his theory incorrect and praying it didn't actually fit. Internal fist pump! I snatched my hand back, tickled at his confused look when he saw the glove was way too small. At almost six feet tall, I didn't have dainty hands. "You were saying, Detective?" I really tried not to be smug. After all, making him mad wouldn't serve any good purpose. But I couldn't help but enjoy his disappointed look.

"Maybe the glove belongs to someone else. Childers probably had other lady friends." Sutter rallied, and his look said he was still determined to pin the crime on me.

"Look, Detective." I backpedaled, trying to regain some sense of dignity and composure. "I'm sure you think you have this all sewn up. But if I had killed Norman, why would I be demanding to speak with him in a loud voice from the hall?"

"Maybe you wanted to throw us off track." *Grunt.* Sutter's eyes gleamed as he worked out his newer theory. "Maybe you thought others would see you pounding and would back up your story that you didn't know he was dead yet. Maybe it was all a part of your plan."

"Sutter, knock it off." Logan stepped into Sutter's line of sight. "Badgering her won't gain anything."

Sutter's face reddened, and his nostrils flared. "You'd do well to remember I'm the senior partner. You don't control how I run an investigation. As long as I'm here, there's no way I'm letting a murderer get away with it." His gaze latched on to me.

I couldn't believe how stupid some people could be. Or maybe I could. I'd seen it up close and personal not too far in the past. Police detectives were supposed to be objective and look at things from all angles until the case was solved, but my previous experience with narrow-minded cops had proven otherwise. "How could I have planned something like this? I've never even been in this hotel before."

"Oh, then how did you get the room number? The front desk doesn't hand those out to whoever walks up and asks for them." Sutter sat back, a self-satisfied smile settling in under the I've-got-you-now look in his eyes.

"I got that information for her, Frank," Rita said from her seat beside me.

Sutter's beady eyes narrowed, and he settled his gaze on Rita. "And exactly how did you manage that?"

"I work here, and you know that. Or did you think I dress like this every day for fun? Jenna's never been here. I can attest to that fact."

"Oh, really?" *Grunt.* Sutter cocked his head and wrinkled his brow. "You're saying you've known this woman for only a few days and you already know for a fact she's never been to this hotel. And how can you be so sure?"

"Because she told me." Rita gave my hand a soft squeeze.

Sutter narrowed his eyes at Rita. "I see." He turned back to me, a speculative look on his face.

When I could speak past the anger choking me, thankful Rita had given me a few precious seconds to regain my composure yet worried she was unintentionally doing more harm than good, I said, "While we had our differences, I would never have killed Norman. Unless you have something proving I did this and plan to arrest me, I'm leaving."

Sutter looked at me and leaned forward, a clear attempt at intimidation. His gaze bored into me when I didn't back away from him but held my ground. "No, you're not under arrest. For now. But stay in town. We may want to talk to you further."

Again with the useless demand that I stay in town. However, as I had no intention of leaving, especially since I could now prove beyond a doubt that Norman wasn't Uncle Paul's son, long-lost or otherwise, I chose not to irritate him simply for the sake of irritation. "Thank you, Detective, for a lovely time," I said as Rita and I rose and started toward the door.

"Miss Quinn, please wait." Detective Logan's softer tones made me stop and turn. "It would really help our investigation if you told us why you came here today." Logan's open expression caught me off guard.

I wanted to believe he wasn't playing the good cop to Sutter's bad again, but I simply couldn't trust it. However, I knew there was a time to protect family from gossip and there was a time to protect my own backside. In this particular instance, my backside definitely came first. "I'll answer if you're actually interested in the truth." I stood with my chin held high, determined not to look intimidated. In the back of my mind, I knew I should be scared I was now being considered a suspect again. However, I could not, would not, believe the universe would make me the victim of blame for a third murder I hadn't committed. No one had luck that bad.

Logan approached and held out his hand to lead me back to the couch. "I'm always interested in the truth."

Instinctively, I placed my hand in his, letting its warmth give me strength. He walked beside me, and a corner of my brain registered that he was a bit taller than I was as Rita and I recrossed the room and sat. "I'd better start at the beginning." I gathered my thoughts as Logan moved to stand behind Sutter.

"Please do," said Sutter, his sarcastic tone briefly shaking my resolve. *Grunt.*

I took a deep breath, chose to ignore him, and focused instead on Logan's kind eyes. "As you know, I came here a week and a half ago, at my uncle's invitation, to stay for a while. As you also know, I inherited most of what Uncle Paul had." I held up a hand as Sutter leaned forward. "Before you get all worked up with the theory that I killed him for an inheritance, let me nip that one in the bud.

I hadn't seen him since I was a teenager, so I had no idea what he owned, much less that I was a beneficiary of some sort of trust he'd put in place." Rita's hand had slipped into mine again as I spoke, and I gripped it tightly. I'd have to apologize later.

"Where does Childers fit into this story?" asked Logan.

"Three days ago, he stormed into my store, insisting he was Uncle Paul's long-lost son and had come to claim the inheritance as his, since the only reason I received everything was because Uncle Paul had no children. I talked to my lawyer, and he said some of the papers looked legitimate."

Grunt. Sutter blinked slowly, giving the impression I was telling him things he already knew. "Continue, please, Miss Quinn. I'm in suspense."

I clamped down on Rita's hand even harder, grateful for the lifeline. "Mr. Childers claimed to be conceived by his mother and Uncle Paul about five years after Uncle Paul and Aunt Irene married. That would have meant Uncle Paul had been unfaithful. It really bothered me, so I phoned my parents. My mother was Aunt Irene's younger sister. They called back this morning and told me what they'd found. The reason Uncle Paul and Aunt Irene never had any children was because Uncle Paul had a bad case of the mumps as a child."

"So?" Sutter quirked up a corner of his mouth and raised an eyebrow.

"The mumps can cause sterility in men." Logan leaned over and spoke quietly near Sutter's ear.

I smiled at him. Maybe he really wasn't in the let's-convict-Jenna camp. "Exactly. Norman Childers couldn't have been Uncle Paul's son, because Uncle Paul couldn't father any children. Neither in nor out of wedlock. Obviously, this little fact had slipped past our Mr. Childers, or he would have tried for a better story."

Sutter sat up and leaned forward. "Why do you think this guy cooked up such an elaborate story?"

"That, Detective Sutter, is the question of the day." I rose once again, pulling Rita along with me, and walked toward the door. I turned and locked gazes with Sutter before sweeping out of the room. "And it's a question to which I full well intend to find an answer." Perry would have been proud.

Chapter
Twenty-One

A gain I stood in the lavish hotel lobby, drooling over its opulence. Rita had left me alone while she went to let someone know she was leaving for lunch. We hoped to come up with a solution together. I was so lost in thought, I didn't hear the man speaking to me until he touched my elbow. Jumping a bit, I turned to look into the bluest eyes I'd ever seen in my life.

"Ma'am?" he questioned, obviously not for the first time.

I mentally shook myself, reminding myself that my last relationship had failed so badly I'd sworn off men. "Yes?"

"I asked if I could assist you in any way." His voice was even smoother than the rest of him. The tag attached to his lapel announced he was the hotel manager.

Great, they'd sent in the big guns to remove the woman who obviously didn't belong in a hotel this expensive. "I'm sorry. I'm waiting for a friend to go to lunch."

His raised eyebrows told me he wasn't sure he believed me. Fortunately, Rita chose that exact moment to reappear.

"Jenna, you ready to go?" Rita did seem to have the best timing. "Oh hello, Elliot. I see you've met my new neighbor."

"Not really," his silken voice replied as he eyed me speculatively.

"Elliot, this is Jenna Quinn." She turned to me. "Jenna, this is Elliot Burke. He runs this little roach motel."

Elliot smiled a slightly stiff smile that didn't completely reach his eyes.

"Jenna and I are running out for a bite to eat. Care to join us?" Rita asked.

"I really shouldn't. I should be here in case . . ." His voice trailed off, his eyes narrowing.

"We already know about the 'little incident' in suite four-twelve. We just came from there," Rita said quietly.

"Then you know why I can't join you today. Another time, maybe?" Elliot turned to leave.

Rita put a hand on his arm to stop him. "Elliot, you can't quit eating every time there's a crisis of some kind at the hotel. You can let the front desk know where you are. We won't go far. As a matter of fact, why don't we eat right here in the hotel dining room?"

I groaned inside, picturing my not-quite-new khakis set against Rita's gorgeous costume. And Elliot was hardly wearing rags himself, dressed in a sack coat, high vest, tie, creased and cuffed pants, and heeled shoes—quite the fashion statement for men from the turn of the twentieth century. I resisted the urge to kick Rita to shut her up.

And shut up Rita did not. "Come on, Elliot. You'll be right here if they need you. Wouldn't you rather eat with two beautiful women and enjoy witty conversation than grab some lunch tray and take it to your office to eat while you worry yourself into an ulcer?"

Elliot looked at me as if he wasn't quite sure about the witty conversation, but he apparently decided to chance it. "All right.

You two go ahead to the dining hall. Tell them you're to be seated at my table. I'll be there as soon as I let my assistant know where to find me." He strode purposefully across the room, down the hall, and around a corner.

Rita grinned. "You'll love our dining room. The food is to die for." Her grin slipped as her words struck home.

"Let's hope I don't get tossed out for being underdressed." I looked at her clothes. "I hardly fit in with the two of you or the surroundings."

"Listen, if Elliot Burke is taking the time to eat with us, then it doesn't matter if you're wearing a Hefty bag. No one is tossing you out."

"I think you're dreaming, but either way, we'll never know if we stand him up while we argue in the lobby."

Rita sighed, threaded her arm through mine, and led me across the hotel to the dining hall. While Rita arranged for us to sit at Elliot's personal lunch table, I soaked up the surroundings, which were as lavish as the rest of the hotel.

Dining hall was an apt name for the long room. Like the lobby, it had a large chandelier hanging from the center of the incredibly high ceiling. At each end of the room, a massive fireplace opened up, tall enough for a man to stand in without bumping his head on the top. Although neither was lit, I could imagine both giving off good cheer on a cold winter's night as huge logs crackled and popped, warming the long room.

Large Oriental rugs lay in front of the fireplaces, covering the highly polished wood floors, and several large tapestries hung on the walls to absorb sound. It was obvious the room had originally been intended to house a very long table for formal dinner parties, but smaller tables now dotted the room instead, letting separate groups have a bit of privacy from the rest of the guests.

I took it all in as I followed Rita to Elliot's table near one of the floor-to-ceiling windows overlooking the terrace. Quite a few tables sat outside, and I sighed with relief when I noticed several guests, both inside and outside, were dressed almost as casually as I was.

Rita nudged me and pointed toward the door. Elliot threaded his way across the room to our table.

"Hello again, ladies." Elliot sat in the empty chair next to Rita.

"Why, fancy meetin' you here, sir." Rita had donned her southern drawl. All she needed was a fan to wave in front of her face.

Elliot grinned at Rita, obviously enjoying the light flirting.

"So, what brings you out to the hotel today, Miss Quinn?" He was the epitome of politeness.

What could I say? *I wanted to talk to this guy who was staying here, but somebody beat me to it and killed him?* "I had personal business with one of your guests."

"Not the one in four-twelve, I hope." Worry lines creased his forehead.

"That very gentleman." Rita gave a slight nod. "Although I do use the term *gentleman* loosely. He was trying to steal Jenna's inheritance. Tell him, Jenna."

Without going into too much detail, I explained to Elliot about my run-ins with the now-deceased Norman Childers. I wrapped up with the tale of my interview with the police detectives upstairs. When I had caught Elliot up to speed, I was pleased to note I hadn't stuttered, stammered, let spittle fly out of my mouth, spilled my drink, which had been ordered and delivered during my speech, knocked my eating utensils on the floor, or used poor grammar, which would have proved I didn't belong in a place this nice. Mom would be proud.

Rita propped her arms on the table and leaned forward. "I have a question. If Paul knew he didn't have any children and that your mom only had one child, why did the trust say something about if he didn't have any birth or adopted children it would go to any children your mom had?"

Not a bad paraphrase. I was glad I'd explained it well enough that she remembered the details. "I asked Mom the same thing. She said while Aunt Irene was alive, they never took the time to update things. What they had was legally binding, and they saw no need to change anything. After her death, he apparently couldn't bring himself to change things because it was how she'd wanted it phrased originally. After he finally started to heal, he probably went back to the whole 'it's legally binding, so why bother' stance."

Elliot seemed to consider my story for a moment. "You know what irritates me the most about the incident upstairs? Other than that a man lost his life, of course." He cleared his throat. "The main door was locked, and the chain was attached. Whoever killed him didn't go out the door into the hall."

"Really?" It sounded like something out of some old-time mystery novel, and I could almost picture Sherlock Holmes smoking a pipe next to the fireplace or Miss Marple sipping tea at one of the tables across the room. "Do the police have any idea how that was managed?"

"The murderer must have been someone who knew about all of the secret passageways originally built into the place." Elliot took a sip of his hot tea.

"Secret passageways?" My ears perked up. This was even better.

"Yes," replied Elliot. "When the hotel conglomerate bought this place, they discovered a whole network of secret passageways designed to allow servants to move in and out of rooms without disturbing guests in the hallways. Since they were trying to be as accurate as possible, they decided to leave them in the plans. I suppose they thought it lent the place an air of authenticity to have our staff use those passageways to service the rooms. Guests seem to love the idea."

"Aren't there locks on the passageway doors?" I asked.

"There are." Elliot wrapped his long fingers around his tea. "And this one was left unlocked. That's the only way the killer could have gotten out of the room."

"Then the person who killed Norman Childers knew enough to use the passageways and therefore be less likely to be seen," Rita added.

Elliot sighed and leaned back in his chair. "Which narrows down the list of possible suspects to every guest and employee at the hotel and everyone in town who has ever taken a tour here and every worker who helped complete the project, changing the original home into a hotel. But the police seem to think it should be narrowed down to the staff, since they are the only ones who know how to navigate the passageways easily. And they have a point, since the passages can get confusing if you don't know where you're going. Lots of the new staffers get lost a few times before getting it all mapped out in their heads."

"No wonder you're so uptight." Rita shook her head. "You've got to help decide which of your employees gets fingered for the murder. Do they think it was a robbery?"

"I'm not sure." Elliot took a sip of his drink before continuing. "I don't think so. There didn't seem to be anything missing from his room. The silver candlesticks were still on the mantel; the crystal vases were still on the bedside tables. He still wore his Rolex, and his wallet—with credit cards and cash—was in his jacket pocket. Unless the killer was after something in particular, robbery doesn't look likely."

Rita piped in again. "Did he have anything in the hotel safe?"

"No, not a thing," said Elliot. "But I understand there were a few personal and business papers in the wall safe in his room."

"Probably his phony papers from his lawyer." I leaned back and crossed my fingers in my lap, hoping Norman had been dumb enough or cocky enough to bring incriminating evidence with him.

"Possibly." Elliot nodded, his hands fiddling with the napkin on the table in front of him. "The police aren't saying, but you might be correct."

"If so, I'd sure love to get a look at them." I fidgeted in my seat, resisting the urge to run upstairs and snatch the papers that could possibly incriminate Norman from Detective Sutter's hands. While I hadn't wished Norman dead, I still relished the thought of destroying his flimsy cover story.

"I doubt that would be possible." Rita sighed and propped her elbows on the table. "Even if they do turn out to be his legal papers. If they are, though, the police will probably have to turn them over to Mr. Grimes, and you'll get to know about them then."

"At least the police have a long list of suspects besides me. Plus, I didn't know about the secret passages." I was reaching for a long shot, but hey, I'd take what I could get.

"Yes, but none of the others had an apparent motive other than Norman being a big jerk." Rita sure knew how to burst a girl's bubble. "The bigger question is, did anyone also have a motive to kill Paul? The two murders have to be connected." She turned to Elliot. "Stan Jergins, the real estate guy, comes here sometimes with Barbie when they need to woo clients. Have they been here in the last few days?"

Elliot pulled out a non-turn-of-the-nineteenth-century iPhone and made a quick call. After he hung up, he said, "It seems Stan and Barbie were here last night."

Rita grabbed his phone and made her own call before adding, "And she wore a navy-blue dress with black lace accents, topped off with black lace gloves." A smug smile crossed her face.

At Elliot's confused look, Rita and I launched into a brief explanation of Stan's possible reasons for wanting Paul dead.

"I'll ensure Detective Sutter knows about their stay," Elliot said as our server brought lunch. He then suggested we change the subject to something less upsetting than murder while we ate, and companionable conversation accompanied the meal. Although consumed with my own thoughts, I did enjoy the light and friendly banter between Rita and Elliot.

As we returned to the lobby after we finished our meals, the conversation returned to the murder.

"How do you plan to keep this incident from the guests?" Rita's brow furrowed.

"I don't really know." Elliot frowned, looking at the guests passing through the lobby on their way to the dining hall or to their rooms. He dropped his voice to almost a whisper and leaned in. "For now, the news media has been kept away, and the police are being very cooperative. They've agreed to wait until dark to bring their car for the body, which will be brought out through the passageways to the service entrance. We've even managed to keep the staff unaware, for the most part, separating the few who do know from everyone else. I know sooner or later the media will find out, but I hope to at least keep them from getting any shots of the actual body on the premises."

"Good luck," I said. "Nosy reporters have to know about everything."

"I know." Elliot sighed and pinched the bridge of his nose with his fingers. "I don't want to give them too much to sensationalize."

"I'll keep my fingers crossed for you." I patted him on the arm, knowing firsthand exactly how persistent the reporters would be once they smelled blood.

By this time we had reached the front desk. Elliot turned to me. "If you'll leave me your telephone number, I promise to call you if I have any other information that might concern you." He dipped a feather quill into a tiny silver inkwell and held it poised over a piece of ivory-colored parchment.

I gave him my number and thanked him for his hospitality. "It's really beautiful here. I wish I could afford to be a paying guest. I'd love to stay in one of those rooms."

"We'll see what we can do." Smiling, he placed my number in his pocket and strode away from us back to his job.

I turned to Rita and winked. "You two seem to have a good thing going."

Rita chuckled. "Oh, there's nothing going on. We only like flirting."

"Looked like something to me."

"Sure, he's eye candy with that silvering hair and great body, not to mention those eyes." Rita fanned herself with her hand. "But he's gay and deeply in love with his long-term partner. So, he's off-limits. He simply doesn't flaunt it so the older women who come here will feel free to flirt and will tip the staff better."

I changed the subject. "Do you think he'll call?"

"He will if he has news. He wouldn't have said so if he didn't mean it." Rita pulled a watch from a hidden pocket in her skirt. "I've got to be off for now too. See you later."

I couldn't stop thinking about Norman's murder as I climbed into the carriage for the ride down the tree-lined drive on the way back to my car. Sutter had already zeroed in on me as his number-one suspect, and if we proved Mason didn't kill my uncle, I'd again be his primary suspect for that as well. My life teetered on the edge of a nightmarish turn.

Chapter
Twenty-Two

As I fit my key into the lock at Baxter's Book Emporium, Olivia Hokes rushed out from next door. *Oh God, what now?* I fervently hoped she wasn't on another pissed-off rant. I much preferred the supportive-neighbor version of Olivia.

"What a pleasant surprise." I'd be in deep trouble if the woman turned out to be a mind reader.

"Good afternoon, Miss Quinn."

"It's Jenna, please." I breathed a sigh of relief.

"Only if you'll call me Livie." She ducked her head in a tiny nod.

I unlocked my door and held it open for her to precede me inside. "All right, Livie. Is there something I can help you with?"

"Yes, there is." Livie seated herself beside the counter. "First, I'd like to apologize for the way I treated you a few days ago. I was having a bad day with the arthritis in my knees. I tend to be snippy on days like that. After our last chat, I realized I hadn't set things straight."

I nodded with sympathy I didn't feel. This lady was way too spry to have arthritis as bad as she claimed, but I'd allow her a way to save face. "Don't think a thing about it. Consider it completely forgotten. Was there anything else?" I genuinely hoped there wasn't. No matter how I looked at it, the older woman got on my nerves, and I hoped my irritation didn't show.

"Actually, there is. Paul sometimes found books that mentioned Hokes Folly or one of its citizens. When he did, he always gave me first chance at buying them. I have quite a collection. It's become sort of a hobby of mine. Would you mind offering me the same service?" Livie was still using her sweet, helpless act.

I wasn't buying it. However, if Livie wanted to purchase books, I'd manage to put on a nice act of my own. "I'd be delighted to help out. Anything for a neighbor." I hoped Livie couldn't see through my forced politeness, but I couldn't resist the opportunity to find out more about the woman who now pretended to like Uncle Paul, a man she had previously implied she despised. "But only if you promise to give me a look at your collection sometime when it's convenient. It sounds fascinating."

"Of course. Anytime you want." A genuine smile crossed Olivia Hokes's face, the first I'd seen since I'd met her in Mr. Grimes's office.

The change was startling. I could now see a strong resemblance between the two sisters, as the smile softened Livie's features and brought a sparkle to her eyes.

"You stop by anytime you want," Livie repeated, continuing to smile. "I love to show off my books and get a chance to teach someone about our town."

"I'll be sure and do that." I couldn't help but wonder at this third version of the woman.

Livie rose and turned toward the door. "I guess I should be getting back next door. Phillie didn't want me gone too long, since she's ready to go home for the day."

I breathed a sigh of relief as the bells tinkled to announce Olivia Hokes's departure and shook my head at the sisters' nicknames for each other. Sure, Phillie fit the sweet Ophelia, but Livie seemed a bit too cute for the usually sour Olivia. Or was it? Livie had shown an unexpected side of herself today. Was the woman as sour as she seemed, or was there still a wholesome and hopeful attitude buried somewhere under all the bitterness she wore like a badge? Would the real Olivia Hokes please step forward?

I pulled my attention back to the bookstore. As I looked down the aisles, I was amazed at how much Mason had accomplished during my absence the previous afternoon. He'd be a true asset while here, and I'd hate to see him go.

I'd given Mason the day off since I'd had no idea what time I'd arrive, so I passed the afternoon alone with my thoughts of murder.

The bells tinkled, and I hoped it was a genuine customer this time. I was pleased to find it was. Thanks to my efforts and the assistance from my new friends, I managed to help my first customer of the day and the subsequent three who entered the store, finding the right book for each and sending them away happy with minimal effort. I was genuinely starting to like this place. Maybe once word got out that things were run a bit differently and Norman Childers could in no way change the store's makeup, more business would roll in. As I eyed the large front windows with the little shelf below them, display possibilities ran through my mind, and I spent the afternoon plotting how to attract more customers.

That evening I replayed the day: the information from my parents, Norman's murder, and the tense-but-not-unpleasant meeting with the newest version of Olivia Hokes. The sales I'd made had definitely made the day's end a success. Yet the shadow of murder and the ordeal I'd suffered through that morning at the hands of Detective Sutter, with his ugly insinuations, pompous assumptions, and rude allegations, cast a pall on what could have been an otherwise good day.

I went into the kitchen to make a pot of tea. At the sight of jumbled kitchen towels in a slightly open drawer, I frowned. Oh well, it wouldn't be the first time I'd left things in a bit of a mess. I wasn't the best housekeeper in the world, much to the disappointment of my mom, who had to be related somehow to Martha Stewart.

I took my tea to the bedroom, turning the lights out and locking up as I went. My eyes sought a book about how to run a business I'd brought home from my store the day before, determined to be successful in this peaceful little town if I stayed—Norman Childers and Detective Sutter aside.

The book lay under my bed, a corner peeking out from under the dust ruffle. My brow furrowed. I could've sworn I'd left it on the nightstand, but I shrugged and got ready for bed, changing into my comfy pajamas, which had somehow managed to work their way onto the floor from the chair I'd thrown them over that morning.

I started reading as I set my tea mug on the nightstand. I turned back the covers and absently propped the pillow against the headboard, sat, and leaned back. A crinkling sound startled me, and I turned to examine my pillow. The business book thudded to the floor as it fell from my numb fingers. I unpinned the note from my pillow and reread it.

Go home! We don't want you here!
If you stay, you'll end up like
Paul Baxter and Norman Childers.
GO HOME BEFORE YOU REGRET IT!

Chapter Twenty-Three

Rita patted me on the back for what must have been the twentieth time in the last thirty minutes. I sat on her couch across from Detective Sutter, while Detective Logan moved restlessly around the room.

"Tell me once more what happened, Miss Quinn. I want to make sure I've written it down correctly. Don't leave anything out, no matter how insignificant you may think it is." Sutter narrowed his eyes, scrutinizing me intensely.

I kept my hands clutched in my lap to keep them from shaking. Too bad it didn't work as well for my voice. "As I said the last two times you asked me to tell you this story, I came home about an hour ago. I went into the kitchen to make tea. The towel drawer was slightly open and messed up. I didn't think anything about it at the time, so I went into my bedroom. I changed into my pajamas, which had somehow managed to get onto the floor instead of still being on the chair where I'd left them. I assumed I had knocked them off myself, but now, of course, I'm sure I didn't. I had left a book on top of the nightstand this morning, but I had to drag it out from under the bed to read it. I sat on the bed and leaned back on my pillow. I heard the paper crinkle and leaned up to see what the noise was. I found the note and called you guys."

"You didn't touch anything else until we arrived?" Sutter had been insistent on this point the first two times I'd told the story.

"No, I didn't." Tired of answering the same questions over and over, I shifted uncomfortably on the couch, which triggered another reflexive pat from Rita. "I told you, I waited until you arrived and did a walk-through to see if anything valuable was missing after you had 'secured the premises.' As you saw, there was evidence the drawers had been rifled through, the mattress moved, and the pantry rearranged. Detective, why do you keep asking the same questions?"

"I want to make sure I've got it all." *Grunt.* Sutter leaned back and closed his little book.

"Baloney," said Rita. "What do you really want?"

"We're simply ensuring we have all the facts so we can pursue a quick closure to the situation." Detective Logan smiled reassuringly.

"And you?" Rita aimed this last directly at Sutter.

He cocked his head at Rita. "To be honest, I'm still not completely convinced your friend here didn't kill her uncle for his estate and kill Childers to keep it."

"Frank, you've already made an arrest. You know that's highly illegal if you think Jenna is guilty. So stop blustering." Rita crossed her arms.

"That doesn't mean she didn't orchestrate the whole thing. I see she's hired Mason Craig, a man we've arrested under suspicion of murdering her uncle, to work in the store that's conveniently hers again. Seems she might know something we don't." Sutter rubbed his chin as if in deep, slow thought. However, the glint in his eyes as he stared at me belied the bumbling gesture. "I'm trying to decide if she planned this whole little scene to try and throw us off. How are we to know if the pantry was rearranged or her nightie wasn't where it was supposed to be? The drawers looked fine to me, and Miss Quinn has admitted to assuming she'd either remembered incorrectly about those things or jumbled them herself. What's to say she didn't write the note herself to make it look like someone was after her?"

I pulled the robe I'd borrowed from Rita tighter, trying to stop my shivering. "Why would I do such a thing when I had nothing to do with either death? I had nothing to gain from Norman's death, since I had legitimate proof he could not have been Uncle Paul's son. Just like I had nothing to gain by dragging the police out here and putting myself at the forefront of your attention again." Anger was becoming a natural reaction around Detective Sutter. He seemed to know exactly how to push all my buttons.

"Oh, you could have gained from old Norman's death, all right. It saved you a lot of court troubles in order to try to prove he was a fraud. Now you don't have to deal with that problem anymore." Sutter stared at me as if he expected me to break down and confess that his astute mind had worked it all out.

"And you really think I would've murdered a man to save myself from taking the time to talk to a couple of lawyers and possibly testify at a hearing? How dumb do you think I am?"

"I've seen people kill for less." Sutter cocked his head, and his calculating gaze raked across me. "You never know what someone might do with little or no provocation."

"Detective." Again I gripped my hands together. "I would have easily won the court case over Norman's claims. While it does seem obvious Norman Childers's murder is tied in with Uncle Paul's somehow, as is evidenced by the note, I can assure you I had nothing to do with either."

"It seems obvious to you?" Sutter's sarcastic tone brought my hackles up. "Listen, lady, I'll tell you what's obvious to me. I would have preferred to discuss this at another time, but we'll lay it all out right here."

My stomach flip-flopped. I looked over at Detective Logan, whose jaw tightened, and his hand clenched into a fist.

"And what do we have to discuss?" I knew he had no proof of anything, but unease slithered up the back of my neck.

Sutter leaned in, his eyes hard and his nostrils flaring. "Let's talk about how you're stone cold broke after paying your lawyers, you have no support since all your friends dumped you, and you lost your home and put all your things in storage. Let's talk about how you used the last of your money to rent a cheap motel room under an assumed name. Let's talk about how inheriting after your uncle's death has kept you from being out on the streets and the threat of a drawn-out court case would upset that apple cart. Yes, Miss Quinn, I've done my homework."

"Enough." Logan stepped forward, glaring at Sutter. It was the first time I'd seen him use his height to tower over Sutter.

"Enough? I'll say when it's enough, and you keep your mouth shut," Sutter snarled, not backing down from Logan's seeming attempt at intimidation.

"I don't work for you, Frank, so you can't bully me." Rita rose and moved toward the door. "Therefore, I can and will say when it is enough, especially in my home. Unless you intend to bring charges of some sort against Jenna right here and now, then I suggest you stop making accusations you cannot prove. If you have any legitimate questions, I'm sure she'll be very happy to answer them. If you only intend to waste her time with unfounded allegations based on circumstantial insinuations, then I believe you know where your car is." Rita swept her front door open, motioning for them to leave.

Sutter stood and stretched, matching Rita's glare with one of his own. "It's been a long day of digging, and I've only scratched the surface. Tomorrow I'll keep digging, and again the day after and next week and for however long it takes. Unlike those big-city detectives with so many cases they can't keep up, I have all the time I need, and when I find what I'm looking for, I'll be back." The man sauntered toward the door.

Rage boiled up within me. Rage against all the accusations, against the loss of my friends, my job, and my home. Rage pulsed through me to the point I could feel nothing, sense nothing, hear nothing else. And then it settled into a low hum, sending strength up my spine. I spit out my words at Sutter's departing back. "If you wish to speak with me again, please feel free to contact my attorney. I'm sure he can help you with whatever you may need."

"Oh?" Sutter turned to face me. "And which attorney might that be?"

I scrambled to come up with a name. My attorney in Charlotte had dumped me as soon as my money ran out. I no longer had a lawyer. Except . . . "Mr. Horace Grimes. I'm sure you can manage to look him up in the book." *And I've got to remember to actually hire him.* I prayed he took murder cases. While I hadn't actually been accused, I knew a contract or estate lawyer would do no good if things came down to that.

Sutter finished his trip to the front door with Logan behind him, and Rita slammed it as they went out. I sank to the couch, my knees completely jellied.

"Care to talk about it yet?" Rita asked gently, patting me on the back again.

I guessed she didn't know what else to do. A tear rolled down my cheek, and I choked back the rest, taking deep breaths to still the screaming in my head. *Not again. Please, God, not again.* "I thought it might be different here, that maybe I could start over. But it's all following me."

"What really happened?" Rita handed me a tissue.

"It was last year." I tore at the tissue in my hands. "I worked for a marketing firm in the accounting department. Money went missing, and the trail seemed to lead to me. Someone had hacked in and used my login to siphon money from several major client accounts. During the investigation, the head of the department was murdered, and the police were sure it was me because he had evidence tying me to the embezzlement."

"Based on the mug shots on TV last week, I take it you were arrested?" Rita asked quietly.

I nodded and took a shuddering breath. "I spent three months in jail with no bail while I waited on the trial because of the murder charge and the assumption I had a ton of cash secreted away that I could use to flee. The jury acquitted me because all the evidence was flimsy and circumstantial. But by the time it was over, I'd already lost my job."

"I'm so sorry." Rita gave my shoulder a gentle squeeze.

"My parents tried to help, but they didn't have a huge amount of money sitting in the bank. I used everything I had to pay attorney fees. None of my 'friends' would help for fear of being dragged into things as accomplices. Even my fiancé dumped me."

"Fiancé?" Rita's eyebrows rose.

"Yeah." I leaned back into the corner of the couch and tucked my feet under me. "Although, in hindsight, I'm better off without him. He was in management, so he didn't want anyone to know we were a couple for fear of sexual harassment or nepotism accusations. We lived together, for crying out loud, but he insisted I keep a post office box and talked me into not telling the company when I moved out of my apartment and into his so no one would know my address. He wouldn't even buy me a ring when he proposed so I wouldn't be tempted to show anyone and let word get around we were engaged. I don't know what he would've done once we actually got married."

"What a jackass." Rita propped her feet on the coffee table.

I snorted. "He was. Once things got ugly, he distanced himself from me. When I was acquitted and finally got out of jail, I took a cab home, only to find the locks had all been changed. He handed me a key to a storage unit where he'd taken my things."

"So that's when you rented the motel room?" Rita asked.

"I had to have somewhere to live." A shudder rippled through me. "I knew the case was all over the papers, and I didn't want reporters hounding me, so I registered under an assumed name and paid cash in advance." I looked down at what was left of my unused, shredded tissue, still clutched in one hand and wadded into a ball.

"And then you inherited Paul's estate." Rita's voice was low.

"And then I inherited Uncle Paul's estate." I nodded, meeting Rita's speculative gaze. "Look, I didn't kill Uncle Paul to get his money. I didn't even know I would inherit anything, much less everything. And I have absolutely no clue who would have wanted to kill him for any reason."

Rita frowned. "I'm worried about what Frank Sutter will try to do with all of this."

Suddenly restless, I rose, picked up my empty tea mug, and started toward the kitchen. "I should go."

"Stay." Rita followed me.

At the firmness in Rita's voice, I turned. "I don't want to put you out." That was a lie. I desperately wanted to put her out. I was terrified to be alone right now, but I wasn't about to wait around to see one more friendly face freeze awkwardly when we spoke. I couldn't handle more uncomfortable silences or inane chitchat about nothing while avoiding anything that might mean something or sensing fear, as if someone thought I might murder them in their sleep and steal away with the silver. Although Rita had been gracious up to now and she had stated she thought I was "one of the good ones," I simply wasn't ready to risk the possibility of a change in her attitude tonight.

"And I don't want to worry all night about you in your house alone with a crazy person threatening you." Rita took my hand and led me back to the living room, pulling me down to sit beside her on the couch. "The bed in the guest room is already made up. It's pretty comfortable. At least you won't be home in case whoever was there earlier comes back."

My throat tightened, another flood of tears pushing at the backs of my eyes. "Are you sure?" I didn't dare to hope.

"Positive. I'd love to have you stay. We can chat as late as we want, tell scary stories, and eat junk food." Rita smiled and patted me again.

The woman really needed to find another comfort gesture, but it was the most awesome sensation I'd ever felt right about then.

"Gee, can we do each other's hair and makeup too?" I wiped my eyes and tried to toss a saucy grin, knowing I had failed miserably.

Rita chuckled. "I guess it does sound like a high school sleepover. But it'll still be fun."

Over the next couple of hours, the heaviness in my chest lightened, and my heart expanded to fully accept the friendship Rita so openly offered. We stopped short of my proposed makeovers, but Rita's suggestions had all been taken. After filling up on ice cream and cookies and being scared out of my skin by a story Rita had heard one year at summer camp, I huddled on the couch.

"I'm glad you stayed," Rita said gently.

An open smile slid across my face. I didn't have to hide any-more. "Me too. Thanks for insisting."

"Even though I scared the liver out of you with that last story?" Rita leaned over and bumped my shoulder with hers.

I sobered. "There's no story scarier than having someone threaten your life."

"We need to prove the two murders are connected and you had nothing to do with either of them." Rita placed her hand on top of mine.

I turned my hand over and squeezed Rita's. "I only hope we can before the body count goes up, especially since my name has now been moved to the top of the list of possible victims."

Chapter
Twenty-Four

Mason's Friday-morning appointment with his court-appointed attorney left me alone at the store. I hadn't been there for more than a few minutes when the door chimes tinkled.

I rose from my seat on the floor, where I had been arranging a stack of books into alphabetical order, stretching as I did so. "Detective Logan. How nice of you to stop by." It was anything but nice, but I couldn't afford to aggravate the one person on the police force who didn't seem already convinced of my guilt. "Is there any special reason you stopped by, or did you want to browse the books? We're rearranging, but I can do my best to help you find a book you'll enjoy."

"No thanks, but maybe next time. I'm here on official business today." He pulled out an ink pad and a fingerprint card. "I need to get your prints so we can compare them to the ones found at your apartment. This should have been done last night, but it seems to have been overlooked." His small smile reeked of exhaustion and frustration.

"I'm sure Detective Sutter already has my prints from that business in Charlotte." I tucked my hands into my jeans pockets reflexively.

Detective Logan sighed and closed his eyes briefly before locking them on to mine. "He does. But he wants to make sure you haven't altered them in some way since then."

"Are you kidding me?" I shook my head, and a disgusted chuckle barked from my chest. My hands slid from my pockets. "Detective Logan, I'll let you take my fingerprints without a warrant, but give me the courtesy of honesty about why you want them. Your boss desperately wants to place me at the crime scene at the hotel, doesn't he?"

His mouth opened and closed, and his brows knit together. At least the detective had the decency to look uncomfortable. "He's not my boss. But yes, Sutter wants to compare them to several sets of prints found at both the murder scene at the inn and the one here in the store. He's trying to straighten out whose prints belong where and what they mean in the timing of both murders."

"Explain, please." I wiped my hands on my jeans to remove most of the dust as I walked to the front of the store, where I leaned a hip on the counter, my hands extended toward him.

Logan took my right hand in his and began the process of inking my fingers and rolling them on the paper. "I really can't say anything, as it's an ongoing investigation."

"I see." I cleared my throat, preparing for an argument if necessary, and withdrew my hands. "Detective Logan—"

"Keith," he interrupted, looking at me.

I searched his eyes, finding only a clear, steady gaze. "Keith, my life has been threatened, whether or not Detective Sutter believes me. I think that entitles me to know what's going on." I wiggled my partially inked fingers at him. "And it's tit for tat. I give you prints, you give me information."

Keith narrowed his eyes and shook his head, a half chuckle, half sigh pushing out of his chest. "Sutter would have my hide if he heard me say this, but for what it's worth, I don't think you did it."

"Did what exactly?"

"Any of it." Keith paused, his deep brown eyes warm, his gaze searching mine. "Not here, and not in Charlotte."

I looked away, determined to keep him from seeing the tears that sprang to my eyes. Gads, I had to get a handle on this whole weepy thing.

"There wasn't enough evidence. It was all so circumstantial, and it was too neat, too clean. Nothing is that clean unless it's fake." He reached for my hand and squeezed my fingers gently. "You do have a friend in all of this."

I turned back to look up into his eyes. "So why is Detective Sutter convinced I had anything to do with any of it?"

Keith propped his bronzed forearms on the counter. "I shouldn't be telling you this, but Sutter is up for a promotion. He's already been passed over once. He needs a big case closed to fill out his résumé, and if he can pin these two murders on you and solve the crimes in Charlotte in the mix, it'll be a massive win for him. I think it's interfering with his judgment."

I took a steadying breath, exhaling slowly. "Then tell me why you're fingerprinting me. The real reason." With my tears now under control, I turned to face him.

He straightened, took my hand again, rolled the next finger in ink, and moved it toward the print card. "When Paul was killed, we found, along with his prints, a very fresh and very clear set of prints on one of his plates, which contained brownie crumbs. The plate was found on the desk in the back room. We assume these are the prints of the person who drugged the brownies we found in his stomach. We found what turned out to be Childers's prints in a few spots in the room, but not on the brownie plate linked directly to

Paul's murder. When the store was broken into a few days ago, we found what turned out to be Childers's prints all over the place—and they hadn't been there when we dusted the place after Paul's murder. Are you with me so far?"

"I think so." I tried to make sense of what he had said. "You mean Norman was the man who broke into the store after Uncle Paul was killed but was probably not the one who killed Uncle Paul in the first place?"

"Exactly." Keith smiled as he started printing my left hand. "The set of prints we found on the brownie plate at Paul's murder scene was also found at the Childers murder scene."

"Was Norman poisoned too?"

"He was, this time with blackberry cobbler."

"With sleeping medications again?" Good Lord, I definitely needed to stay away from baked goods for a while.

"It's still under investigation, and I really can't say any more."

"Can't? Or won't?" I looked at my fingers, now sticky with ink.

"Can't." He handed me a wet wipe from his kit. "I've already said enough to get me fired if Sutter found out."

"Detective Sutter implied I'm a suspect in Norman's murder and I might still be a suspect in Uncle Paul's murder." I finished cleaning off the ink and tossed the wipe into the trash.

Keith turned to pack his fingerprinting supplies. "He wanted to see how much you knew about either death. Don't worry, you passed with flying colors. You're still a suspect in his eyes, but I think these babies should clear it right up." He patted his fingerprint kit.

"How?" When he hesitated, I added, "You've already told me a lot about the prints, so you might as well tell me the rest."

"We picked up five distinct sets of prints at your house last night. We've already printed Ms. Wallace, who has been a recent guest in your home; Ms. Washburn, who cleans up the store and your apartment; and Mr. Grimes, who showed you around the property when you came to town, and have eliminated their three sets of prints. That leaves two to go."

"What does that have to do with the prints at the two murder scenes?"

"Are you sure you want to know?" Keith gently asked.

"Of course I'm sure. After all, my uncle was the first victim, and I'm suspected of having something to do with both his and Norman's murders. If we can believe the note left on my pillow, someone may want to make me the third victim. Who else could have more of a right to know?" My hands gripped the edge of the counter as I steeled myself for the answer I suspected was coming. It was the only logical thing he could say.

The detective nodded his head. "If you insist. Of the two sets of unidentified prints upstairs, one of them exactly matches the set found on Mr. Baxter's brownie plate and Mr. Childers's cobbler plate. So, if it wasn't you who killed the two men, then the real killer left you that note last night." His quick reflexes allowed him to catch me as my knees wobbled, and he gently helped me to the chair at the end of the counter and knelt in front of me.

"I knew that was probably true, but it's unnerving to have it confirmed." I sucked in a long, shaky breath. "What about Mason Craig's fingerprints? Do they match either set?" My heart squeezed, and my stomach rolled. I couldn't have been wrong about him. I just couldn't.

"No. And they don't match any prints found at either crime scene. I think we're about to drop the charges against him. It was an awfully weak case to begin with, but Sutter was determined to get that win."

Relief poured through me, and I would have sagged to the floor if I hadn't already been sitting in a chair, practically held in place by Keith, who still knelt in front of me. "Finally, some good news out of all of this."

Keith stood. "Are you going to be okay?"

"I think so." I took another steadying breath and also stood, determined not to let my shaky knees take me back down.

"Please be careful." Keith picked up his fingerprint case. "Whoever did this has already killed twice. Don't let yourself think they won't try it a third time if they feel you're a threat. Whatever you do, be careful who you trust."

"I promise."

He walked out of my store. The bells tinkled over the doorway, but this time they didn't sound happy. Instead they sounded sinister, reminding me I was alone with a murderer lurking nearby.

Chapter
Twenty-Five

S till thinking about my conversation with Keith, I looked up when Mason arrived. He whistled a happy tune and seemed more relaxed than I'd seen him since we first met.

"What's got you in such a fine mood this afternoon?" I already knew but wanted to give him a chance to tell his good news.

"I've been officially let off the hook about Paul's murder. They found evidence that couldn't possibly have anything to do with me, so they let me go. No trial, I get my bail money back, and I'm free as a bird." To illustrate his point, he jumped into the air and flapped his arms.

I laughed at his antics. "I heard about the fingerprints."

"Who told you?" He stopped midflap.

"Let's say it was a different little birdie than you." The memory of Keith's gentleness sparked a warmth in my chest. I had to keep his confidence. I couldn't get him into trouble for his honesty.

"Well, they almost kept me," he said. "That stupid Detective Sutter was determined to pin it on me because of the sleeping medication connection. I'm just glad the second murder was different. He tried to connect me to the hydrangea too, saying I could buy them. But so could anyone, so he let me go."

"Hydrangea?" I poured a fortifying cup of coffee and sat on a stool behind the counter.

"Yeah, it seems old Norman was poisoned with hydrangea flower petals baked up in blackberry cobbler. Apparently they're deadly." Mason walked to the coffee table and picked up a Styrofoam cup.

"Wait. I thought the fingerprints were the same on the plates at both murders. Are they now thinking it wasn't the same person after all?" Should I be worried about two killers coming after me instead of only one?

Mason grinned. "Confusing, I know. They think it was the same person who poisoned both of them, but with different things. I guess the killer ran out of sleeping pills."

"Hmm. Could be. But how would he know about hydrangea? That's not exactly common knowledge." I sipped my coffee, letting the hot liquid burn down my throat. I grimaced at the flat taste. The coffee hadn't been too bad at first, but the longer the old can of Folgers was open, the more stale it tasted in the pot. I made a mental note to add fresh coffee to the grocery list. No telling how long that old can had been hiding in the back room before we found it.

"You can research anything on the internet if you know how and where to look." Mason turned and leaned his elbows on the counter. "It's the only thing that really makes any sense. Maybe he didn't have a whole lot of money to waste on medications, so he wanted to use something else the second time." Mason was silent for a second. "Or maybe he didn't want anyone noticing he'd refilled his prescription too soon."

"I hope the police figure it out." Pouring coffee into my Styrofoam cup, I added real mugs to my list so we could have more than a few sips at a time.

"Me too," agreed Mason. "But either way, I'm glad it lets me off the hook."

"Will you go back home now?" I turned and leaned on the counter.

Mason's head ducked and his shoulders slumped. He had apparently been going over and over the same things in his own mind, because the words gushed out. "I guess I should. I mean, I've got a job there, an apartment, a few new friends. Granted, the job's nothing great. Oh, sure, I bragged about it to everyone here, but that was when I felt I had to impress everyone with how well I was doing without any help. But if you want to know the truth, I'm a janitor for an office complex. I'm barely making minimum wage cleaning up other people's messes. But here, I guess nobody would ever hire me. There will always be someone who thinks I might steal again. You know how it would go. Mr. Owner drops a twenty without realizing it and kicks it under the counter, and the next thing I know I'm out on my ear, or worse, arrested for stealing. Who would believe I didn't do it? I can't say I'd blame them, but still, it's not very fair." Mason flopped down in the chair by the counter and raked his hands through his hair.

"You'd really like to come back to Hokes Folly, wouldn't you?" I knew the answer, but Mason needed to finish this argument he'd begun with himself, and I let him do so.

Although he hesitated, it was easy to see he was talking more to himself than to anyone else. "I'd like to come back, but I don't know if people would accept me. And where would I stay? I can't keep mooching off of folks indefinitely. I'd have to get a place of my own. But with what money? Everything I've made has gone toward a car payment on the junker I drive, rent for a dumpy apartment, cheap food, and gas money to get back and forth to work. I have no savings of any kind. I looked around here and found a cheap studio apartment close by, but how would I pay first and last month's rent or utility deposits?

"If I lived close enough, I guess I could sell the car, but who would buy it? I only bought it because it was the cheapest thing I could find that was still drivable. Maybe someone else would be as desperate for wheels as I was when I bought that lemon, but what if they weren't? Then what? I'll tell you what. I'd be stuck with a car I couldn't afford to put gas in. I'd have no job, no place to stay, and would end up living in some cardboard box or at the mission downtown. Maybe I could sleep in the car. At least then it would be good for something." He crossed his arms on the counter and rested his forehead on them, sighing deeply.

My motherly instincts, such as they were, shoved their way to the forefront. I'd been where this kid was not too long ago. Knowing how frightening it was to realize you had nothing, I reached out a hand and squeezed his shoulder to get his attention. "Might I suggest a viable option before you start looking at your future real estate out back by the cardboard recycling bin?"

Mason raised his head. His sad eyes and solemn face reminded me of a lost puppy, and I resisted the impulse to pat him on the head or scratch him behind the ears.

I did a bit of quick mental math. "I've been thinking I could use some help around here on a more permanent basis."

Mason jumped up and whooped with delight. "You mean you would let me keep working here? Really? You'd trust me that much?" He grabbed me in a big hug and nearly squeezed my breath away.

I managed to disengage myself from his exuberant embrace, rubbing my sides and chuckling. Guess I wasn't the only one prone to random hugging. "You shouldn't agree until you've heard the entire offer. You might not want to stay after you've listened to the whole thing."

"I don't think anything you could suggest would make me say no." Mason looked like he was about to hug me again.

I stepped around the counter to protect my ribs. "As a part of your job description, you'll work full-time on an ongoing basis, but you'll need to be here extra hours until we can get a handle on not only this front room, but also the inventory in the back. You'll need to assist with pricing decisions, so you'll need to start educating yourself on antique books."

Mason's jaw dropped, and out of his open mouth came another whoop of delight. Suddenly sobering, he said, "I guess I can talk my friends into a couple more months on couches until I can save enough for deposits and all."

"Oh, did I forget to mention the relocation bonus?"

A crease crossed his brow. "You don't have to do that. I'll manage."

I nudged him on the shoulder. "Stop it. Uncle Paul would have wanted me to take care of this for you." After all, I had a nice nest egg now, and I knew Uncle Paul would have agreed this was a worthy cause.

Mason blinked a few times and cleared his throat before standing and straightening his shoulders. "I'll do a good job for you, Jenna, I swear. After the next few weeks, you'll realize you can't do without me. I'll be the best employee you could ever wish for. You'll never have to hire anyone else again as long as you live. You'll see." And with that pronouncement, Mason went back to whistling the happy tune he'd been whistling when he came through the front door. Marching up the aisle, he tackled the book stacks with renewed enthusiasm.

I watched him for a few minutes, amazed and somewhat envious that he could change his outlook so drastically in such a short time. I pitched in, and we worked efficiently for a while before the phone rang.

"Baxter's Book Emporium." I really needed to come up with a better name. Maybe I could hold a contest. Ten free books to the winner.

"Hello, Jenna," came Horace Grimes's mellow voice. "I received a call from a Detective Sutter. Is there something I should know?"

"Oh no!" I cringed. "I am so sorry. I forgot to call and ask if you take on criminal cases. It's been a rough twenty-four hours."

"It's all right. I don't normally practice criminal law, but I think I can help you temporarily until you find an attorney who does."

"Thank you so much." *Mental list item number . . . however many: add Horace Grimes to my Christmas list.* "What did Sutter want?"

"He wanted us to meet him downtown. He said he had some questions for you. However, I don't have time for a downtown junket right now. I told him if he would like to speak to my client, he could meet us both here at three thirty."

I looked at my watch, and my stomach sank. "That's in ten minutes!"

"Yes, it is. Can you make it?" he asked.

"I'll be there." I hung up, snatched my purse, and rushed out the door, calling out to Mason as I left, "I've got to go for a while. I should be back before closing."

Chapter
Twenty-Six

The receptionist ushered me into Horace's office immediately upon arrival, and I barely had time to sit before Detective Sutter was announced.

"Frank." Horace held out his hand.

"Horace." The detective shook it and sat in the chair next to mine.

They were on a first-name basis. For some reason, this startled me. I covered my surprise and turned toward the detective. "Why did you ask to see me?"

Sutter laid a folder on the attorney's desk then asked me, "Did your uncle keep a diary?"

I blinked. "What? Why would I know that?"

Sutter stared at me as if trying to mesmerize me into giving him the information he wanted.

"Frank, if you have a legitimate question, ask it. Otherwise, I have pressing appointments." Mr. Grimes rose.

"Sit down, Horace." Sutter gestured with his hand then turned to me again. "We found a diary among the papers in the safe in Childers's hotel room. We believe it belonged to Paul Baxter. Do you know anything about that?"

Mr. Grimes interrupted before I could speak. "My client has already stated she had no knowledge of whether or not her uncle even kept a diary. She would therefore have no knowledge of why Mr. Childers might have a diary possibly belonging to her uncle. Next question."

I flashed the attorney a questioning glance, receiving a tiny smile and nod in response. Go, Horace Grimes!

Frank Sutter's jaw clenched and relaxed. "Do you know any reason why someone might want to steal your uncle's diary?"

Mr. Grimes answered for me again. "My client has already stated she had no knowledge—"

"I got it," Sutter interrupted, glaring at the attorney.

"Detective, why do you think someone stole a diary that supposedly belonged to Uncle Paul?" I was proud I managed to keep my voice even.

"When we autopsied the body, we discovered leather particles under your uncle's fingernails."

"And?" I prompted when he didn't continue.

"There are claw marks in the leather cover of your uncle's diary found in Childers's safe, and the lab has confirmed the leather scrapings under Baxter's nails exactly match the leather on the diary. We think it was stolen the night of Baxter's murder."

I caught myself before I blurted out that it hadn't been Norman's fingerprints on Uncle Paul's brownie plate. Innocently I asked, "Do you think Norman killed my uncle to steal it?"

"No, we don't. Gladys Washburn has identified Childers as the man who argued with your uncle on the day of his murder, although she says his hair was a different color that day, but his fingerprints didn't match those on a plate we discovered which contained crumbs from poisoned brownies. We feel your uncle was drugged with these brownies. However, it's possible Childers was partnered with whoever did kill Baxter. Maybe that partner killed Childers but didn't get a chance to grab the diary from his safe before she had to leave. Maybe she returned a little while later, hoping to recover it." Sutter narrowed his eyes, and a small, predatory smile tugged at his mouth.

"My client has already stated she had no knowledge of the diary, nor do you have any proof of her involvement in any crime, nor involvement with Norman Childers in any way," Mr. Grimes cut in before I could give a scathing retort. "Was there anything else you needed of Miss Quinn?"

Sutter opened the folder on the desk. "We have found evidence that implicates Norman Childers in the break-in at your uncle's store. We think we have discovered what he may have been looking for. It could be a motive for his murder as well." He handed the attorney a sheet of paper.

Mr. Grimes scanned the page and passed it to me. I scanned it while Sutter continued.

"From other papers, we know this letter is from John Hokes, the town's founder, written in 1934 to his lawyer, Granford Childers, who was Norman's great-great-great-grandfather. It mentions some sort of treasure Hokes apparently found and intended to use to finish building his home. He mentioned making a diary entry so he wouldn't forget where he'd hidden the evidence."

"It says the evidence, whatever it was, was hidden somewhere on the estate." I handed the letter back to the detective.

Sutter slid the sheet back into his folder. "Nobody's ever found any kind of treasure, so it's probably still there somewhere. Do you know anything about that, Miss Quinn?"

Was he for real? How many times did I have to tell him I didn't know anything about this stuff? I took the higher road, though, and ignored his question. "You think the killer wasn't after Uncle

Paul's diary but was trying to grab John Hokes's diary instead." I tilted my head at Sutter. "And you still think I had something to do with it."

The predatory smile slid fully across his face, his eyes cold. "I think you and Norman Childers wanted that diary, but you had a falling-out among thieves. When Norman couldn't talk Baxter out of the diary, you killed him to steal it. The argument over your failed attempt, which got you nothing but your uncle's own diary, led you to kill Norman, so you would have time to search your uncle's holdings to find where he'd hidden John Hokes's diary."

"My client has already stated—"

"I know, I know." Sutter picked up his folder and stood. "I also know you're not telling me everything."

I remained silent. I didn't really have anything I could add, but I also didn't want to accidentally say anything that would give Sutter any more fodder for his idiotic idea that I had killed my uncle or Norman Childers.

He glared at me, his voice sliding out in a slimy rasp. "I'll be watching you, and when you make a mistake, as all criminals do at some point, I'll be there to catch you."

When Sutter had been ushered from the law offices, Mr. Grimes sat in the seat vacated by the detective. "Jenna, can you think of anywhere your uncle might have hidden something that valuable?"

"You know, Norman asked the same question as we went through the store. I should have known he was the one who broke in. He was too familiar with everything. He even knew where the light switches were in the back-room bathroom. They're in a really odd, out-of-the-way place, but he went right to them. I can't believe I didn't pick up on that before now."

"Don't feel badly," replied the attorney. "I missed that too."

I racked my brain. I'd been all through the store and the apartment. I'd talked to two of Uncle Paul's ex-girlfriends, an ex-employee, and an ex-enemy. Blending in all the vast stores of almost-nothing I could remember about him from my childhood, I still came up with nada. "As for where valuables might be hidden, I didn't know then, and I still have no idea. But I'm sure going to find out."

Mr. Grimes laid a hand on my arm. "Jenna, please be careful. Whoever wants that diary wants it badly enough to kill for it."

Chapter
Twenty-Seven

I n an attempt to fill my mind with something other than Detective Sutter and my utter frustration at his bullheaded determination to pin some sort of crime on me, when I returned from my meeting with Horace I approached the bookstore—legally *my* bookstore again—from across the street. I looked again at the plain sign, brainstorming new names, and I let my mind run with creative ideas for the empty front-window display. I might as well try to beef up business. Even if I didn't stay, it would help increase the selling price and lure prospective buyers. And who knew? Maybe I'd stay.

If I was being honest with myself, the longer I remained here, the less appealing it was to return to Charlotte to clear my name. For whom? I had no real life there, no real friends. For ego? I just wasn't sure ego was a good enough reason to give up what I had gained in Hokes Folly. My chest heaved a deep sigh. I'd have to make some sort of decision eventually.

I squared my shoulders and focused on the storefront, letting various holiday and seasonal themes run through my head, all lending themselves to book displays. With a few solid ideas for late summer, I stepped toward the curb to cross the street to the bookstore and almost jumped out of my skin when a hand clamped down on my shoulder.

"Ms. Quinn, wait." Stan Jergins pulled his hand back. "Would you mind having a drink with me? I'd really like to talk to you for a moment, if you have time."

His open smile won me over, and we walked to the pub where Rita and I had eaten the day Mason was arrested. He shifted the large shopping bag he carried to his other hand so he could hold the door for me. We settled into a booth and ordered drinks: coffee for me and a Scotch for him.

"May I call you Jenna?" At my nod, he continued. "Jenna, it seems we got off on the wrong foot. I know I was a bit insensitive the day we met to confer on a possible sale of your uncle's business and apartment, and I wanted to apologize. I do get somewhat passionate when I talk about my mall deal."

I was sure he intended for his sympathetic tone to seem apologetic and honest, but it came off as forced as it had the first day we met. Did the man have a sincere bone in his body about anything other than his real estate deals?

I aimed for a sweet and understanding smile and hoped it didn't look as false as his expression. "I understand. It's okay. Really."

Stan flashed a bright grin and leaned back as the server delivered our beverages. "I knew you'd get it." Once the server left, Stan leaned forward, his forearms braced on the table. "Listen, I also want to apologize for the whole issue with who inherited from your uncle. Now that you're the only heir again, I still want to help you sell."

I shifted uncomfortably. "I wasn't aware Mr. Childers's death had been made public knowledge."

"Oh, it hasn't. I have a cousin who works as a dispatcher. She hears things." Another wide grin spread across his face, although this time it seemed more ominous than friendly.

Or maybe that was my imagination. "I see."

"I wanted to make sure I talked to you before you offered the sale to another agent."

My shoulders had tensed into knots, and I forced them to relax and drop a bit. I was only being paranoid. I couldn't see everyone as a possible killer. "I'm sure we can work something out."

Stan slapped a palm on the table, making me jump a bit. "Fantastic! That store? We could put a little shine and polish on it and sell it to someone wanting to get into this hot market. Hell, maybe I'll buy it myself and add it to my personal business ventures. I'm sure that old building has a ton of secrets she'll give up to the right owner. Who knows what treasures are stashed within those walls?"

The tension yanked my shoulders up again. "Yes, I'm sure she does. I'll let you know if I choose to sell and move away." I took a quick sip from my coffee so I wouldn't appear rude and reached for my purse. "If there's nothing else, I do need to get back across the street."

His expression sobered. "In that case, there is another matter I'd like to discuss if you have a few more minutes."

I didn't loosen my grip on my purse but stayed perched on the edge of the booth bench. "I'm listening."

"If you do consider staying on in Hokes Folly to run Paul's store, a younger store owner in the district might bring fresh insights to the community."

"Is this about your mall effort?"

He chuckled. "Is it that obvious?" At my nod, he reached into his bag and pulled out a stack of papers. "Well, no sense in pussyfooting around it then."

A glossy folder slid across the table to me, but Stan kept his palm on top, his gaze boring into mine. "I did respect your uncle. I hope you understand that. But he was a shortsighted man who couldn't see past how things have always been done to embrace the future. I hope you're a bit more forward thinking."

He released the folder, and I opened it slowly. It contained a prospectus for his new mall, which included mock-up drawings of the front, back, and side elevations; a map of the inside for both floors; a listing of potential stores, some of which had tentatively agreed to move in if the deal went through; a timeline showing when each phase would be completed; and a business plan, laying out investors, market research, competitors, expected revenue, and more.

After I had flipped through what was there, giving it a cursory perusal, I picked it up and tucked it into my purse. "I promise I'll read over this and get back to you." I stood.

Stan popped up from the booth. "Please look at it with an open mind. I'll be honest. Your uncle was the deciding vote with the Hokes Folly Merchants Association, and their vote always sways the city council's approval. Now your vote could make or break this deal. I hope you'll give it a fair chance and not automatically side with Paul Baxter."

I leveled a stare at him. "Mr. Jergins, I can assure you, I will give it my full attention as soon as I have time."

His hand grabbed mine and pumped it in a hearty handshake. "I knew I could count on you." He released my hand. "Oh, before I forget. I brought you a store-warming gift to help seal the deal, so to speak." He reached into his bag, removed a small, potted hydrangea with one large flower cluster, and thrust the plant toward me. "I grow these in my greenhouse. Most of the time I stick to roses, but recently I've been playing with species of hydrangea, and I have a few promising hybrids I'm working on."

"Thank you. It's lovely." I took it, praying he didn't notice my shaking hands. "I really do have to get to the store now."

Stan nodded. "Remember what we talked about. And enjoy the plant." He smiled and settled into the booth once more, picking up his drink and taking a sizable swallow.

I rushed toward the door, my instinct to escape outweighing my good manners. As I stumbled out onto the sidewalk, I turned and looked back over my shoulder at Stan. He watched me with an odd glint in his eyes, and he raised his glass to me before taking another drink. The hair on my neck stood on end, and I turned and hurried across to the bookstore, not stopping until I was in the back room and the sinister plant sat on the back desk. Had a killer just threatened me with a potted plant? Or was I being fanciful and making something menacing out of an innocent albeit coincidental gift? I couldn't be sure as I stared at the plant, its lavender-blue blooms mocking my confusion.

Chapter
Twenty-Eight

After taking a few cleansing breaths, I peeked out of the back room. At almost closing time, three customers wandered the aisles and Mason was ringing up a fourth. Pushing my paranoia to the back of my mind, I slid into my brand-new store-owner persona. With Mason's help, we found books for each customer, rang them up, and ushered them out amid promises they would come back and buy more.

After I locked the door and flipped the sign to Closed, I announced, "Mason, we're going on a treasure hunt." That got his attention. I filled him in on the conversation in the attorney's office. "It would be nice to have your help, but with or without, I've got to find that diary, if it exists. If I don't, whoever is after it will never stop coming after me." Until I could process it fully, I chose to keep my conversation with Stan to myself.

"Of course I'll help." Mason jumped up and brandished the duster he'd picked up like a sword. "I'll be your knight in shining armor and will come and rescue yon fair maiden."

"Knight in shining armor?" I chuckled at his attempt at theatrics.

"Okay." Mason rolled his eyes. "So the armor is pretty dinged up in places and has a few rust spots. But!" He ran and hopped up on the chair by the counter and waved the duster in the air once more, letting a dust cloud rain down. "Who would cross me with my trusty weapon at my side?"

I laughed and sneezed at the same time. "Don't you mean *dusty* weapon? Put that weapon down, sir knight, before you choke us both to death."

Mason obediently dropped it on the counter, letting fly another small puff, and stepped down from the chair. "What's our first move, boss lady?"

I surveyed the room, my brain processing any likely hiding spots. "There's no reason to check the front. Uncle Paul wouldn't have left it out here and risked anyone trying to buy it or shoplift it out from under his nose. Let's start with the back room."

Determined to succeed, we were even more thorough than Norman had been when he'd demanded to see the store. I went over the back-room shelves, opening every book to double-check, and reached into each desk drawer, while Mason riffled through the file cabinets and the book stacks on the tables. Once the logical places had been eliminated, we got more creative.

Taking a cue from Norman, I got a chair and, with a flashlight in hand, raised a few of the ceiling tiles, sweeping the light around in the attic space, searching in the dust and dark for the outline of the missing book and praying I didn't discover a nest of God only knew what. No nest, but no diary either. Next came the refrigerator. Nothing. Mason emptied the bathroom cabinets, and I pawed through the supply cabinets in the kitchen area. Still nothing. Mason even looked under all the tables to see if Uncle Paul had mounted a hidden compartment under one. No luck anywhere.

After a couple of hours, we had nothing to show for our efforts except dust clumps in my hair from when I stuck my head in the ceiling gap and a bump on Mason's head from when he poked it under the bathroom counter to look for loose flooring in the cabinet space. I finally declared the back room thoroughly searched and the book officially not there.

"I really didn't expect it to be here, but we couldn't take the chance I was wrong." I sighed heavily as we headed to the front to gather our things to go home.

"We could always search your apartment next," suggested the inexhaustible Mason.

At that moment, I wished I had half Mason's energy. Instead, my back ached, I'd sprained my ankle getting off the chair after I'd peeked above the ceiling tiles, and I had a massive sinus headache blossoming, thanks to all the dust we'd stirred up. "I don't think so. I think we've done enough for tonight. I'll search the apartment tomorrow."

Mason grinned, and his eyes sparkled. "I'll meet you there." He nodded firmly, as if it were a foregone conclusion that he would be included in any further search efforts.

"No. You won't. You'll be here working on the books and running the store." I handed Mason a store key.

"You trust me with the key to your store?" he asked solemnly.

"Of course. And I expect to come in here later and find this place all cleaned up."

"Hey," said Mason, with mutiny in his voice. "No fair."

"What?" I gave what I hoped was a boss-type look as I walked with him to the door. "Complaints to the management already?"

"You'll have all the fun while I'll be stuck here slaving away," Mason grumbled under his breath, crossing his arms.

"That's the beauty of being the boss," I responded in a singsong voice as I ushered him outside before locking up and heading up the spiral stairs, intentionally ignoring the potted plant in the back room of the store.

Chapter
Twenty-Nine

Someone pounded on my door. Pounded again. I glanced at the clock as I rolled out of bed. Seven AM. This had better be good. "I'm coming!" I stumbled down the hall on my sore ankle, pulling on a robe over my pajamas, and yanked open the front door.

"Oh, good, you're awake. I only have fifteen minutes before I need to head to work." Rita swept past me to the kitchen and plopped down on one of the barstools.

I stared blankly at her, willing my brain to wake up without the coffee it was now demanding, even if it was way too early on a Saturday morning. I stumbled to the coffeepot and started it up. With the aroma of the heavenly brew reviving me a tad, I turned to Rita.

Her expectant look sagged, and she rolled her eyes, turning to prop her elbows on the counter. "Oh for heaven's sake, spill it, woman. I want to know what you found out yesterday. I heard you went to Horace's office to see Frank. I just didn't get home early enough to come ask last night."

I snagged the pot off the coffeemaker and poured a cup before filling her in. Trying to cram all the information in and not make her too late for work, I quickly told Rita what had happened yesterday. Rita made the appropriate noises at the pertinent parts in the story, as any good friend should do, and I wrapped it up nicely with my plans to search the apartment. "Any suggestions as to where I should look?"

She slung her purse over her shoulder and headed toward the door. "Not really. I never asked him about where he'd hide things. I'd guess somewhere in his room, though."

I followed as far as the front door, not wanting the rest of the neighbors to see me in my bathrobe. If people kept showing up when I was still in my nightclothes, I would need to invest in something more attractive. "I haven't even been in there yet. It just seems so intrusive."

Rita turned at the threshold and gave me a quick hug. "I wish I could help, but I have a huge gaggle of octogenarians who have come for the week, and they're throwing a midmorning tea on the lawn. Gotta make them look elegant, or Elliot will have my hide."

I chuckled, knowing good and well that Elliot would do no such thing but appreciating Rita's attempt to give me something else to focus on, even if only for a moment. "Thanks. I'll manage."

"Gotta run."

"Hey, before you leave, can I ask you an odd question?" I hoped I could ask about Stan without too much of an explanation. I still needed to run things through my own head.

"Sure." She paused by the front door. "What's up?"

"Does Stan or Barbie bake?" I sipped my coffee, hoping the question didn't sound as weird as I thought it did.

"Yes, Stan loves to cook, and he bakes quite a lot. He even enters the town's annual pie contest. Wins sometimes too. Remember I told you he'd baked a cake for your aunt's birthday?"

I nodded slowly, letting the information churn through my thoughts.

Rita wrinkled her forehead. "I'd love to stay and hear why you wanted to know, but I really do have to scoot. Just take Detective Logan's advice. Be careful who you trust." She rushed down the walkway toward the stairs.

"I will," I called after her retreating back. I had no desire to be the next victim on a growing list.

The rest of my morning routine flowed smoothly, and by the time I was showered and dressed, I'd come up with a way to temporarily avoid the painful task of searching Uncle Paul's private belongings. Stan's involvement aside, I needed to find that diary. Who better to ask about an old book on local history than the local expert? Olivia Hokes was the foremost authority on Hokes Folly and John Hokes, at least according to herself. Maybe she could shed a bit of light on the whole diary issue and at least give me an idea of what I was looking for.

Over the past week, I'd seen the sisters come and go from the store enough that I had a pretty good idea of their schedule. The friendly Phillie worked in the mornings, with her not-always-so-friendly older sister coming in the afternoons. This meant Livie was more than likely still at home. I'd also learned the Hokes sisters lived in a grand old mansion in the historic neighborhood a couple of blocks away.

I walked to Livie's house, and after ringing the doorbell, I was surprised to see it opened by Livie herself. I guess I'd expected a housekeeper.

"Can I help you?" Livie pursed her lips and glanced back over her shoulder.

I put on my friendly-neighbor smile. "Hi. I hope I'm not interrupting something. I can come back if you're busy."

"I'm always busy." Livie's clipped tone and narrowed eyes told me which version of Olivia Hokes I'd see today. "What do you want?"

I tried another route. "Since you're the expert on local history, I wondered if I might talk to you for a moment."

This seemed to relax her, and she opened the door wider. "I would be delighted to talk about the town's history. Was there anything specific you wanted to know?"

"It's about one of John Hokes's old diaries."

At the mention of an old book, the woman's face lit up like the sun coming out from behind a cloud. "I was about to have my morning tea. Will you join me?" She stepped back so I could enter.

"That would be wonderful." I marveled at the mood swing. Maybe she was bipolar. Or maybe Livie was simply really into this old-book thing. I made a mental note in case I needed to butter the woman up for something else.

As we walked through the house, I looked around at the treasures the two sisters had saved over a lifetime. Every room had a lived-in feel, with what appeared to be handwoven rugs lying on the floors and countless pieces of bric-a-brac on several shelves and in every nook available. Lace doilies adorned the tabletops under family photographs that looked extremely old.

I followed Livie down a long hall and into what would have been called a family room in a more contemporary home. An unlit fireplace graced one wall, surrounded by two chairs with deep cushions, a small, flower-patterned couch, and a coffee table with dainty legs. The main feature of the room, however, was the floor-to-ceiling bookshelf that spanned one entire wall. Livie placed herself in front of the shelves and proudly pointed out various books concerning this prominent citizen or that town landmark. Her pride in her knowledge of the subject was obvious.

After twenty minutes of the woman's interesting yet seemingly unending lecture, I finally managed to get a chance to speak. "Livie, about the diary?"

"Oh, yes." She settled herself into one of the chairs, indicating I should take its twin. "My great-great-great-uncle John died almost twenty years or so before I was born, so I don't really have any memories of him personally. I do remember my grandmother talking about how he always kept a diary. She peeked in one of them once while he was still living, and she said most of what he wrote was pure rubbish."

"What happened to the diaries after he died?" They couldn't be only gibberish if one was worth killing over. At least I hoped not.

"Most of his things were packed up and auctioned off. Although I can't imagine what someone would want with them, since they were only his personal notes to himself. Some of the diaries probably went to auction with all the other books he had collected. Book collecting seems to run in the family." She smiled and looked at her bookcase.

I jumped in to keep the other woman from starting off on her beloved hobby once more. "What about his personal papers? Could the diaries have been packed in with those and stored or sent off somewhere?"

Livie concentrated for a moment. "I do think I remember hearing many of his papers were sent to his solicitor to be gone through for family records. But I don't know what would've happened to them after that. They probably got thrown out or burned. There would've been no reason to keep them. Nothing of value could've been in the ramblings of a senile old man."

"Senile?" My stomach bottomed out, and my hope of increasing my chances of survival by finding the diary faded. Rita had said everyone thought he was senile. What if it was true?

"Oh yes. It was rumored that, in the several years before his death, John was literally bonkers."

"I heard everyone in town thought he was crazy, but did the family think so too?"

"Some did, but others simply thought he was pitiful to cling to his dreams so long when it was obvious he could never reach them. He could've made a good life for himself if he'd sold off part of his land and moved into town. Maybe he'd have married and had children, run a business, farmed, whatever he wanted. Instead, he hung on to his fantasy of regaining his fortune." Livie shook her head.

"That's a shame." Once again I found myself pulling for the underdog, hoping beyond hope that he really hadn't been crazy.

"Yes, it was." Livie narrowed her eyes at me as if trying to guess my secret. "You seem very interested in the history of John Hokes. Why do you want to know so much about him?"

I wasn't sure I wanted anyone else, especially someone with a low opinion of John Hokes's ideas, to know what the diary might lead to. "Uncle Paul might have had one of John Hokes's diaries. I wanted to see what the history of the thing might be."

"Oh," gasped Livie, as a hand fluttered to her chest. "I would love to get a chance to buy that book from you. If you have it, may I have first chance at it? It would mean so much to me, since my sister and I are the last of the Hokes family."

"Of course." I smiled in response to her unbridled enthusiasm. "He may not have had it, but if he did, I'll let you know. I thought you said his diaries were nothing but rubbish, though. Why would you want it?"

"They were, mostly, but consider what they could mean, simply from a historical standpoint. I'd have the only known volume from his diaries, making me the envy of every book collector in North Carolina." Livie's eyes sparkled with excitement.

"As I said, I'll let you know if I find it, and we'll try to put a price on history." *Right after I have a good look to see if there's any truth to this hidden-treasure thing.*

Chapter Thirty

I stood in the center of the apartment, my mind running in circles thinking about hiding places and old diaries. Logically, I should look in Uncle Paul's room first. However, knowing didn't equate to doing. I chose instead to go through the main living area first. Avoidance was bliss.

Even though whoever had broken into my apartment had probably searched this area, I repeated the process, just in case he or she had missed something. I started in the living room, lifting couch cushions and running my hands down into the cracks in the couch base, looking under the couch with the light on my phone, and running my hands over the underside of the coffee table in search of a tucked-away book.

Next I moved to the dining table, again checking to see if a book had been attached to the underside of the table or chairs and finishing with knocking across its surface, seeking a hidden compartment. Nothing.

Kitchen cabinets were next, followed by drawers, knocking around to look for hidden compartments. Appliances were overturned or peeked into, and stools were checked. The pantry held no secrets either, other than a few outdated items, which went into the trash. I even pulled bags out of cereal boxes to see if the book had been hidden underneath.

The laundry room and guest bath held equally few secrets, and although I'd already checked my room for storage space, I spent forty-five minutes scouring every drawer, looking under the bed, even lifting up the mattress to check between it and the box spring beneath. Short of cutting into the mattress or the couch cushions in the living room, I had exhausted every possibility.

Resignedly, I moved to Uncle Paul's door and stood. I knew I was being ridiculous, but it still seemed like it was *his* room. Whispering an apology to him for invading his private space, I stepped across the threshold.

The room embodied the uncle—and the aunt—I remembered. Though not overtly feminine, I could see Aunt Irene's little touches here and there—a dainty crocheted doily on the dresser, delicate yellow curtains hung over the window facing the cobbled street below, and a cross-stitch of lavender roses with the initials IEB for Irene Elaine Baxter stitched in the lower corner. Uncle Paul had never stopped loving her or missing her.

Deciding I didn't want to have to do this again, I retrieved a Hefty bag from the pantry—if I went to get a box from the store, I'd find an excuse to put it all off again—and began to sort their clothes into it, destined for donation. Along with the contents of Uncle Paul's sock and underwear drawers, I also emptied lacy underthings I assumed had been Aunt Irene's. I folded each item carefully and packed it into the rapidly filling black bag. I moved all of their non-clothing items into two drawers to go through later.

Having exhausted the dresser, I moved to the nightstands, again treating each item with respect but taking time to double-check for hidden compartments. Nothing. The closet was next, and another Hefty bag was retrieved. When I had nothing left but a line of hangers, I dragged the bags out beside the front door and returned to the closet. Here I tapped on walls, tugged at carpet for loose segments, and shoved on ceiling tiles to see if there was a loose one. Nothing again.

Realizing it was already afternoon, I headed downstairs to check in on Mason's progress and to see if he wanted to grab a quick lunch with me. However, the store sat empty, and on the door hung an Out to Lunch sign, which Mason must have found tucked under the counter. I stepped outside, contemplating where to go eat.

As I stood there, I noticed Phillie in the window of the antique clothing store and waved a friendly hand in greeting. Phillie waved back, signaling for me to come inside.

"I'm awfully dusty," I said as I entered the store, brushing off a spider web I'd apparently picked up from under a piece of furniture. "Are you sure you want me to come in?"

"Yes," replied the sweet voice. "I wanted to thank you for making peace so nicely with Livie. She was very happy to have her new book."

"She really gets into her subject, doesn't she?" I remembered the lengthy tour and the animated lecture with the older Hokes sister that morning.

"Yes, she does. She's considered somewhat of an expert on the subject. Hers is the most extensive collection of its kind outside a library." Phillie's pride in her older sister's accomplishments shone from her eyes.

"Do you have any hobbies?" I remembered the bric-a-brac and decorative touches in the big house Phillie shared with her sister, and I wondered if that was all the younger sister had to occupy her time when not at their clothing store.

"No, not really. I crochet a bit and have quilted a few times, but I guess the closest thing you could say I have to a hobby would be gardening. I especially love to grow roses and flowering bulbs." The woman's face took on a dreamy quality. "I have a few very rare species of lilies and irises, some varieties with extremely large flowers, and I have quite a few miniature rosebushes. They're all out back behind the house. I'd love to show them to you sometime when you're out our way."

"I'd like that too." I honestly wished I'd been able to see them that morning on my visit to the Hokes house. It simply proved the older sister didn't take as much pride in her younger sibling's accomplishments as Phillie took in hers. "I've never been able to grow much of anything. Everything seems to die on me. I either overwater or underwater. I overfeed or underfeed. I get the soil too rich or too poor. I can't seem to get it right. And now I've got a lovely front window where I could have plants inside but no idea which ones to buy or how to keep them alive."

The tiny woman was truly animated for the first time since I'd met her. "I remember those amazingly sunny windows. Mostly morning sun, very little hot afternoon sun. If you really want to grow plants . . ." Phillie launched herself into a fifteen-minute dissertation on how to grow plants and how to tell which ones needed which kind of soil and which kind of food. Grabbing a dainty pad of paper with flowers printed around its border, Phillie listed several gardening books for me to read and told me which nurseries sold the best plants, bulbs, seeds, and gardening supplies.

Finally, I managed to get a word in. "Have you ever thought about teaching a gardening class? You'd be a natural." I grinned, thrilled to have found another side to Ophelia Hokes.

Phillie blushed and waved the suggestion away with a dismissive hand. "I'm no teacher. Livie would laugh her backside off if she heard you."

"I'm serious. You should talk to some of the greenhouses you like and see what they say. I'll bet at least one of them would love to have someone come in and give classes to their customers once a week or so on how to grow plants and which tools are the best to use for each purpose. It would save them some time explaining so much to customers, and it would probably draw more customers into their store. What do you have to lose?"

The woman genuinely had a knack for imparting gardening knowledge. After only fifteen minutes with her, I was almost tempted to try my hand at keeping plants of some sort again. Almost.

Phillie snorted under her breath, but her eyes held a speculative gleam, and I fist pumped inwardly.

"Well, I'd better get back to it." I stepped toward the door to leave. "We've managed to put most of the store back in order, and I'd better grab some lunch so I can help Mason this afternoon. At least we can make it through the next couple of months without buying any more books, thanks to the surplus in the back room."

Phillie chuckled. "With all he had in the warehouse, I'm sure you'll be up to your ears in plenty of books for a while to come."

I froze halfway out the door and turned. "Warehouse?"

"Yes." A crease deepened in her forehead as she drew her brows together. "Paul had been to a couple of rather large estate sales lately. I'm assuming the surplus is in one of the storage slots he kept out at Hokes Folly Mini Storage. I doubt he'd had time to catalog all of it and bring it to the store. He didn't make a big deal about having those spaces, but didn't you know?"

I shook my head. "Nope, but I'll definitely check them out. Thanks."

"Just keep an eye out for books for Livie," she called.

I left with a bounce in my step. I'd helped Phillie find something new to delve into, and I'd taken one more step to ensure good relations with my bookstore's neighbors. If I could keep the well-known and well-respected Hokes sisters shopping at my store, others might follow their example.

I rushed back into my store and rummaged for a phone book. I found the number and called, finding out what papers I needed to show to place the storage units in my name instead of Uncle Paul's. Excitement skittered through me at the hope that the diary might be there.

After grabbing a quick bite from a drive-through window, I arrived at the storage place and soon stood in a quiet indoor hallway in front of two ten-by-ten spaces with spare keys in hand, provided by the management. With a grin on my face, I stepped forward and threw up the rolling door on the first unit. My smile fell to the floor as I took in the space. The unit was full of boxes stacked head-high with only a few tiny gaps—walkways, I assumed—between the rows. With a sense of dread, I stepped to the second unit, unlocked it, and slid the door up. As with the other unit, I discovered more stacks of boxes, but this unit was only two-thirds full, leaving at least a little room to move around.

Before delving into the stacks, I stepped back and snapped a picture, texting it to Rita and Mason. *Looks like we have more books to catalog.* I added a wide-eyed emoji face with raised brows, hit send, and stuffed my phone in my pocket, ready to get to work. I spent the rest of the afternoon going through books of all shapes and sizes and subjects, stopping every once in a while to lay aside a book for Livie or a gardening book to ask Phillie about when I saw her next. Over the next few hours, I made it through almost half of the emptier unit without finding the elusive diary.

I only hoped I could locate it in time to keep anyone else from dying.

Chapter
Thirty-One

The weekend proved to be a busy one. While I was at the warehouse on Saturday, Mason had finished reorganizing the books, and he floated through the store on Sunday, assisting customers with selections while I manned the register. With so many customers in and out, which delighted me to no end, I didn't feel right leaving Mason to deal with it alone.

When Monday dawned, I rose with the chickens, determined to get an early start on the warehouse spaces, and hurried away from the apartment long before anyone else seemed to be awake in Hokes Folly.

Since I had decided to follow the trend of the other historic district store owners and keep the bookstore closed on Mondays, I stood looking over the boxes of books once more. Frustration bubbled to the surface, and I pushed it aside. Sure, I'd found a few gardening and local history books and little else worth noting, but I refused to let that get me down.

Instead, I tackled yet another box, then another and another. "It's got to be here somewhere," I whispered, almost dropping a heavy encyclopedia when a voice answered.

"No luck yet?"

I scrambled out from behind a stack of boxes to see Rita coming down the hallway. Setting the large book aside, I grinned and wiped dust from my hands onto the legs of my jeans. "What are you doing here?"

"Asks the woman with the secret warehouse."

I chuckled and shrugged. "How'd you know to look for me here?"

"It wasn't exactly hard to figure out. When you weren't at the bookstore, I figured this was the only other place you could be. There are only two storage places in Hokes Folly, and I knew Paul would go for the only one with climate control to preserve his books. He'd never allow them to be at the mercy of heat and cold and damp. I saw your car outside and knew I was right. You know, they really should have better security. I found the front gate open. You never know who might come wandering in."

"Like you did?" I quirked an eyebrow at her and stood, remembering the manager giving me the code but telling me the gate had a short in it and wouldn't be fixed until the following week.

"Hey," Rita protested. "I'm one of the good guys."

"I sure hope so." I flashed a quick grin.

"You'd better do more than hope. If I'm the killer, then you're in trouble, cookie." Rita moved toward me in a mock-vicious manner, her arms and hands outstretched as if to strangle her victim.

I crossed my arms and leaned back against a wall. "The other two victims were poisoned."

"Oh, yeah." Rita let her arms fall to her sides. "I guess you'd better not eat the lunch I brought." She surveyed the boxes, her eyes sad and a small wistful smile playing at the corners of her mouth. "I can almost see him digging through the boxes, excited over this or that book."

"I can do this myself, if this is too difficult for you." Dealing with my own emotional roller coaster this past week and a half had been a huge strain, and I didn't want to put anyone else through emotional trauma if I could help it.

"No. I'm okay. Where do we start?" Rita straightened her spine and smiled.

"If you're sure, pick a box." I swept my arm toward the unfinished portion of the smaller unit. "There's more than enough to go around."

We started in on the boxes I'd not gotten to before the weekend, chatting while we sorted.

"So, what's the deal with you and the hot detective?" Rita's voice was nonchalant.

I almost dropped the books I was pulling out of a box. "What?" An image flashed through my mind of dark hair, tight abs, bronzed skin, long legs, a tight butt—

"You heard me. Spill it." Rita tilted her head and gave me a no-nonsense look.

"Why do you think there's something?" I stabilized my stack and flipped through the first one, making sure the diary wasn't hidden in another book jacket.

"Oh, come on. I'm not blind. I've seen the way the man looks at you."

"Well, stop wondering. There's nothing. And I'm not sure I want something to be there either. I may not even stay here once things are settled." Warm brown eyes and a gentle touch popped into my mind next, and I almost wished there really could be something there.

"Why not?" Rita flipped a book open and closed and put it back into her own emptied box.

"Why not what? Why am I possibly not staying, or why isn't there something there with Keith Logan?" I plopped three books back into the box and folded the lid closed.

"Either. Both." Rita shrugged. "First, tell me why you may not stay."

I stood and piled the box on a growing stack of those already sorted. "I really like it here, and I think I might be good at running the bookstore. But I'm not sure if this is where I need to be."

"Do you want to go back to accounting?" Rita pulled the tape from another box and flipped it open.

"Maybe." I'd opened another as well, and my fingers slid over the tooled-leather cover on the top book. "I don't know. With my history, I'm not sure anyone would hire me."

Rita stopped working and gave me a searching look. "Did you really love it so much?"

I sighed. How could I answer that when I wasn't really sure? "It was challenging. I met interesting people. It was steady and stable."

"But somewhere along the way it changed?" Rita offered gently.

"You could say that." I nodded. "I'm not even sure when it changed. I only know one day I looked up and it wasn't so fun anymore. I guess it was about the time I realized my only steady relationship in years was with a guy who didn't want anyone to know we were dating. I couldn't make friends with anyone at work because they might find out, and I didn't have time to make friends elsewhere." It had been a lonely life, and I'd been too blind to notice.

"I'm sure you mattered to your clients." Rita's voice softened, the books forgotten for now.

"My clients, with rare exception, probably couldn't have cared less." I looked back, assessing, processing. "Their only concern if I disappeared off the face of the earth would have been how it affected their marketing timetables and budgets." I heaved a deep sigh and leaned back, slid the box to the floor, and plopped down beside it.

"I care," Rita said gently.

"I know." I smiled at my new friend. "I've only been here two weeks, but I've made more real friends in these few days than I have in the last five years."

Rita picked up a book and resumed our task. "What's so hard about deciding to stay where you're happy?"

"I guess there's a determination to prove everyone wrong, to prove I'm capable of bouncing back from all that happened." To prove to myself I wasn't the loser I'd felt like when everything collapsed like the proverbial house of cards. I slid a leather tome from my lap onto a pile and brushed off my hands.

"But couldn't your bounce back be through running a successful bookstore?" Rita wiggled a couple of volumes at me.

"I'll think about it." Honestly, I didn't know how I'd manage to think about much else. "At least I'll be here long enough to get it all sorted out. Can't sell something in this much of a mess. After that, we'll see."

Rita apparently sensed the subject was closed and changed topics. "So, what about you and the sexy cop?"

I shrugged and picked up another book, absently opening the cover and running my fingers across the aging page. "Nothing to tell."

Rita rolled her eyes. "Don't tell me you're still mooning over a man who hid you like some nasty secret and dumped you at the first sign of trouble."

"No, not really." The past played across my eyes like a B-grade movie. The pain, the hurt, the anger. "It still hurts, but not like it should."

"What do you mean?"

"We were engaged. We lived together. I thought I was in love with him." I blinked, cutting off the movie rerun of my love life. "After things ended, I realized I had loved the idea of the relationship more than I had loved him. I simply never had the opportunity to find someone else."

"Has it occurred to you that Keith Logan might be your someone else?"

I pictured spending time with the detective and his warm smiles, the soft squeeze of his hand, and the way he'd stood up for me when his partner went too far. "What makes you so sure he's even interested? Not that I'm ready for it anyway, but I'm curious." I placed a gardening book to the side for Phillie.

"Let me tell you something, girl." Rita scooted closer and pulled my hands into hers. "I haven't lived this long not to learn a few things. When a man looks at a woman the way he looks at you, he's interested. When a man looks like he's ready to knock another man's teeth down his throat for upsetting you, he's not just interested, he's serious."

"As nice as it might be, I'm not sure I want a relationship right now."

"Well, I don't want you talking yourself into becoming a hermit. You need to get out there and realize that good men do exist." She squeezed my fingers and scooted back to her own box.

"We'll see." I closed the subject for the time being and opened another box. "I'll tell you one thing, Uncle Paul sure was a bookaholic."

"Seems that way, doesn't it? Whenever I came over, he was always researching some book or other, trying to figure out if he should send it to auction or put it on the shelf for the average collector. Sometimes it really panned out for him. One time he found a book that went to auction and sold for about fifty thousand dollars. That made him all the more determined to see if there was another like it in every batch he bought."

"I could see why he would take the time. It seemed to pay off for him." I eyed the stacks of boxes and wondered what treasures, other than the frustratingly elusive diary, I might eventually discover in here.

"In that instance it did, but mostly he found the books he had were nothing really special."

I looked around at the boxes we'd managed to go through. "It's those times he did find a gem that I wonder about. Where did he keep the really valuable ones until he could sell them?"

"That, my friend"—Rita stood to look around the room as she stretched her cramped muscles—"is a question we'd better find an answer to pretty soon."

Chapter
Thirty-Two

Rita had thought to pack a cooler before she came that morning, and as we laid out paper plates and took the food out, I remembered our earlier teasing.

"I thought I wasn't supposed to let you fix the food, in case you're the killer." I opened a container of potato salad and sniffed it.

"Shoot." Rita shook her red tresses. "You caught me." Sighing, she began putting part of the food back into the cooler.

"Hey, what are you doing?"

"Since you won't be eating any, I thought I'd put the poisoned stuff back in the cooler so I won't accidentally eat any of it. I wouldn't want to kill myself, now would I?" With one corner of her mouth turned up impishly, Rita calmly continued to pack away my part of the lunch.

"I was kidding. Right now, I wouldn't mind if it was poisoned. I'm too hungry to care." I grabbed the sandwich Rita was putting away, slid it from its baggie, and took a huge bite. "There. It's too late now. I'm already contaminated. I might as well enjoy my last meal. Besides, you probably wouldn't poison me before we find the diary. You need access to Uncle Paul's stuff."

Rita laughed and set the food back on the makeshift table we'd made from stacked boxes. We settled onto the floor to eat, and Rita took a bite of her sandwich, chewed, and swallowed.

"Hey, I was joking about poisoning the food. You're not eating."

I stopped stirring my fork in the potato salad on my plate. "Can I ask you something?"

Rita put down her sandwich and gave me her full attention. "Sure, what's up?"

I explained about my run-in with Stan and his gift of a potted hydrangea.

"Why didn't you tell me about this before?" She leaned in, pinning me with her gaze.

I shook my head. "I don't know. I just wanted to think about it for a while, to make sure I wasn't overreacting. But I can't help feeling like maybe there's something there. Maybe he really did do it."

Rita shrugged. "There's always that possibility."

"I guess so." I ate a bite of the potato salad then listed my concerns. "He obviously has hydrangea available. But then, so does a huge portion of the world. It's a popular plant. And he did know about Norman's murder. I know it's all over the news now, but it wasn't on the day after the murder when he talked to me."

Rita had picked up her sandwich again, and she wiped her mouth before speaking. "Oh, he really does have a cousin who works as a dispatcher. She's quite the busybody and a gossip to boot. It's a miracle the newswires hadn't already picked up the story. The only reason they hadn't is we're too small of a town for the TV stations to notice."

"But would he have known about the secret passages at the hotel?"

Rita nodded. "He was a junior agent at the real estate company that brokered the sale to the hotel. He was very familiar with the plans and was even inside a couple of times while it was being built. Plus he and Barbie were there the night Norman was killed."

"Hmm." I ate some more potato salad. I needed to get her recipe. "I guess the brownie and cobbler angle fit too."

"So that's why you asked me if he liked to bake." Rita had polished off the last of her lunch, leaving me with half a plate to go. She grabbed a plastic bag from the cooler and began to put the lunch trash into it.

My brows knit together. "Yeah, I was trying to fit the pieces into something that made sense. But we'll probably never know if he used sleeping pills for anything." Whether we found that connection or not, a lot of other evidence was piling up that Stan might have killed my uncle and Norman Childers. "I guess the big question remains: how would he have known about the diary?"

"Who knows? But until we find it and can turn it over to the police, whoever wants it still has you in his cross hairs."

I ate the last of my sandwich while Rita packed the leftovers neatly in the cooler. We'd just finished as the door at the end of the hall opened and two figures entered, shadowed by the light behind them. I jumped to my feet, relieved when I saw not only Mason Craig but Keith Logan exiting as well. I quickly asked Rita to keep our conversation about Stan private for now. I didn't want to point a finger at a possibly innocent man simply because he'd been nice enough to give me a potted plant.

"Hi, Jenna, Rita. We thought you guys might need some help." Mason walked up the hallway with a bounce in his step.

"Sure. We'd love it," replied Rita.

I looked at Keith, trying to figure out why he had come. I was pretty sure he wasn't there in an official capacity, so maybe Rita was right about him. I narrowed my eyes. "You do know I haven't told Detective Sutter about this place yet, right?"

"I know nothing, see nothing, hear nothing." Keith winked and walked past me into the almost completed unit.

Mason grinned. "I had to stop by the store to pick up my jacket, and he was looking in the windows." He gestured toward Keith. "I told him we were closed on Mondays, and he asked if I knew where you were today. I figured it was the place with the heat and air."

"Don't worry," Keith interrupted. "He swore me to secrecy."

"Won't you get in trouble if someone else official shows up and catches you here helping me? Isn't this a conflict of interest or something?" I crossed my arms and tilted my head.

"Nah," Keith replied, his face serious. "I'll tell them I was patrolling and caught everyone here, and I'm arresting you all."

My breath caught in my throat, my stomach tightened, and my knees sagged.

"I'm kidding." Keith helped me sit on a box. "I swear. I'm so sorry. I didn't think."

Rita punched him on the arm. "Well, think next time."

I stopped her before she could chastise him further. "I'm okay. It brought back a few memories I'd rather not have." I pushed away thoughts of handcuffs and jail cell bars, breathing slowly and thinking instead about what plants I'd put in the bright windows in the apartment.

Keith knelt in front of me, taking one of my hands into his own. "I really am sorry. I promise."

"I'm fine." I squeezed his hand softly. "Why are you really here?"

Keith grinned boyishly. "I wanted to take you up on your offer of helping me find a good book to read."

Uh-huh. Sure. I wanted to give him the benefit of the doubt that maybe he wasn't there undercover to help Sutter prove his case against me. "I have several thousand you can choose from." I rolled my shoulders and forced myself to relax. "Care to join us?"

"I'd like nothing better." Keith helped me to my feet.

"Boy, it's as big a mess down here as it was at the store." Mason had stepped to the second unit, and he whistled low and shook his head.

Rita spoke up in Paul's defense. "It wasn't always this bad. Not until Jenna got ahold of it."

Way to throw me under the bus! I shoulder-bumped her. "Hey, remember you helped with a great deal of this mess. I'm trying to make sure we go through each book to see if the diary's hidden in another book jacket."

"Oh." Mason surveyed the mess. "I guess it's like the 'You've got to break a few eggs to make an omelet' thing."

Rita threw a wadded paper towel at Mason, making him duck. "You behave, or you'll be kicked out of the fun of going through all these boxes of books."

"Okay, okay." He grinned and grabbed a box. "No need to be pushy."

I pointed out what I'd already gone through and showed them how I wanted things restacked, and we got to work. After five hours, we'd gone through the rest of the first unit and much of the second.

"I give up." Rita placed her current box with the others we'd completed.

"Me too." Mason sank to the floor and leaned against the wall. "I'm worn out."

"We've been at this a long time." I dusted off my hands, feeling as frustrated and clueless as I had that morning. "I guess we should call it a day."

"Let's regroup here tomorrow morning and go at it again," Mason suggested, a hopeful look on his face.

231

I hated to pop his bubble, but it couldn't be helped. "You've got to run the store tomorrow and go through the books in the back room."

"And I have a date to help a group of rich women learn how to primp, early-1900s style." Rita looked about as excited as someone announcing an appointment to have a root canal.

When I looked over at him, Keith raised his hands in surrender. "Don't look at me. I have to work a double shift starting at six in the morning."

"I guess it'll be little ol' me here tomorrow," I said more cheerfully than I felt. "But I swear I'll let you know if I find anything."

"Jenna, one more thing." Keith caught my arm before we got into our cars, a look of worry etched on his face.

My heart fluttered at his warm touch. "What's that?" Good God, I sounded like a breathless teenager. Maybe I needed to stop hanging around Rita. She was putting goofy ideas in my head.

"Promise me you'll keep an eye out while you're here alone."

There was no way he was interested. I was a suspect in a crime. He was only being nice. "I promise. I don't want to get this close only to be caught unaware by the police."

"I wasn't thinking of the police." Keith squeezed my arm gently then let go. "I'm worried about whoever wants the diary badly enough to kill for it. They've already threatened you and seem prepared to kill someone else to get what they want. I don't want that someone to be you."

Chapter
Thirty-Three

Tuesday morning brought much-needed showers to Hokes Folly, leaving puddles everywhere and giving the air a clean, fresh smell. I didn't let the dreary skies spoil my good mood or dampen my determination to find the diary. I bounded down the stairs and headed to the back room to grab a couple of empty boxes from Uncle Paul's stash so I could bring back the growing stacks I had set aside for Phillie and Livie.

As I came back into the front room, I ducked behind a shelf. Stan Jergins stood outside, an umbrella in one hand while his other hand cupped his eyes, peering intently into the closed store. I was pretty sure he hadn't seen me, and I flinched when I heard him rattle the front door as if trying to pull it open in spite of the Closed sign and the posted hours. I refused to get up and let him in while I was there by myself, especially since Mason wouldn't arrive for another hour and a half.

I stayed hidden for ten minutes or more before daring to peek out around the shelves, relieved to see only rain sliding across the windows. Boxes under my arm and a roll of packing tape on my wrist, I scurried across the room and up the stairs to grab my purse.

Outside again, I splashed through the puddles to my car, waving to Rita, who was leaving for work.

Rita rolled down her window. "Please be careful."

"I promise." I waved again, sliding into my car quickly to keep from getting too wet. In spite of the rain, I enjoyed the drive over to the warehouse. As I passed through a historic neighborhood, I mentally took a step back in time to a day when neighbors knew one another and hours in the evenings were spent sitting on the front porch waving to passersby. A hushed sense of time slowing down settled over me as I drove along the street in front of the older manor houses. Moving past the Hokeses' home, I marveled at the differences between their house and the ones on either side. Each home, like all the others on the street, had its own unique personality, unlike the cookie-cutter housing developments cropping up these days.

Still wondering what it would be like to live in one of those grand old homes, I pulled into the warehouse lot and pulled around to the building that housed my units. I rushed inside, holding my raincoat up to shield myself from the rain, which had begun to blow at an angle in the increasing wind.

I set the hallway lights and stepped to my units, opening both. I mentally mapped out what was left to go through and got to work. Slowly I filled the two boxes for the Hokes sisters, gardening books to ask Phillie about and Hokes Folly books for Livie, a testament to how many more boxes I'd scoured looking for the elusive diary.

As I moved down the final row of books, I hit pay dirt: a small safe tucked in among the boxes. A safe with a combination. I groaned. I couldn't get this close only to be stopped by three little numbers. I racked my brain, trying to figure out what Uncle Paul might have used. A number popped into my head, and I grinned. It couldn't be that easy. I quickly turned the dial to the day, month, and year of my aunt and uncle's wedding and felt the door give as the last tumbler fell. Giddy with excitement, I pulled it open and pulled out a book-shaped item wrapped in a cloth.

After brushing dust from my T-shirt and jeans, I slid back against the wall and gently slid the cloth away. *Oh my God oh my God oh my God.* My hands trembled as I opened the aged leather cover. There, on the first page, were the words "John Jacob Hokes, Diary, Volume 47, 1934." The handwriting was elegant but a bit spidery.

Filled with a sense of awe mixed with urgency, I sank down onto the cold floor, turned the page, and began to read about the last year of John Jacob Hokes's life.

January 1, 1934

The new year has begun. With each year that rolls around, I fall further into despair, knowing my time grows shorter and shorter in which to find a way to regain my wealth. I will be seventy years of age next month, and death creeps up on me with each passing moment.

Daily I search for ways to build a fortune. Nightly I pray to God for guidance. Nothing I have done has yet worked out, but I must continue to hope. It is all I have left.

His despair leapt off the page at me, but I also sensed he had been truly hopeful. I remembered Livie's statements about how John Hokes could have had more in life and wondered if there were times he regretted his obsessions. I skimmed through quite a few entries and stopped when another caught my eye.

February 23, 1934

Today is my seventieth birthday. Although I do not like to face it, my age shows itself in many ways. I can no longer move as easily as I once could, nor can I hear the birds outside my window as loudly as before. My eyes grow dim, and at times I have trouble reading in the evening in front of the fire, even with my spectacles. I find I even have to climb the ladder in my study to get to the books on the top shelves before I can make out their titles.

Age. It is a blessing and a curse. A blessing to those who can see their lives come full circle, reaping what they have sown in their younger years. A curse to those who have lived in seclusion with no one to keep them company in their dying years.

I saw her today. She is a grandmother again. Her oldest daughter had another child yesterday evening. A boy this time. I envy her the laughter and, yes, even the tears of family life. I sometimes wonder if I should have gone with her, marrying her and working in the mill she inherited from her first husband upon his death. We would have been married for twenty-five years now. I might have children and possibly grandchildren of my own. But those decisions were made a lifetime ago. I chose this solitary life, and I cannot second guess myself now.

I become more determined each time I see her to show her I was not wrong to continue my search. None of the others matter. Only she and her opinion of me matter. I cannot fail.

I dabbed at the tears that stung my eyes, unable to imagine going through life alone and unhappy when obviously there had been another choice. Then it hit me. That's exactly what would happen if I chased after my old life, only so I could prove everyone wrong, especially now when I had another opportunity. Especially now when there might be Keith. Pushing those thoughts aside for the time being and promising myself I'd examine them later, I continued through the lengthy, morose diary entries. Several months of entries went by before I ran across one that made me sit up and take notice.

July 12, 1934

I am redeemed! I talked with a man today who told me where to find my fortune. He gave exact directions for a pittance of a price, considering what he sold me. It is there. I know it is. Now all I have to do is find the proper spot. He had no maps and claimed not to remember the exact location, but he did show me a sample. It took my breath away. Tomorrow I begin down the road back to riches.

My first real clue to what someone had resorted to murder to obtain. I skimmed through entries about purchasing tools and working out a search pattern for the new piece of land he'd bought from a stranger. Other entries detailed his search, acre by acre, and his overwhelming disappointment at his failure to find his life-redeeming treasure. I struggled to keep my mind from wandering.

I sat up straighter, and my eyes became riveted to the page as I read the first sentence of the next entry.

November 30, 1934

I found it! It is truly there! I cannot quite believe my good fortune. I had almost given up hope. The search seemed almost endless. I have brought a piece of my future back with me to

*take to the bank. This should get their attention. I do not,
however, feel safe having it lying around waiting for some ruf-
fian to come along and take it from me. With the economy in
its present shape, you cannot trust people to be honest. As a
precautionary measure, I have hidden my treasure, along with
a detailed map. It can be found twisted up under Bartholomew's
watchful eye.*

*I am sending a detailed letter to my solicitor of old. He will be
an elderly man now, as I am. But he will remember his first client.
He will help a friend find his way. I know he is still respected by
the banking and legal community. With his assistance, I will
regain a bit of respect for myself as I go through the process of
rebuilding. It is only a matter of time. And time, for once, seems to
be on my side.*

This was the last entry in the diary. I flipped through several
more pages to make sure, but it seemed there was nothing else. I
reread the last entry twice, picking it apart each time, trying to
absorb its meaning. It was obvious John Hokes had found something of great value. But he'd hidden it. He also referred to the
letter sent to his solicitor, which verified the information on the
papers found in Norman Childers's safe after his death. Norman
had been onto something, as had Uncle Paul. That left three big
questions. What had John Hokes found? Where had he hidden it?
And who had killed twice to get it?

Chapter
Thirty-Four

My legs were stiff from sitting on the concrete floor for what must have been hours. I hadn't even considered moving to the comfort of my car. I'd been too engrossed in reliving John Hokes's life to care about the cold seeping in or the hardness of the floor. I stood and took a few minutes to stretch before grabbing my phone to call everyone, as I'd promised to do if I found anything.

Damn. Dead battery. Had I forgotten to charge it again? Maybe I should start carrying an extra charger, just in case. For now, my phone was about as useful as an attempt at smoke signals in the rain that continued to pour.

I made sure all the boxes were inside, except the two I'd take to the Hokes sisters, and rolled down the doors, locking them and dropping the keys into my pocket. I rewrapped the diary and stuck it inside my raincoat, which I'd retrieved from the corner where I'd laid it while I worked, and loaded the two boxes into the car.

As I approached the Hokes sisters' house on my way back through town, I decided to stop. Livie would love the books, and she might be able to shed some light on the weird clue. It was already midafternoon, and I crossed my fingers that Livie would still be home. I didn't want to walk from the historic district's car park all the way to her store in this pouring rain with fragile books to catch her there if she'd already left the house. The diary was too important to risk.

Once on her porch, I stood, Livie's box in my arms and the diary still tucked into the inside pocket of my coat, crammed up against the door to keep the rain from hitting me under the tiny overhang. I jumped as the door swung open before I'd even had the chance to ring the doorbell.

Livie stood there with her coat on and her purse over one arm. Her eyes widened, and she jumped back, opening the door wider and gesturing for me to come inside. "Good Lord, child. What on earth are you doing here?"

Inwardly, I thanked my fairy godmother or whoever it was who looked out for me, since Livie seemed to be in the best of the several moods she regularly displayed.

I held out the box. "I found some books in Uncle Paul's warehouse I thought you might want to look at. I haven't set a price yet, but if you want any of them, I'll make pricing them my top priority." I smiled and held out the books. All except the diary, which stayed inside my coat.

Livie's voice raised a few notches and took on a breathy quality. "How absolutely wonderful." She moved down the hallway to her library, cradling the antique books as tenderly and gently as if they were newborn babies.

I followed her into the room and watched as Livie removed her raincoat and tossed it aside to land in a messy heap on the floor by the doorway. My eyebrows shot up. I hadn't seen Livie as the clutter-bug type. Guess I knew who did the housekeeping as well as the gardening.

"Am I keeping you?" I didn't want to delay the other woman from relieving her sister.

"No, not at all." Livie waved a dismissive hand in my general direction without looking up. "Phillie can wait a bit. She'll understand."

I took off my wet coat and draped it across the other chair, watching as Livie laid out the books on a table near the tall windows. Putting on reading glasses, Livie first put the books in order by author. Then she referred to her shelves, also in alphabetical order, I assumed to ensure she didn't already own these volumes. Finally, she opened each book, running her fingers across the date and author's credentials if there, then reading a passage or two within the text.

Through all of this process, I waited patiently. Okay, maybe not so patiently, but I needed the sales if Livie decided to buy, and I also needed the Hokes sisters' goodwill, as they were important members of the community. While I waited, I walked to the windows and looked out across the backyard. Flowers in every hue held faces toward the slowing rain. Enjoying the riot of color, I let my mind drift, wondering if I should show Livie the diary before the police had had a chance to look at it. When Livie spoke, bringing my thoughts back to the present, my heart jumped, as I hadn't heard her move up behind me.

"I'll take all of them," Olivia said firmly. "There's not a bad one in the lot."

Yay for me! "That's great." I slid into my bookseller persona. "I'll get them priced as soon as possible. Please bear with me, though. I'm not likely to be as fast at that as Uncle Paul was. But I'll do my best for you."

"See that you do," came the crisp reply. "I hope I can assume you won't try to gouge me for a higher price." Livie raised her eyebrows and leveled a piercing stare at me.

I stood my ground and matched her stare, although I was oddly intimidated by this tiny woman. "I can assure you I would never price a book higher than its value, regardless of the identity of the buyer."

Livie maintained her intense gaze for a moment longer before finally relaxing. "Good, then. If there's nothing else, I need to get to the store. Phillie will expect me to come and relieve her."

It was now or never. I took a deep breath. "Actually, there is one more thing."

Livie turned expectantly, her gaze following my movements as I walked to the chair and brought the small diary out of my coat. "It's John Hokes's diary." I extended the book toward the other woman. "I found it among Uncle Paul's books today."

Livie's eyes widened as she reached for the diary. "Have you read it?" she asked in a breathy voice, not taking her eyes from the book.

I hoped she wasn't about to have a heart attack or anything, because she had paled drastically. I led her to one of the high-backed chairs, settling her in one and sitting in another opposite her. "I read the whole thing, and I didn't think it was rubbish. Actually, I thought it was fascinating. This is only the last year he lived, but it tells so much about his entire life. I almost cried in several spots." I stopped, not wanting to seem too sentimental.

Livie patted my arm gently. "I understand. Sometimes these things get to me too." She smiled reassuringly at me.

I relaxed as more color returned to Livie's face. This time I truly was patient as Livie settled herself back onto her chair and read a few of the entries.

"May I keep this a while?" Livie didn't look up from the page she was reading.

"I don't think so. The police want to see this. They think Uncle Paul's murder may have something to do with this diary."

Livie almost dropped the book. Her hand fluttered to her chest as she gasped. "What?"

Oh Lord, if she wasn't having a heart attack, I might give her one if I wasn't careful. "I'm sorry to blurt it out like that. I didn't think."

"It's all right." The strained look slowly left Livie's face. "You simply startled me. That was definitely not what I expected you to say."

"No, I guess it wasn't." What would Sutter say if I actually did cause a death? He'd have a field day with this one. I'd probably end up with the death penalty before he was done.

The older woman read a bit more. "What makes the police think this book had anything to do with Paul's death?" She looked up, her brow furrowed and her eyes concerned.

I hesitated. I really hadn't thought this through, had I? "I'm not sure how much I can say, but I can tell you this much. The police have found evidence that makes them believe Uncle Paul was killed by someone trying to steal this diary. They've also linked it to Norman Childers's death."

"That nasty man who tried to take your bookstore?" Livie's mouth pursed with obvious distaste.

"Yep, that's the one."

"What could be in this diary that someone would kill over?" A frown crossed Livie's face, and she shook her head. "It's only an old man's rantings."

I wrestled again with how much to reveal. Well, as they always said, in for a penny, in for a pound. "It seems your ancestor found some kind of treasure right before he died. He hid a piece of it and a map to find the rest. Then he left a clue at the end of the diary, telling where he hid them."

"This sounds like it might take some time to sort out. I'll make tea." She stood and moved toward the kitchen. "I'll be back shortly."

After a few minutes, I got up and made my way to the kitchen. The teapot heated water on the stove, and teacups and saucers for two already sat on a tray to be brought into the den. Stepping back into the hallway, I caught sight of Livie entering the hall from a door halfway down its length. The woman jumped but recovered her composure as she came toward me.

"Was there something you needed?" Livie asked sweetly.

I held out my dusty hands. "Yes. I was hoping to find a bathroom. I've been handling old books all day. I'd like to wash up, if you don't mind."

"Of course. It's down the hall, the first door on the right." Livie brushed past me and into the kitchen.

I strode down the hall to the indicated doorway. I hesitated. This was the door Livie had come out of. Shrugging, I walked through, closed the door behind me, and walked the length of the room to the sink. I reached to turn on the water, but before I could pump any soap from the dispenser, a small pink pill caught my eye.

It had rolled behind the trash can next to the sink, and I bent down to pick it up. It wasn't the only one of its kind on the floor. Two more like it lay halfway under the skirt of the sink. I picked up all three pills and straightened.

Intending to put them back where they came from, I opened the mirrored door on the wall above the sink, revealing an organized cabinet. Mom would have been in heaven. Except for that one bottle. The lid wasn't put on properly, and it stood out of line on the perfectly ordered shelf. I pushed it back into place and laid the pink pills next to it on the shelf. The label caught my eye. "One pill to be taken at bedtime as needed for sleep."

The hair on the back of my neck stood up. The bottle had obviously been closed and put away in a hasty manner, and the pills on the floor suggested someone had been in too much of a hurry to notice they had fallen out. I reached out as if in slow motion and slowly picked up the bottle, fully opening it once I held it. The little pink pills inside matched the ones from the floor. The name on the bottle was Ophelia Hokes.

Bile rose in my throat, and my heart squeezed then pounded as if desperate to get out of my chest. My hands trembled as I replaced the cap on the bottle and put it back into the cabinet. I all but ran out of the bathroom, hoping to get to the den to grab my coat, my car keys, and the diary before Livie could return with the tea tray. I groaned under my breath when I found Livie seated under the windows, pouring tea into two cups.

"Oh, just in time." She smiled her sweet smile.

I hesitated. Maybe my overactive imagination had gotten the better of me. Maybe I was wrong. I swallowed back a scream when I realized I hadn't been wrong, as Livie extended a small plate.

"I made a blackberry cobbler a few days ago. I thought you might enjoy a piece or two with your tea."

I glanced at my watch and shook my head. "I'm so sorry." I prayed my voice sounded sincere. "I've remembered another appointment I made. I'll barely make it in time as it is, so I'll have to come back later to talk about the diary."

My raincoat was on the chair beside me, and I bent to retrieve it, checking for the keys in my pocket as I strode across to the little table to snag the diary. I slipped the coat on, easing the book into a pocket and breathing another silent prayer that Livie wouldn't sense anything was wrong. I turned . . . and stared straight into the barrel of a gun.

Chapter Thirty-Five

My mouth dropped open. In the few seconds it had taken me to grab everything, Livie had silently moved across the room. She stood in the doorway, barring my only escape route. A large revolver, pointed at my chest, rested in her hands.

"I knew you were trouble the first time I saw you." The woman sighed deeply. "Why wouldn't you go away?" She sounded like she was bargaining with a toddler who refused to wash his hands for dinner rather than contemplating murder.

I quickly scoped out the room. It had one door, which left only the tall windows, and I wondered if I had the body weight to break through one if I tossed myself at it. Considering my recent luck, that would be one of those movie things that didn't happen in real life and I'd bounce off the glass like a bird, too stunned to defend myself. "I have every right to be here." I struggled to keep my voice calm and soothing. "Uncle Paul did leave all of his possessions to me."

"I know." Livie looked genuinely regretful. "I wish you hadn't become mixed up in all of this."

Her patient, grandmotherly tone sent chills up my spine, but a question burned its way into my brain, and I had to ask it, even though I knew it was stupid to antagonize her. "Did you kill Uncle Paul and Norman Childers?"

"Yes. Yes, of course." Livie waved mention of the dead men away with a flick of her wrist, as if they were completely unimportant to her, slightly wobbling the barrel of the gun before leveling it at me again. "I poisoned them both. I would have poisoned you too. Why didn't you drink the tea and eat some cobbler? It would have been so much neater that way."

No point in lying. I sucked at lying, and she'd see right through me. "You dropped a few of the pills on the bathroom floor. I saw the bottle and suspected. The plate of cobbler confirmed it."

Livie shook her head and huffed out a sigh. "It never pays to be in a rush with important things. But I didn't have time to plan."

I took a deep breath, scrambling to come up with a plan of my own. "Weren't you worried you or Ophelia might accidentally eat the cobbler with the hydrangea petals?"

"Oh no, dear." Livie shook her head. "I tossed that out. This cobbler isn't poisoned. I only needed it to help cover up the taste of the medicine in the tea."

My mind screamed. Desperate to keep the woman talking, I watched for any chance to overpower Livie. Escape was everything. As calmly as I could, I asked, "Since I won't be around to tell anyone, would you answer a few questions?"

Livie hesitated. "I don't see why not." She nodded her head once.

I released the breath I'd been holding. Chalk one up to TV. At least the shows had gotten something right. "Why did you kill Uncle Paul?"

Livie frowned, and the barrel of the gun dipped a fraction of an inch. "He was an accident. I simply wanted the diary. I only meant to put him to sleep for a while so I could get away without him knowing. But he woke up too soon and tried to chase me up the stairs. He grabbed the diary, but I held on tightly." She stretched and smiled, a proud glint in her eyes before the smile faded into a frown. "He tugged so hard he lost his balance and fell backward down the stairs. I didn't know until later that he'd been killed by the fall. I was very sorry, but he shouldn't have tried to keep the Hokes treasure from me. After all, my family would have inherited it all if John Hokes had been successful in finding it."

I thought of the book in Norman's room safe. "But you got the wrong diary."

"Yes, I did, and it made me furious. All of that for nothing." Livie looked like she was coming to the end of her tell-all session.

I quickly asked another question. "How did you find out about the diary in the first place?"

"Your stupid uncle gave the secret away." She pursed her lips, a sneer of distaste crossing her face. "He came to me, asking questions about John Hokes, trying to figure out about the clue you mentioned. Oh, he didn't come right out and tell me about it, but he said enough that I put two and two together and decided I wanted the diary for myself."

"What about Norman?" When her gun dipped a bit lower, I edged closer to the door. "How did he fit in?"

"That idiot?" Livie's jaw tightened. "He found out about the diary also. Crazy John sent Norman's great-great"—she waved her hand—"however many great grandfather a letter about it. Norman found it in some papers in the basement after his mother died. He came into town planning to steal the diary and the treasure out from under my nose. He'd been to see Paul the same day I went to get the diary. But Paul refused to sell it to him. Then, after Paul died, Norman came to me, because my sister and I are the last of the Hokes family, and he thought I'd have the knowledge he needed. He offered to help me get the diary if we split the treasure evenly."

"That's when he broke into my store?" Slowly, bit by bit, I inched closer to the older woman.

"Yes. He came up with that harebrained idea all on his own." Livie snorted. "He couldn't even get that right."

"Why did you kill him?" I was almost close enough to leap at Livie and knock her down.

"He was going to cut me out of the deal." Livie spoke through gritted teeth. "Actually, you let me in on that part of his scheme when you told me about him trying to take your inheritance. I almost didn't recognize him with his changed hair color. My eyes aren't what they used to be. After that, I confronted him. He'd decided he didn't need my expertise after all. He called me . . . a . . . crazy old bat." She blurted the words out as if they still stung a great deal.

Only a few more inches. "But you showed him."

"Yes, I did." She nodded her head, and a gleeful smile, which gave her an oddly sinister look, crossed her face. "I poisoned him on purpose, using some of Phillie's stupid flowers. Took me a couple of days with her boring gardening books to find one that said which plants were poisonous. But I wasn't going to be cheated by a man again. And now, I have the diary."

"Actually, I have the diary." My stomach tightened, and I clenched my jaw. That was really moronic. Was I trying to piss her off? "And several people knew I was coming here. They'll look for me if I go missing." *Please don't see through my lie.*

"Well, then, that does change things. I'll have to find a cleaner way to deal with this." Livie paused. "Outside with you." She waved her gun for me to precede her out of the room.

I stayed rooted to the spot. I was almost close enough to jump the "crazy old bat." Norman had been right. It turned out to be an apt title.

Livie pointed the gun at me, taking a more careful aim this time and backing away from the door. "I would prefer to do this outside, as I honestly don't want to spend hours getting bloodstains out of my rugs. But I'll shoot you in here if I have to. And don't think I can't. This old gun belonged to Daddy. He taught me to shoot when I was young. Although the only things I've ever shot have been squirrels in my attic, I'm quite accurate and won't hesitate to pull the trigger."

Hysterical laughter threatened to bubble up within me. She had squirrels in her attic, all right, and not the one attached to the house. I swallowed back the hysteria and looked at where Livie stood now, too far away for me to grab before she could pull the trigger. Going outside might be the better choice. There were no doors to be blocked outside, so maybe I'd have a greater chance of escaping. I moved across the room and went through the door and across to the kitchen. Livie ushered me out the back door and into the beautifully landscaped garden area.

"These must be your sister's flowers." I pointed at a section of rosebushes with blooms still wet from the recent rain, hoping to distract Livie by changing the subject.

"Yes, they are. And you'll make wonderful food for them. We're turning up a new bed over there. Please go stand next to it." She waved the gun in the general direction of a freshly turned, although slightly muddy, patch of ground.

Sweat dripped down my back in spite of the breezy, early fall evening. My heart plummeted when I looked around for a way out but found the entire yard surrounded by a privacy fence with a closed gate as the only exit. Livie stood between me and my chance of escape, effectively blocking both the gate and the door back into the house.

It was time to change tactics. The rain had stopped, but the air still hung heavy with moisture, making sound more likely to carry on the wind. I raised my voice, hoping a neighbor might hear. "You don't really want to do this. You've already killed two people. If you turn yourself in, they might go easier on you."

"Turn myself in?" Livie furrowed her brow and tilted her head. "For what? I've done nothing wrong. Paul's death was an accident, and Norman deserved to die. He tried to cheat me."

"What about me, Livie?" I fought the urge to throw up, struggling to keep my tone gentle and wistful, hoping to soften the woman a bit. "Why do I have to die?"

Livie scowled. "You'd tell everyone what's in the diary and would try to make them think I had done something wrong. You want to keep the treasure all for yourself." Her expression lightened as she said this, obviously relieved to have found a way to put me into a category that, to her mixed-up mind, deserved to die.

"No. I'll share it with you." Desperate times called for desperate measures. "It will be you and me. We'll find the treasure together. After all, I came to you for help in the first place, didn't I?"

Doubt flickered behind Livie's eyes before her expression hardened once more. "No. I don't think so. Paul came to me for help too, but he had no intention of sharing the treasure. Norman asked him about sharing, and Paul said he wanted to find it, but it would belong to the hotel, since they bought the land and house. I'd be left with nothing. And you're his niece. You want to do the same thing, don't you?" Livie raised the gun and aimed.

The gate burst open, and Phillie rushed into the backyard. "Livie, what is going on?" she gasped, coming to a halt when she caught sight of the gun in her sister's hand.

"Phillie!" Livie's aim faltered, and she took a step back. "What are you doing home?"

"You were two hours late coming to the store," replied Ophelia. "I thought something might have happened to you. I tried to call, but the phone lines are down on the entire street. So, I came home. I heard raised voices back here."

Thank God for acoustics and drama club in high school, where I'd learned to push my voice out.

Livie shook her head and sighed heavily. "I had hoped to keep you out of this, but since you're here, I can use the help burying the body under the new daffodil bed." Livie turned back to me.

"The what?" Phillie's eyes widened in horror.

"Oh, Phillie, grow a spine." Livie glanced over her shoulder at her sister.

"But why?" Phillie asked.

"She knows too much about Paul and Norman," came the terse reply as Livie leveled the gun at me again, taking careful aim.

I clenched my fists, my gaze locked on Phillie, desperately hoping she could talk her older sister down.

Phillie paled even further, and her hand went to her throat. "Paul? And Norman?"

A defensive pout crossed Livie's face, and she waved another dismissive hand. "Yes. I killed them. They deserved it. They tried to cheat me." With her back to Phillie, she missed the determined straightening of her sister's spine.

"I won't let you do it." Phillie's voice took on an edge of steel.

Livie's voice rose to a screech, and the gun trembled in her hands. "Won't let me? I've taken care of you all of your life. I've kept you from making mistakes and kept your life on track. And now you won't 'let' me keep things as they should be by getting rid of this troublemaker? I think you'll do what I tell you to do. And

I'm telling you to go get the shovel from the shed." Livie planted her feet and raised the gun, taking aim a third time in the increasing drizzle as the rain threatened to fall once more.

My stomach dropped, and my throat closed over the scream threatening to fly out. I couldn't tell if the dampness on my cheeks was from my tears or the misting rain that fell from the sky.

Without warning, Phillie threw herself at her sister, catching Livie by surprise as she pulled the trigger. I had flinched away from the shot, reflexively holding up my hands as if that might stop a bullet going however many feet per second those things flew. But the bullet never hit me.

I turned back to see the surprise on Livie's face turn to horror as she realized her sister had taken the bullet meant for me. Dropping the gun on the wet ground at her feet, Livie crumpled into a pile next to Phillie, carefully scooping her into trembling arms, weeping and rocking her sister back and forth as two police cars pulled into the driveway, their red and blue twirling lights creating eerie patterns in the falling drizzle.

Chapter
Thirty-Six

"So, Livie killed them both?" Rita knelt in front of my TV, checking the channel guide.

"Yep." I'd spent two days talking with the detestable Detective Sutter about Tuesday's events, as he had remained determined to pin at least one of the murders on me, if only as an accomplice. The fact that Keith had also been present had softened things, but it still had been an ordeal, even though I'd rather enjoyed Sutter's disappointment when he realized I wasn't guilty of murdering anyone. I'd then taken a day to myself, soaking in my spa bathtub, taking naps, and binge-watching TV, just to let go of it all.

Now that I felt more like myself, I'd let Rita and Mason talk me into taking one more day off. I'd chosen to keep the store closed, although it was Saturday and would be a good sales day, so I wouldn't feel bad about not working.

Rita and Mason had taken over my living room, demanding answers of their own, soon followed by Keith, who claimed he had come to return the book he'd borrowed the day we searched for the diary together.

"But why?" Mason helped himself to the potato chips he had brought.

It seemed I needed to go over it one more time. At least Mason and Rita were both there and it would be only once. "Livie convinced herself she would've inherited John Hokes's money if he'd found the treasure; therefore, she was the only one truly entitled to the diary. Because of her past experiences with men, she felt Uncle Paul was trying to cheat her out of something rightfully hers. She thought she was clever to steal the diary out from under his nose." I stretched my legs out and propped my feet on the coffee table.

"But Paul died, even if she hadn't meant to kill him." Mason popped a few more chips into his mouth.

I nodded. "He did. Livie figured he deserved it since he didn't willingly give her the diary. She figured it was Uncle Paul's own fault that he died. If he'd given her the diary, or if he'd at least stayed asleep, he'd still be alive."

"What about Norman?" Rita rose from her position in front of the television set, where she'd found the channel for the North Carolina State football game.

I shifted on the couch to make room for her so she could prop up her feet as well. Truthfully, I was glad they were here, even if I was missing out on my bath and nap. "Norman actually did try to cheat her. He wanted to cut her out with his scam to get my inheritance and thereby the diary. She got mad and killed him intentionally."

"So, the glove they found in Norman's room that Detective Sutter tried to prove was yours was actually hers?" asked Rita.

"Yes." Keith slid onto the couch on my other side. "It fits her exactly, and we found its mate in her dresser drawer when we searched her house."

"That would explain the use of the passageways." Rita reached for Mason's chip bowl. "Livie and Phillie were both in and out of the inn as it was being finished. They inherited the plans for the mansion, and both knew every inch of those passageways."

"How did the police know it was Livie?" Mason aimed his question at Keith, swiping his salty fingers on his shorts and drawing a whack from Rita, who handed him a napkin. He glared at her before obediently wiping his hands on the paper square and turning back to Keith. "I mean, you guys showed up right as she shot her sister, didn't you?"

"Yes," replied Keith. "But we were coming to question Phillie, not Livie."

"Why?" Rita's eyebrows rose.

He stretched, easing his legs onto the coffee table and fully sandwiching me between him and Rita. "The prescription angle finally paid off. Phillie was on a list of people who were prescribed the sleeping medication used in Paul's death. We had also checked with the local garden centers to see if anyone had purchased hydrangea plants around the time of Norman's death. Livie had come in recently, stating her sister's hydrangea bushes had died due to a severe aphid infestation. She said Phillie had asked her to pick up new plants on her way home to replace the lost ones.

"The salesgirl thought it was odd, since Livie so rarely darkened their door and she didn't buy any pesticides so Phillie's other flowers wouldn't become infested. Plus, the salesgirl and Phillie had talked about flowers often enough that she was pretty sure Phillie didn't grow hydrangea bushes. It sounded suspicious, so we obtained warrants to search their store and house for evidence. It was just lucky timing we got there when we did." Keith reached for my hand and wrapped it in his. "I'm glad you weren't victim number three."

I stared at our hands twined together. His was warm and strong, and the feel of his body against mine, from hip to ankle, caused my heart to pitter-patter in a way it hadn't in a very long time. Maybe Rita was right and I should give Keith a shot.

Rita dragged me back into the conversation. "I think we have Phillie to thank for that one. How is she, by the way?"

I squelched thoughts of snuggling with Keith. "I went by the hospital this morning. She's doing fine. It was only a shoulder wound, no major organs, and no major tissue damage. They expect her to recover enough for discharge within the week. The only problem they're having is keeping her still and in bed." I smiled, remembering the argument Phillie had had with a nurse over whether or not she, Phillie, should be allowed to go down to the hospital's flower shop. Phillie wanted to tell them what they were doing wrong and why the mums she received looked half dead.

Mason washed down his latest mouthful of chips with a soft drink. "What's she going to do with her store while she recovers?"

"When I talked to her, she said she might sell the store and open her own greenhouse." I reached for a soft drink of my own then realized I couldn't open it while still holding hands with Keith.

I didn't want to let go, but the problem was solved when he squeezed my fingers, winked at me, and reached to pop the top with his free hand. God, this man was going to turn me to mush.

I struggled to keep a waver out of my voice. "She says the more she thought about the clothing store, the more she realized the reason she loved it was because Livie expected her to love it. She and I had talked recently about her working part-time for a nursery somewhere, but now she says she doesn't think that will be enough for her. She's too used to being her own boss."

"Will she stay here in town to run her business, or will she move to where nobody knows her?" Concern shone from Rita's eyes.

"She'll stay." I took a sip of my Coke. "She says she figures the town has a bad enough opinion of the Hokes family, what with John's crazy talk and now Livie's murderous streak. She wants to stay and prove not everyone in the Hokes family is insane."

"At least her new business will get off to a roaring start," Keith said. "Everyone will either go there to show sympathy or out of morbid curiosity. But at least they'll go."

"That's a mean thing to say. Possibly true, but mean." I bumped my shoulder into his, shoving him a bit, and he mock-swooned.

Rita chuckled. "I have a question. How did Norman get ahold of the letter John Hokes wrote to his solicitor?"

"Norman was a descendant of John's solicitor," I answered. "He had told Livie his family still owned and lived in the original solicitor's house. And when Norman's mother died, he decided to sell. He found the letter while going through old papers in preparation for putting the house on the market."

"I've got a question too," piped in Mason. "How did Livie get into your apartment to leave that note? There were no signs of forced entry, and Livie doesn't seem like the type to be able to pick a lock."

"According to Phillie, she and Uncle Paul used to come here to have some private time away from Livie. No, not for any hanky-panky." I stopped the question I knew was getting ready to pop out of Mason's mouth. "Phillie said they liked to be here alone to talk and plan and simply be together in peace and quiet. She still had the key as a memento and had no idea Livie had found it, or even knew what it opened, until this was all over."

"What about Stan? Wasn't he a suspect too?" Rita leaned forward and looked across me at Keith. "He baked, grew hydrangeas, and knew the passages in the inn."

Keith shrugged, rubbing his shoulder against mine in the process. "All coincidence. Sure, we were keeping an eye on him, but he had no connection to the sleeping medication that we could find."

I looked across the room at the potted hydrangea sitting on my kitchen counter. "He was apparently just trying to be nice in his own odd way."

"Wasn't he trying to get into the store the day you found the diary?" Mason took another swig of his soda.

"He was here that day trying to get another look at the layout to see if he wanted to make an offer, prior to any repairs." I shook my head. "It seems he may actually want to buy the store and use it as a rental property, although he still wanted me to vote for his mall deal if I chose not to sell. And in case anyone wonders, this morning I voted no."

"Oh, thank God!" Rita stood and moved to the kitchen table, where she picked up one of the little quarter sandwiches she'd made. "So, what's going to happen to Livie?"

"They're keeping her at the North Carolina Correctional Institution for Women in Raleigh until the trial," answered Keith.

With Rita gone, I now had room to slide over and give Keith some space, but I couldn't bring myself to do it. Instead, I concentrated on Rita's question. "The DA said she'd probably be put in a mental institution, since she obviously can't tell right from wrong. Livie still doesn't see anything wrong with what she did."

"I feel sorry for her," said Mason. "She had a rough history with men."

"True," agreed Rita. "But she shouldn't have been trying to steal something that didn't belong to her, no matter what the treasure was. And she shouldn't have killed for it."

"Speaking of treasure." Keith sat forward and dropped his feet to the floor, although his fingers still clasped mine tightly. "Does anyone know what that turned out to be?"

"I almost forgot." I stood and tugged my fingers from Keith's, but not before I received another wink. *Be still, my heart.* I walked to the kitchen bar and picked up a piece of paper then returned to offer it to Rita. "Here's what the last entry said. I copied it at the police station before I turned the diary over as evidence. They say I'll get it back when the trial is done."

Everyone read the entry in turn, and when the paper made it back to me, Mason's greasy-chip fingerprints and all, Rita broke the silence.

"Does anyone have any idea who Bartholomew was?"

Mason swallowed yet another mouthful of chips. "And what does it mean that something is twisted up under his watchful eye?"

"I honestly don't have any idea. But I think I might know who would." I pulled my phone out of my pocket, placed a call, and spoke quietly with the other party for a few moments before disconnecting.

"Well?" Keith leaned forward, his elbows on his knees.

"Well." I paused for effect, earning a get-on-with-it glare from Rita. "Phillie says John Hokes used to have a stuffed crow named Bartholomew. It was rumored that he talked to it all the time. He kept it in his cottage as part of the decor."

Rita set her plate on the table, her eyes wide and her words tumbling out. "The cottage is still as it was back then. That was one of the stipulations the Hokes sisters required, along with a healthy sum for the house plans, before the inn was allowed to use their family name. And there's an old stuffed crow in the study. I remember seeing it the last time I was over there."

"What are we waiting for?" Mason stood and rushed toward the door.

The rest of us hesitated only a fraction of a second before following.

Mason was trying to unlock his car door when we got to the parking lot. "Come on." He opened his door.

"Mason, wait." Keith clapped a hand on the boy's shoulder. "Why don't we all go in my car?"

Mason looked at his beat-up subcompact car. Then he turned his gaze to the much nicer and more spacious sedan Keith drove. "Fine by me." Mason shrugged and sauntered toward Keith's car. "I'll ride in the back." He opened the door and climbed in.

"I'll ride in back with Mason," volunteered Rita, sliding in beside him, maintaining an innocent look as I got in the front next to Keith.

After buckling up, I placed my arm on the console between us. I felt like a teenager waiting to see if he'd hold my hand again. What was wrong with me? I didn't usually act this goofy.

Keith hesitated only a second then placed his arm beside mine and laced his fingers through mine. "Will you stay long in Hokes Folly?" he asked casually.

I studied the way our hands fit together. "I'll be here at least long enough to finish sorting things out and possibly sell the business."

"That could take a while." Keith gave my fingers a tiny squeeze.

My heart performed its new pitter-patter rhythm again, and I fought to keep my voice from sounding breathy. "Yes, it could at that." I studied him as we drove in silence to the inn and pulled into the parking lot. What was going on behind those chocolate eyes?

As we moved from his car into a horse-drawn carriage—Keith and I still in the front and Mason and Rita in the back—for the ride onto the estate, Keith casually asked another question. "Do you think we could do this sometime without chaperones?" He averted his gaze, busily watching the tree-lined road.

This time my heart stopped for an instant then pounded hard. "Are you asking me out?" I turned toward him, my eyebrows raised.

Keith blushed. He actually blushed. I tried not to giggle.

"I guess I am," he said quietly, before returning his gaze to the street ahead.

Before I could chicken out, I blurted, "Then I accept." Now that it was too late to take it back, the idea both terrified and excited me.

"You guys are going out? Cool," Mason's voice sounded from the back seat of the carriage. A muffled thud preceded his next words. "Ow! What did you do that for?"

"Shut up, Mason," hissed Rita.

Well, that wasn't awkward at all. I rolled my eyes, stole a look at Keith, and grinned at another faint blush staining his cheeks, which matched my own, if the warm sensation in my face was any indication.

"So, neighbor, when are you going to come over for tea again?" Rita to the rescue! Her voice had never sounded so good.

I chuckled. "How about tomorrow morning?"

Before she could answer, Mason jumped in. "Speaking of schedules, is anyone available Monday to help me move into my new apartment?"

We all agreed, but Mason's exuberant reply was cut off as the carriage stopped in front of the little cottage that had once been John Hokes's residence. We tumbled out in haste, rushing as a group to the front door, where Elliot waited. The attendant was locking up and putting the sign out that gave the hours for the next day.

"I'll close up, Mrs. Brattle. I have a private party I want to take through the cottage." Elliot spoke with authority to the plump woman who oversaw the little building.

"Of course, Mr. Burke." She handed him the keys. "Where shall I collect the keys in the morning?"

"I'll leave them for you at the front desk. Thank you, Mrs. Brattle," came his crisp and businesslike reply.

"Very well, sir. Enjoy your tour." Mrs. Brattle shot one last glance our way before she shuffled off to the waiting carriage for the trip to her car.

Rita patted the hotel manager on the arm and tossed me a smug grin. "I texted Elliot on the drive over while you two were making goo-goo eyes at one another." She stepped briskly into the cottage, the smile still playing at the corners of her mouth.

So much for her rescue. Heat crept over my cheeks again, and I couldn't make myself look at Keith to see his reaction. Instead, I followed Rita into the little house.

Elliot led us down a short hallway to the study, one of the larger rooms in the house. A fireplace took up most of the far wall. Bookcases filled the other two longer walls, reminding me of Livie's favorite room. A worn-leather wingback chair sat in front of the fireplace, and a small table stood beside its arm with a brandy snifter on its surface, waiting to be filled.

Rita pointed toward the ceiling. "There it is."

I looked up at a large, stuffed crow mounted on the top shelf above the books. A rolling ladder used to gain access to the higher books leaned down from the top shelf, and Mason pulled it over to the section with the bird.

Keith stopped Mason before he could climb the ladder. "I think Jenna should be the one to do the honors," he said quietly, after a nod of approval from Elliot. "After all, she's the one who almost died for the diary."

"You're right." Mason backed away from the ladder.

Gingerly I placed my foot on the bottom rung, testing it to see if the wood was still strong enough to bear weight. Finding it in good shape, I climbed, stopping at eye level with the bird. How had the entry read? Something about being twisted up under Bartholomew's watchful eye. I looked for a twisted piece of paper jammed between the books or under the stuffed bird. Nothing. I spent several minutes poking and prodding, but still nothing.

It wasn't here. Someone had probably already found it and . . . The title of the book directly under the bird caught my eye. *Oliver Twist*. It couldn't be that simple. Or could it? Gently I removed the book from the shelf and opened the cover. There, in a carved-out hollow in the middle of the pages, lay a small cheesecloth bag and a folded piece of paper.

My heart raced as I closed the book and carefully brought it down the ladder. The others crowded around as I walked to the wingback chair and sat with the book on my lap. I opened it and removed the little bag and paper. Slowly I unfolded a hand-drawn map. Laying it aside, I loosened the drawstring at the top of the age-yellowed bag and turned it up on end, letting the contents fall into my waiting hand.

"It's gold," gasped Mason, going down on one knee to get a closer look.

I turned the chunk of metal in my hands. "No, Mason. It's not." I fought the disbelieving laughter that bubbled up in my throat.

"How do you know?" Mason obviously wasn't convinced.

"Dad used to collect rocks. I remember when he brought home a piece like this. I was twelve. I was also convinced we were rich, and I was so disappointed when he told me it wasn't gold. This piece is definitely pyrite, also known as fool's gold because it looks similar to the real thing." I offered the piece to Mason.

"Is it valuable?" He turned the mineral in his hands.

I shook my head. "Not really. It has a few uses, but compared to gold, it's pretty much worthless."

"You mean John Hokes's treasure was fool's gold?" Rita let out the laugh I'd been suppressing. "I guess the town was named well after all."

"What about Phillie?" asked Keith. "If this gets out, then, just like before, John Hokes will be a laughingstock. Phillie has enough to deal with, living down her sister's crimes, without adding this."

"We could put the book back and pretend we never found it." Mason handed me the chunk of metal.

"We could." Rita scowled. "But what if the police try to find the treasure as evidence, or what if some reporter gets the information and tries to find it? Then where would she be?"

"I think the hotel doesn't really need this book on the shelf for the cottage to be authentic," interjected Elliot, who had been quiet since we'd found the clues to the treasure's location. "Can anyone think of someone who might like to have it?"

I shot a look at Elliot. Who were these people? Did everyone in small towns watch out for each other, or had I truly stumbled into Mayberry after all? "You mean you'd let us give the book to Phillie and not tell the hotel about it?"

"I don't see why the hotel should know about this." Elliot gestured at the items in my lap. "There's no point in further troubling a woman's life over a worthless chunk of metal."

"The book is worthless too, now that it's been cut up," I added.

We agreed to take the book and its hidden contents to Phillie for her to dispose of in any way she saw fit. Keith climbed the ladder, rearranging the books to keep anyone from noticing one had been removed. I carefully replaced the pyrite into its bag, drawing the string closed and placing it in the book. Mason folded the map and tucked it inside as well. Elliot took upon himself the task of carrying the book out of the cottage and up to the hotel to get us a carriage ride to the parking lot, in case we crossed paths with someone from security. That way, if any questions arose, he could say he was taking the book in for repair.

Leaving Elliot behind, we climbed into a carriage and rode down the tree-lined drive leading off the estate. I studied my companions. In two and a half weeks, these three had become a very important part of my life. I'd found friendship and true companionship, and they impressed me with their integrity and honesty, something that had been sorely lacking in the people with whom I had previously surrounded myself. I thought about my life in Charlotte, so different from the one I knew I could have here in Hokes Folly.

Charlotte meant incredibly hectic work, if I could find work at all, with little or no time for social activities of any kind. Yes, I still needed to prove myself, but in Charlotte my success would be filled with loneliness and tainted by the knowledge that others would always see me as a possible criminal.

Hokes Folly, however, was much simpler and brimmed with exciting, endless possibilities. I could stand on my own, run my own business any way I wished, and order my own life, one full of friendship and hope for true romance. Maybe I'd stay after all.

Rita interrupted my rambling thoughts. "You know, you've been in your new house for almost three weeks, and we have yet to throw you a housewarming party."

"That's right," agreed Mason.

"How about tomorrow afternoon?" suggested Keith. "I'm off that day."

"It's settled, then," said Rita. "Now, Mason, you bring drinks, and Keith, you bring a salad of some kind. I'll take care of the rest."

"What about gifts?" asked Mason. "Aren't you supposed to bring presents to a housewarming party?"

"That's right," exclaimed Rita. "I'd almost forgotten. Now, let's see. What could we bring?"

"I don't know. Maybe a gift card?" Mason suggested.

"What about a nice bottle of wine?" Keith leaned in closer and whispered softly, "We could drink it one evening in front of the fire."

He winked as he leaned back, and I was pretty sure I blushed again.

"I know, how about a diary?" Rita's voice brimmed with humor.

I cringed. I'd been silent up to that point, enjoying listening to my friends plan a party around me, but . . . "Not a diary. Please. Anything but a diary."

Acknowledgments

Thank you to my husband, George. Your encouragement, support, brainstorming sessions, willingness to answer odd questions at even odder moments, and your unwavering belief in me are invaluable. I love you. Thank you to my sons, David and Will Johnson. All the years you gave me uninterrupted time to write and edit, as well as all the offered ideas, have paid off. You guys are awesome. Thank you to my sister, Ginni Myers, for your joy at my success. You've shouted about my book from the rooftops to anyone who will listen, generating excitement and becoming the inaugural member of my street team. Thank you to my network of writing friends: Pat Rohner, Sarah Wolf, Pamela Reese, Sheryl Torres, and Charlotte Parker. You read my book as it morphed from rough draft to finished product, and your brainstorming sessions, encouragement, and feedback helped me make the book stronger and tighter. Thank you to Dawn Dowdle, agent extraordinaire. Your skills as an editor and agent, as well as your encouragement and support, have made this an amazing process. Lastly, thank you to my wonderful team at Crooked Lane Books for giving me the opportunity to share my stories with the world.

Read an excerpt from

MURDER BY THE BOOKEND

the next

ANTIQUE BOOKSHOP MYSTERY

by LAURA GAIL BLACK

available soon in hardcover from
Crooked Lane Books

CROOKED
LANE

NEW YORK

Chapter One

"How do you think it's going?" I peeked out through the curtained doorway from the back room.

I'd inherited the bookstore three months ago from my uncle, Paul Baxter, who had not quite creatively named it Baxter's Book Emporium. Two months of soul-searching and intense waffling had finally forced me to admit I had fallen in love with the small, quaint town of Hokes Folly. The people had accepted me with open arms, and I was pretty sure I'd finally found a place I belonged, a place I could truly call home. As a result, I had taken it upon myself to rename the bookstore, but I had rejected the idea of putting my own last name on it, since Quinn's Book Emporium wouldn't have been much better.

Rita Wallace rolled her green eyes at me as she snagged two fresh pots of coffee, one decaf and one regular. My friend and next-door neighbor had offered to help with tonight's grand reopening event. "Jenna, it's only been twenty minutes since folks started coming in. Why don't you ask me when it's all over?"

I sighed, resisting the urge to grumble about how friends were supposed to lie to you at times like this in order to make you feel better. After grabbing another box of the commemorative coffee mugs I'd splurged on as giveaways for the guests, I followed the chuckling redhead as we threaded our way toward the coffee station at the front of the store.

Rita leaned toward me as she poured the coffee into the urns. "Take a deep breath and chill out a bit, hon. It'll be fine," she whispered before easing her way through the crowd to return the empty pots to the back room.

I smiled as I pulled a mug from the box and ran my thumb over the store's new name, printed in a deep smoky-gray-blue on one side of the mug. "Twice Upon a Time." Uncle Paul would have approved. I'd come to Hokes Folly, nestled high in the mountains of North Carolina, at his invitation. He had offered to help me get back on my feet after recent trauma in my life. I had arrived, looking forward to reconnecting with an uncle I hadn't seen in almost a decade, only to find him dead.

Before I let my thoughts move in a too morbid direction, I took a steadying breath and finished unpacking. As I turned back to the crowd, I scanned the faces, recognizing some. A handsome form in a black tux held up a couple of plastic shopping bags as he walked in the front door. Keith winked a chocolate-brown eye at me, and my heart pitter-pattered like a tap-dancing poodle. I just hoped it wasn't wearing a tutu. In the aftermath of solving not only my uncle's murder but also a second murder, I'd begun dating Detective Keith Logan, and I shot him a playful grin. At least I hoped it looked playful rather than somewhat nauseous, which was how I felt. After all that had happened, I needed this to go well.

Keith set his bags behind the counter and planted a chaste kiss on my cheek. "I bought three of each, so there is no way we can run out of coffee tonight."

I had brought in enough sparkling wine for everyone to celebrate, but I hadn't thought to replenish my dwindling supply of coffee. Before I could thank Keith for stepping in and saving the day with his emergency run to the grocery store, a lithe brunette in an elegant, black evening gown stepped in front of us and held out her champagne flute to Keith for a refill.

"What a charming little party this is." The woman's bored expression made a mockery of her words, but her husband's firm grip on her elbow made her clamp her lips shut before she said more.

"Now, Selina, dear, I think Miss Quinn has done a truly delightful job of bringing together those truly interested in books." He turned to me. "I must apologize for my wife's rudeness."

I'd been mentally counting to ten, and I took a slow breath before responding to the director of the Hokes Folly Community Library. "That's okay, Mr. March." I nodded slightly at him, again hoping my true feelings didn't show through.

In contrast to his wife's obviously expensive gown, he wore a cheap, brown suit that clashed with his ruddy complexion and dirt-colored hair. Although his tone and face had remained calm, I noticed he didn't release the tight hold on his wife's arm.

To help smooth things over, I turned a tentative smile to his much-younger wife. "That's a lovely gown, Mrs. March."

Selina slid her hands down the black, sequined material. "Yes, isn't it? I've always liked wearing Vera Wang. Haven't you?" She narrowed her eyes, and her mouth took on the tiniest hint of a sneer.

My teeth ground together as I choked back the catty response I wanted to blurt out. Her dress may have cost more than a month's take-home pay from my store, but that was no reason for me to be rude. Okay, maybe I could be a little catty.

"When it's all I can find." I tilted my head and smiled sweetly, ignoring the frown that whipped across Selina's delicate features.

Keith stepped forward with the refilled flute. "Both dresses are equally stunning, though everyone knows it's the woman who makes the dress beautiful, not the other way around." He smiled and handed Selina her glass.

Selina's mouth opened in a small "O," and a gasp left her lips. However, before she could speak, her husband tightened his grip on her elbow and led her away through the crowd.

As they moved away, Selina ranted at her husband. "Did you hear what he said to me? The gall! Anyone can see that thing she has on came straight off the sale rack at K-Mart."

Douglas's jaw tightened, but his response was too softly spoken for me to hear.

I glanced down at my own far less expensive dress, which I had purchased from Kohl's, thank you very much. I'd spent too much on the black sheath dress, but the sleeveless gown hugged me in all the right places, and I hadn't been able to resist buying it. And the fact that Keith couldn't keep his eyes off me tonight made it worth every penny.

A glass of sparkling wine was pressed into my hand, and I turned to look into Keith's eyes. "I can't drink this. The last thing I need is for it to go straight to my head. It's all I can do to keep track of who's who as it is."

"Oh yes, you can. You look like you need it." He placed a hand on the small of my back, gently guiding me toward a quiet corner. Once in a slightly less crowded spot in the store, he blocked my view of the room for a moment, giving me a bit of a break from the crowd.

I tensed and relaxed my shoulders a few times and rolled my neck to loosen the tightness. "I just want everyone to have a good time."

Keith shifted a bit, unblocking my view. "Sweetheart, look around you." He gestured with his glass at laughing couples, several people contentedly browsing the shelves, and small conversation groups, which had sprung up around the room. "Everyone *is* having a good time."

I inwardly winced at Selina March's rudeness. "Some don't seem to be."

Keith chuckled. "Don't worry about Selina. Tomorrow, you'll probably be her best friend. She's just in one of her moods. From what I hear, she's pouting because Douglas put his foot down and wouldn't let her stage a late-nineteenth-century ball at the inn."

A picture of the elegant turn-of-the-twentieth-century mansion, which was now the five-star Hokes Bluff Inn, popped into my head. Built in the early 1900s and intended to outshine Biltmore in Asheville, the estate had over three hundred rooms, a bowling alley, two indoor swimming pools, and more. I could just see a ball in the grand ballroom, a stringed orchestra playing period pieces while ladies in beautiful dresses danced with dashing men, all in period dress.

My eyes wandered over my own little soirée, with my new coffee mugs and my rented but inexpensive champagne flutes. I took in my guests, dressed in everything from nice dresses and suits to true formal wear. Next to the image of a late-1800s ball, I could see why Selina would see this as a bit of a letdown.

Keith slipped his arm around my waist and gave me a little squeeze. "Your grand reopening is a smashing success."

I smiled up at him, relaxing at his warm touch, and paraphrased Rita's words. "Let's just hope you can still say that when it's all over."

Soft strains of classical music wafted from the stereo my only employee, Mason Craig, had set up behind the front counter, the soothing notes relaxing me further. I took a small sip of the sparkling wine, enjoying the way it tickled across my tongue.

Keith stroked the back of my neck softly, his warm finger-tips drawing random patterns across my skin. "You look beautiful tonight. You should wear your hair up like that more often."

"Stop that." I reached a hand up to check the artful twist Rita had arranged in my shoulder-length, dark blonde hair, hoping to bluff my way past the warmth that signaled a blush creeping across my face. Yep, all still in place since the last time I'd nervously checked it.

I once again scanned the room, and as I was about to take another sip of the wine, I saw Mason Craig frantically waving at me from the front door. I'd hired him during the investigation into Uncle Paul's murder, and in spite of his personal past with my uncle, I hadn't regretted the decision.

I nodded at Mason and handed my glass to Keith. "No rest for the weary. I need to go see what's happening."

This time, I traversed the store more quickly, sidestepping guests' questions and well-meant compliments. I reached the door to find a flustered twenty-year-old Mason blocking the entrance. I placed my hand on his arm. "Is there a problem?"

"This is Linus Talbot."

Smiling warmly, I extended my hand in welcome to the tuxedoed man, recognizing the name as belonging to the town's Director of Antique Books at the library. Hokes Folly might be a small town, but due to the historical significance of the Hokes Bluff Inn, the library had a rare book section that was the envy of many larger cities. "I'm so glad you could make it, Mr. Talbot."

I turned back to Mason. "Is his name not on the list? If it's not, it was an oversight. I did send Mr. Talbot an invitation." Again, I shot a warm smile at the older gentleman.

Mason looked down at the clipboard in his hand. "Yes, ma'am, his name's here. But—"

"But," Linus interrupted, "I don't go places that don't also allow Eddy to come."

My gaze followed Linus's gesture, and I noted the medium-sized dog sitting quietly beside his master, his head barely reaching Linus's knee. The wavy, golden-red coat and white chest were well groomed, and deep-brown eyes returned my stare. A giggle burbled up when I noticed the black bow tie around the dog's neck, which exactly matched the one Linus wore.

"He's well trained, he's dressed formally for the occasion, and your invitation did say 'Linus Talbot and guest.'" Linus raised his hand. "We solemnly swear that Eddy will not chew anything, disturb other guests, or make a mess in any way."

My heart melted for the dog when I saw Eddy sitting with right paw raised, his eyes glued to Linus. Why the heck not? I preferred not to alienate someone who had been helpful to me in the past and whose assistance I was likely to need again. "All right, you can both come in. But I'll hold you to that promise." I tore two tickets off the roll on a stool beside Mason and handed them to the librarian. "One for you and one for Eddy. You'll need them for tonight's drawings."

Linus and I walked into the store, leaving Mason to cover the door.

"You've really done a lot with this place in the last couple of months," Linus said, his brows up and a speculative gleam in his eyes.

I nodded slowly. "It took us weeks, but we finally organized everything. Thank goodness I had Rita and Mason to help, or I'd probably still be working on it."

Linus chuckled. "I do remember the mess in which Paul kept things. It's amazing he could ever find anything in here, but he seemed to know where every book was hidden. Are those refreshments?"

I blinked, startled by his abrupt change of subject, but I understood when I followed his line of sight to the table I'd set up. "Yes, we have coffee and sparkling wine. If you'd like, I can scare up a bowl for Eddy to have some water." I reached down and stroked the dog's head, receiving a tail wag in response.

"There's no need. Eddy loves to drink from those little Styrofoam cups. If he gets thirsty, I'll make sure he has something. But I think I'll go help myself, if you'll excuse me."

I smiled and watched the book specialist walk away, Eddy trotting beside him, never moving more than a foot from his master. What would it be like to have a pet that devoted to me? Maybe I should consider getting a kitten or puppy now that I'd decided to give living in Hokes Folly a try.

Rita waved from across the room and pointed at her watch. I glanced down at mine and realized it was time for my welcome speech.

I stepped to the front counter and cleared my throat. "Excuse me. May I have everyone's attention, please?"

The sounds of conversation slowly died as faces turned to me expectantly.

I tamped down the butterflies in my stomach and took a deep breath. "I'd like to thank you all for coming tonight. As you know, Uncle Paul loved this store and this town." As I continued my speech, the nervousness left me. This was my town now. I belonged here. "In the past few months, I've come to love them too. You've all opened your hearts to me, and I hope to serve the community as well as my uncle did."

Determined not to bore anyone with a long speech, I wrapped up. "So please, everyone enjoy your time here tonight, and don't forget to take a commemorative mug home with you."

A brief round of applause echoed through the room before guests turned back to their conversations. A man stopped to give Eddy a quick pat before chatting with Linus. Again, I wondered if a pet might be a good idea, as the guests seemed content having the dog in the store.

"Ms. Quinn."

My daydream about pets ended, and I turned to see who had spoken.

"Bradford Prescott." A man extended his hand, his other resting at the waist of the woman beside him.

"Mr. Prescott, I'm so glad you could make it tonight." I took his hand momentarily, recognizing the candidate for state legislature from a speech I'd watched him give recently. "How is your campaign going?"

"Beautifully, thank you." He gently nudged the woman forward with his hand. "This is my wife Becky."

Bradford and Becky? Their matching shades of blond hair and their elegantly coordinated attire marked them as one of the few couples in Hokes Folly that could be considered our version of a power couple, and I remembered Bradford's wife worked at the district attorney's office, although I had her listed in my records as Rebecca. Their almost alliterative names were a bit cutesy, but I figured no one would dare say so and risk offending them. I shook the perfectly manicured hand the petite Becky held out.

"I'm so glad to see you allow animals in your store." Bradford gestured toward Eddy, who sat patiently at Linus's side as the librarian talked to another guest.

I smiled again at the odd pair, the proverbial man and his best friend. "Consider this a trial run."

"As you know, stronger animal cruelty laws are part of what I hope to accomplish should I be elected to the North Carolina House of Representatives next month."

Stifling a groan, I turned the smile toward Bradford. "Oh?" How could I get out of this? I really had no desire whatsoever to listen to his mini-stump speech, as I'd already heard much of his political opinions at the town meeting Rita had forced me to attend with her. He'd verbally danced circles around his opponent, his political savvy and intelligence impressing me even when I had disagreed with a few of his stances, although I thought he was spot-on regarding animal welfare. After the Howell bribery scandal had broken last week, completely discrediting Bradford's opponent, I figured Bradford was a shoo-in for the position. No one wanted to reelect a corrupt official.

I tuned him out as I subtly searched the crowd for Keith's dark head over the crowd. *Darn.* He was deep in conversation with Phillie Hokes, the last member of the Hokes family still living in Hokes Folly. She and her sister had owned a vintage and antique clothing store next to my bookstore. Phillie had recently closed the store, although she was still disposing of the remaining inventory and fixtures and had thrown herself more fully into her love of gardening. I thought of the gorgeous flower beds I'd seen in her backyard. She was probably filling Keith's ear with information on what plants she thought I should include in my display windows as we approached the holiday season, ignoring her knowledge of my completely brown thumb. Plants and I did not get along.

Next, I scanned for Rita's flaming hair. No luck there either. I caught a glimpse of her back as she walked into the back room, probably to make more coffee or grab more sparkling wine. Mason was a bust, too, as he still had his hands full at the front door.

Resigning myself to a political chat, I returned my attention to Bradford as he droned on about his agenda.

"I do feel more funding of the animal shelter could stop this problem, don't you?"

Uh-oh. I had no clue what he was talking about, and I racked my brain for a vague way to answer that wouldn't let him know I'd been ignoring him. "I think any extra money the shelter receives would help every problem they face, Mr. Prescott."

He nodded as if I'd just said something extremely wise, and I wondered if he really thought I was that smart or, more likely, if he was too seasoned a politician to risk making a constituent feel foolish by pointing out her lack of attention based on her weak answer.

When he took a deep breath, as if to launch into another speech on his platform, I jumped in, cutting him off. "Here comes Mr. Talbot now with Eddy. I'm sure he'd love to hear about your ideas on animal rights." I gestured toward the approaching duo.

Bradford turned to see Linus approaching, and he paled a bit and took a step back when Eddy raised his hackles. A low, humming growl rumbled in the dog's chest.

Linus knelt and spoke softly, settling Eddy before rising to speak to the politician, a cold look on his face. "I see you're still using that hypocritical platform to get elected."

Fire flashed in Bradford's eyes, and his jaw clenched for a brief moment. He seemed to gather himself, relaxing his jaw and smiling before speaking in the silky tones he used to sway others to his point of view. "I would have hoped by now you would either have taught that dog manners or put him down."

My brows shot up, my moth dropped open, and a gasp burst from my throat. What the hell?

Bradford turned and placed a hand on my arm in a way I assumed he meant to be comforting rather than sending an icky chill up my spine. "This animal's a known danger to others. I hadn't realized it was this particular dog when I saw him across the room. I truly hate to see any animal put to sleep, which is why I adamantly support having no-kill animal shelters. However, dangerous animals, such as this dog, should not be allowed to threaten the safety and security of the good people of this city."

Linus's voice came out in a low rumble, sounding remarkably like Eddy's growl. "You lying sack of slime. We both know where this dog came from, and after tomorrow, so will a great many more people."

Chapter Two

B radford blanched again, a light sweat breaking out on his forehead. "Now see here! You have no right to slander me publicly!"

Oh crap! The loud voices were drawing people's attention. This was *not* how I wanted the evening to go. A spectacle had definitely not been on the agenda.

"I have every right, especially when it's not slander." Linus reached down to stroke Eddy and moved off into the crowd, leaving me to pacify the agitated politician.

At least it was over for now. I scanned the crowd, saw Keith making his way toward me through the onlookers, and shook my head. He stopped, eyebrows raised. I mouthed, *I've got this,* and he nodded once and stopped to talk to someone who seemed to want to gossip about what had just happened as she gestured wildly in our direction.

I refocused my attention on Bradford, who had returned to a more normal color and was blotting the light sheen of sweat from his forehead. Becky patted his arm, cooing words I couldn't hear, and he seemed to take strength from them.

"Mr. Prescott, since I run a bookstore, I'd like to hear more about what you might do for small business owners if you're elected to the legislature." Thank goodness I'd come up with something that might pull his attention away from the run-in with Linus.

A few other guests moved closer, and the suave politician persona came to the fore, his dulcet tones instilling confidence in the listener. I listened long enough to be polite before I moved away, rolling my eyes when I heard someone who apparently had no clue what had just happened drag him back into talking about his shelter policies by saying, "Isn't it wonderful the owner allows dogs into her store?" I hoped it didn't trigger another scene.

I eased my way through the room to the refreshment table, jonesing for a cup of java. I arrived at the same time as Rita, who was bringing two fresh pots of coffee from the back, and I held the urn open while she poured in the aromatic liquid. "Thanks. I don't know what I'd do without you tonight."

"That's what friends are for." Rita smiled, took the empty coffeepots, and grabbed a couple of empty wine bottles, careful to hold them away from the emerald-green dress that emphasized her voluptuous curves. "Go mingle. I've got this covered."

"I owe you one," I said as she walked away.

I smiled at the "Oh yeah, in a big way" she tossed over her shoulder on her way to the back room.

Holding a Twice Upon a Time mug under the spigot, I let the aromatic brew flow. I'd used beans from a local company, figuring if I wanted them to buy my books, I needed to support their business as well. The little bit extra I paid for the coffee turned out to be more than worth it. The smell and taste were out of this world. I blew across the hot liquid until it cooled enough to take a tiny sip without peeling my tongue, and the flavor slid through my mouth, awakening my senses and giving me just the pick-me-up I needed.

I sighed, wishing I could simply stand here a while and enjoy the sensations, but I was a hostess tonight, and I had guests to keep happy. I turned and scanned the room and noticed a woman standing alone, looking uncomfortable in her baby-pink dress. Her full figure was not flattered by the profusion of ruffles or the puffy sleeves on the outdated style, and her frizzy, mousy-brown hair showed streaks of gray. As I approached, she stared deeply into her own coffee cup, her eyebrows pulled together in concentration.

When I was close enough, I cleared my throat, hoping not to startle her into sloshing her coffee all over the books. "Is there a specific area of interest I could show you? Things are arranged a bit differently from when Uncle Paul was here."

"You must be Jenna Quinn." The woman's face erupted into a smile that brought beauty to her round face. "I'm Alice King. And yes, Paul did keep things in a piled heap. It's why I never came into the shop just to browse. I couldn't stand the mess. He would call me if he found something he knew I'd want, and I'd pop over to pick it up."

"I'm glad you joined us tonight, Ms. King." I racked my brain, and while I remembered the name from the card file Uncle Paul had kept on his best customers, I couldn't recall what types of books the plump woman preferred. "I hope you'll visit more often now that things are a bit more neat and orderly."

"I will, thanks. But it's just Alice. 'Ms. King' makes me remember how old I am. I prefer to think of myself as much younger." She giggled, making the rows and rows of ruffles bounce up and down like a swarm of butterflies.

Well, at least one person seemed to be having a nice time. "Is there anything I can help you find?"

"Poetry."

"Right this way." I led the woman to the correct section and pointed out shelves containing such authors as Tennyson,

Shakespeare, Byron, and Shelley. "We do also have a few nice editions on an endcap."

Alice followed me to the end of one row where I'd set up a display of elegantly bound antique books. As I reached and pulled a book from its shelf, a flurry of movement caught my eye. A woman swept past, and her swinging purse strap snagged the corner of the book in my hand and sent it flying to the floor, where it landed on its edge.

I gently picked up the book, eyeing its damaged spine, and whirled to see who had been responsible. I should've known. Selina March. Before I could say anything, the woman whirled on me.

"How dare you stick that book out in my way! It could have damaged my Gucci handbag. Do you know how much this would have cost you to replace if it had?" The woman's voice carried through the store as she shook her handbag at me.

I drew on my mother's lessons in manners and counted to ten before I replied. "Mrs. March, you knocked the book out of my hand, and I would appreciate it if you would pay for the damage."

"Pay for it? You must be joking. I have absolutely no intention of paying for that piece of junk." She rounded on Alice and sneered. "Why don't you buy it? Maybe you could pawn it off on someone else and make a few bucks."

Alice's face lost all color, and she took a step back. "How dare you?" Her voice came out in a raspy whisper.

"I'm terribly sorry." Douglas stepped from behind the shelf. "I'll pay for the book. How much is it?" He pulled his wallet from his jacket pocket.

I peeked inside the cover for the cost code I'd lightly penciled in a corner. Although not a low price, at least it wasn't hugely expensive. "Mr. March, it's—"

"You will *not* buy that book!" Selina's screech silenced the whispers of the crowd that had gathered. "I did nothing wrong."

Linus pushed his way through the crowd that had gathered to see the spectacle. "I may be able to fix the book. It won't be the first one I've had to repair due to this woman. However, as always, it will drop the value."

"Those were not my fault!" Selina's voice continued to rise in pitch and volume. "I'll have you fired if you keep saying they were!"

Eddy stepped between Linus and Selina, a low growl rumbling in his chest.

Good grief, first the state legislature candidate and now Selina March? Was it a good idea to have animals in the store? I looked up to see Keith working his way through the crowd, and this time I didn't wave him away. I might need backup, although I did wonder whether I should ask Linus to take the dog home or ask Douglas to take his wife home. After all, the dog was simply protecting his master from a screaming banshee.

Selina took a step back, her voice rising yet again. "Keep that mangy mutt away from me! He's probably the one who tore up those books, and you're trying to blame it on me!"

Linus reached to stroke Eddy's head, calming the dog, and gave him a quiet command to sit. The dog immediately obeyed, and Linus focused on Selina. "If they weren't your fault, why did your husband pay out of his pocket to have them repaired?"

Ouch. I knew I should step in, as this was not the memory I wanted people to have of my store, but my inner nosiness pushed to the fore. I know it was petty, but the woman had been catty with me, and a small part of me, a part my mother would have condemned as unladylike, wanted to see Selina put in her place.

Selina's face reddened, her fists clenching and unclenching as she stared daggers at her husband. "*What?* You *paid* for them? You know damned good and well any damage was *your* fault, not mine!

How *dare* you humiliate me like that?" Selina stormed out of the store, with a groveling Douglas trailing pitifully behind her.

Stunned, I stood holding the damaged book as Keith finally made it to my side. I opened my mouth to speak to him, but I honestly had no clue what to say.

Keith put his arm around my waist and gave me a squeeze, dropping a kiss on my hair in front of the gathered crowd. "It's okay, sweetheart. With a gathering of this size, there are bound to be personality clashes."

Linus gently took the book from my hands. "I'm sorry there was such a scene."

"I'm still not quite sure what just happened." I relinquished the damaged tome, glad to have Keith's support.

Linus chuckled. "No one ever is when she's around. Now, if you'll show me to your back room, I think I can repair this with a bit of book glue. I know Paul used to keep some on hand for such emergencies."

I shook my head and motioned toward the back room. "This way." I led him through the dispersing crowd and into the small storage and office area at the back of the store. "You'll find everything you need in the top desk drawer. And thank you."

"No problem. I'll let you know when I'm done." He settled himself at the desk, and Eddy curled up at his feet.

Pasting a smile I didn't feel on my face, I moved back out into the store, determined to put the remaining guests at ease and ensure the mood lightened after the disastrous display. Noticing a familiar pink-clad form, I eased my way through the crowd.

"Alice, I am so sorry about that incident. I apologize for Mrs. March's rudeness."

"What an awful woman." Tears glittered in Alice's eyes. "Some people just won't let things die."

Not knowing what else to do, I patted her shoulder. "I'm sure she didn't mean to upset you so badly."

"Yes, she did." The plump woman took a deep shuddering breath. "And she succeeded." She closed her eyes and swallowed hard. Abruptly, she changed the subject. "I'm not interested in that book."

It took me a second to make the mental leap. "If Mr. Talbot can't repair it properly, I can knock a bit off the price for you. But he seems to know what he's doing, so I'm sure it will be as nice as it was before. If you'd like, I can go ask him how it's coming."

"Linus Talbot is a pompous, self-righteous jackass who thinks everyone is beneath him. Just the fact that he's touched the book ruins it for me. He's another one who won't let things die. One day, if he keeps destroying people's dreams, someone will put him in his place for good."

I barely managed to keep from taking a step back at the vicious fervor in Alice's voice. Before I could think of how to respond, the plump woman swept down the aisle toward the poetry section in the rear of the store. I hoped she intended to pick another book to purchase, but I didn't follow her to find out. At least she hadn't run from the store in a huff like Selina March had.

As that thought passed through my head, I caught sight of the woman herself. Selina had returned to the store and was slipping into the back room.

I all but ran through the store, hoping to stop any more altercations before they happened. Enough was enough.

"Is there something I can do for you?" I asked as Selina exited the back room. Although I forced myself to smile sweetly, I hoped my firm tone left no room for doubt that I wasn't really pleased to see her back in my store.

"I left my fur." Selina's reply was equally aloof as she gestured to the mink coat draped across her arm. "Don't worry. I'm not staying in your nasty little flea-infested store any longer than it will take me to get to the door again."

"I'll see you out." I followed her to the front to ensure she was truly gone this time.

Selina flew through the store, almost dislodging several more books as she swung the arm holding her coat. I breathed a massive sigh of relief as the door closed behind her.

"I'm sorry, Jenna. I couldn't stop her from getting her coat." Mason clutched his clipboard tightly.

"It's okay." I rested a hand on Mason's shoulder and felt him relax a bit at the friendly gesture. "You did the right thing. She's gone now, and I'm glad, although I wonder where Douglas was."

Mason pointed to The Weeping Willow, the small pub across the street. "They argued on the sidewalk after they left. Then she stormed off, and he went in there. I can't say I blame him. That woman would drive any man to drink." As we watched, the library director stepped through the pub's door, shoulders slumped, trailing after his wife as she plowed down the sidewalk on the other side of the cobbled street.

"Poor guy," I muttered under my breath, looking toward the parking lot at one end of the historic district. "I'd hate to be in that car on the drive home."

"Ain't that the truth?" Mason shook his head.

I inhaled deeply and let the breath out slowly, to clear my head, as I took in the picturesque historic street. The Hokes Bluff Inn drew guests to the town, and the historic district completed that step-back-in-time feel the Town Council wanted. The district had been rezoned years before, ensuring only businesses that could have been present at the turn of the twentieth century could inhabit the spaces along the cobblestone street. The ends of Center Street were blocked, allowing only foot traffic down the sidewalks. Long warehouses, once used as part of the cannery that had supported the town decades ago, had been converted into stores with apartments above. Tourists loved the quaint feel, and locals appreciated the number of customers the historic district drew to the area.

I squared my own shoulders, giving Mason's a final squeeze before letting go. "You're doing a great job. Keep it up."

"Yes, ma'am. I'll do my best."

I steeled myself for another round of damage control as I eyed the whispering groups, obviously gossiping about Selina's flamboyant return and departure. *Please don't let anything else happen tonight.*

I moved deeper into the store, mingled with guests, answered questions as tactfully as I could, and made small talk, hoping to soothe any jangled nerves, especially my own. Things settled down, and laughter and merriment flowed as everyone seemed to let go of the night's previous drama in favor of enjoying the free alcohol and opportunity to socialize.

As the evening wore on, so did the blisters forming on the backs of my heels. I hadn't worn shoes like these in months, and my feet were not happy about being forced to remain in the black pumps with three-inch heels for the last few hours.

At nine PM, I moved to the front of the store and again requested everyone's attention. "It's time for the drawing, folks!" I shouted over the crowd. My mother's voice rang in my head, berating me that a lady did not bellow. Well, this lady's feet hurt too badly to care at the moment.

Mason stepped behind the counter and began moving the items into view. He placed a vintage set of blown-glass bookends and an antique reading lamp on the counter and brought a three-foot-tall, solid wood bookshelf around to sit on the floor in front of them. Lastly, he pulled a one-hundred-dollar store gift certificate from the cash drawer and laid it on the counter near the other items.

All but the gift certificate had been donated by Phillie as she cleared out her vintage store. Since she didn't want the items back and hadn't taken a ticket, she had offered to help with the drawing.

Rita moved through the crowd with coffeepots, pouring refills, and Keith did the same with a bottle of sparkling wine.

"The first item tonight is this lovely antique reading lamp." I gently held up the delicate brass lamp, its shade the shape of a large bluebell flower, the petals made of translucent mother of pearl edged in brass.

Phillie reached into the bowl and read out the number on the ticket. An excited patron came forward to claim the gift, and Mason packed it gently into a box he'd brought from the back room.

"Next is a beautiful set of bookends made of hand-blown glass." I picked one up, its tall glass spire twisted gracefully over a glass block base. As I turned it in the light, its interior prisms sent rainbows of color across the room.

Again, Phillie read the number, and this time Linus Talbot stepped forward as winner, Eddy close at heel. I hadn't seen them exit the back room, and I smiled at the loyal dog while his owner happily accepted the open box bottom Mason had found to hold the bookends.

Two more patrons happily won the ornately carved bookcase and gift certificate, and congratulations were extended to each winner as everyone headed out to the parking lots at either end of the historic district, commemorative mugs in hand.

A touch on my arm caught my attention, and I turned.

"I've repaired the book as best I could with what you have in the back room. The fact that it's now been damaged and repaired will devalue it somewhat." Linus shook his head. "It's a shame too. It was a lovely copy."

I followed the librarian back through the store to the back room and stood gazing at the repaired book. To my untrained eye, I couldn't see any remaining damage. However, I knew I couldn't sell something to a customer without disclosing the damage and repair.

My fingers trailed across the brass binding surrounding a white cover with black and gold scroll work, an ornate cutout in the center. Green grosgrain material backed the cutout, on which "MILTON" was stamped in gold lettering, matching the gold gilt edging on the pages. Who had read this book over almost two centuries since its publication in 1853?

"It's still in wonderful condition, in spite of the repair."

Linus's words pulled me from my walk into the past, and I turned as he headed into the front room.

"How long until I can safely put it back out on the shelf?" Even knocking down the price a bit, I could still get a nice sum for the book.

Linus furrowed his brow. "I'd say around two days. That should be sufficient time for it to set."

I thanked him profusely for his time, since he had been here as a guest, not to work on my books, and waved to him as he left, the faithful Eddy at his side.

"Well, that was sure a party." Rita leaned on the front counter and slipped her heels off. "At least I wasn't wearing a hoop skirt and crinoline, not to mention a corset." She rubbed her hands down her ribs.

I joined her, both at the counter and in her barefoot state. "We did have folks dressed from informal to formal. You would have fit right in with one of your work outfits."

Rita worked at the inn as head of the makeup and hair artistry department. People who visited the inn were swept back in time with period events, formal dinners, and more. Each guest was dressed and coiffed in period style, and the staff, including Rita, dressed the part as well.

I sagged against the counter, taking weight off one of my tired feet. "All drama aside, I think it went reasonably well."

Warm arms snaked around me from behind. "It went beautifully." Keith planted a kiss on the back of my head. "You'll be the talk of the town."

Mason exited the back room with one of the rental glassware racks in his hands. "Especially if everyone hears about all the brouhaha that went on." He set the rack on the counter and moved about the room, picking up half-empty champagne flutes.

Rita threw a balled-up napkin at Mason. "It all smoothed out in the end." She leaned over, put an arm around me, elbowing Keith aside, and squeezed my shoulders. "For now, we can relax. Mason can do a little bit of the cleanup tonight, but we can leave most of it for tomorrow. I have the morning off and can help out."

Too exhausted to care, I nodded and walked to the front door. As I checked the lock, a red and white streak ran past the front windows. Eddy?

Without thought for my stockings, I unlocked the door and yanked it open. "Eddy!"

Keith followed me out the door. "You saw Linus's dog?"

"Yes, he ran past as if the boogeyman was after him." I pointed down the street in the direction I'd seen the animal run.

Keith took off at a jog, calling softly, while I ran through the store to the fridge in the back, hoping I could find treats to coax the frightened dog. What had scared him so badly? And where was Linus?

Pushing that thought out of my mind, I raced out the door again, lunchmeat in my hands, to see Keith walking toward the store, a large bundle in his arms wrapped in his jacket. I held the door open, and he brought the terrified dog inside.

Carefully Keith set the dog on the floor, and I knelt to soothe Eddy, offering him a treat. A dark stain covered his feet.

"Keith, is that . . ."

Keith knelt beside me and picked up a paw. "Blood."

"Linus . . ." My stomach tightened.

Keith stood and strode out the door. I jumped up, jammed my feet back into my high heels, my aching feet forgotten, and raced after Keith in the direction we'd seen Linus go when he left the store.

As we neared the parking lot, I could see a lone car in the lot, its passenger door open and the dome light on, the soft dinging of the door chime echoing through the air.

Keith's stride took him to the car considerably faster than I could run in high heels if I didn't want to risk breaking an ankle. I skittered around the open door to see Keith kneeling beside a still body. A shattered blown-glass bookend lay on the asphalt, shards immersed in the dark puddle that oozed out from under Linus's head.

Keith turned. "Go call the police. Tell them I'm here securing the scene."

"Is he . . .?" I couldn't finish the sentence as a lump rose in my throat.

Keith's jaw clenched. "Tell them we'll need the coroner."